MW01102220

ALSO BY JERENA TOBIASEN

THE PROPHECY SAGA
The Emerald
The Destiny

December 2018

THE
CREST

THE PROPHECY BOOK I

For my amazing doctor,
Teresa Cordoni.

With gratitude for
all you do.

Jerena

JERENA TOBIASEN

The Crest
Copyright © 2018 by Jerena Tobiasen

This is a work of fiction. The plot and the
characters are a product of the author's
imagination, and any similarity in names
is a coincidence only. While real places and
establishments have been used to create an illusion
of authenticity, they are used fictitiously. Facts have
been altered for the purpose of the story.

Cover Design: Ana Chabrand,
Chabrand Design House
www.anachabrand.com

Author Photo: Robert M. Douglas,
Copyright © 2018

Interior Formatting: Iryna Spica, Spica Book Design
www.spicabookdesign.com

ISBNs:
978-1-77374-033-1 (Print)
978-1-77374-034-8 (E-book)

This book is for
Ilse-Renata Schickor,
who generously shared her wartime
experiences, and allowed me
to write them.

ACKNOWLEDGEMENTS

While the seed of my saga began with the kidnapping of a friend's son some thirty years ago, this story is my own. Along the way, I have been inspired by others and wish to acknowledge their contributions, including:

- Ilse-Renata Schickor, who told me how, as a young woman, she put her trust in her employer so that he could lead her to safety in the spring of 1945, barely escaping the Russian invasion.
- Gerd, Ilse-Renata's son, who shared tales of life in post-World War II, Germany, and the shenanigans that can occur in an all-boys private school. Together, Gerd and Ilse-Renata told me the story of his father's escape from a prisoner of war camp.

- My parents, from whom I learned the art of storytelling.
- Konstantin Kobelev, who shared tales of life in a communist country and of attending school with children of displaced Roma families, and for the use of his name by two of my characters: Captain Konstantin Anker and Prow Kobelev.
- Henry Fast, who edited my use of the German language.
- Brie Wells, Gaelle Planchenault and Julie Griffiths, who read the rough work and helped me keep the faith.
- Ben Coles of Cascadia Author Services, who read my manuscripts and gave me hope, and his gang of talent, who helped turn my manuscripts into novels.
- And last, but certainly not least, my wonderful husband, Robert McKellar Douglas, an artist with vision. He not only encouraged me while I wrote, but helped me with research, travelled

with me, listened as I bounced ideas around, read my scenes when requested, and provided feedback when I needed it; he is the one who inspired me to keep writing better. "Good photographs are images of the exceptional," he says. "A great painting highlights the universal." I sincerely hope that my readers feel *The Prophecy* delivers an exceptional image that highlights the universal.

CHAPTER ONE

His hands shook with anticipation as he read his name, *Gerhard Lange,* written in a neat hand on the front of the envelope. He turned it over. Embedded in the flap was the insignia of the *Kaiserliche Deutsche Armee.*

From the doorway of the dining room, where the blended aromas of their midday meal faded, Gerhard's family looked on in earnest.

"Open it, son!" Michael's impatience belied his pride in his son's accomplishments.

Gerhard was startled from his motionless reverie by his father's baritone voice. He reached for the letter opener on the hall table. It was shaped like a crane, with a pointed bill protruding from an outstretched neck, wings tucked close to the body, legs striding slightly beneath it, and webbed feet perched on the hilt's guard.

The closed crane's bill trembled slightly as it entered the folded space between the flap and the pocket. With a flick of his wrist, Gerhard ripped the bird's beak through the snow-white field and broke the blood-red seal of the *Kaiser*. His mind racing with anticipation, he replaced the opener on the table.

The wounded envelope gaped to reveal a crisp sheet of folded paper. Gerhard pinched the fold and tugged gently. He grinned mischievously at his father as he unfolded the paper, then lowered his eyes and read silently.

"Well?" Michael encouraged. "Don't keep us waiting!"

Gerhard took a deep breath and relaxed his shoulders. "I am to report for duty Monday next." Smiling with satisfaction and excitement, he waved the page at his onlookers as if it were a flag of truce.

"Oh, Gerhard. How exciting!" Marie skipped forward, snatching the paper from Gerhard's hand. She read the message aloud and began dancing twirls around him, her glossy straw-coloured hair bouncing off the shoulders of her lithe body. "You will finally join the mighty Kaiserliche Deutsche Armee. Does this mean you'll be sent to the Russian Front?"

Marie raised her arms in a high-fifth position and continued twirling along the hall. The duty notice fluttered from her finely-shaped fingers, trailing in elegant circles above her golden tresses.

Gerhard resisted her enthusiasm for all of one minute, then joined in her excitement.

"You're crushing me!" she squealed when he scooped her into his arms and danced with her. Her legs swung together like a pendulum while he held her firm and twisted one way and then another.

At eighteen, Gerhard stood as tall as his father, and would soon surpass that, but his sister was fourteen and had the slender body of the dancer she dreamt of being. His strength and surety were a product of helping his father maintain the estate and working alongside his friend, Otto, on *Herr* Schmidt's farm.

"Perhaps," he said, hugging her firmly before setting her feet to the floor. "It doesn't really matter where I'm sent. Wherever I go, it will be far from home and family. I want to serve my country; but, at the same time, I'll miss all of you." His eyes rose to meet his mother's, and saw worry and fear etched in her youthful face.

"Enough Marie!" Michael barked, interrupting the celebration. "Help your mother and Cook clear the table. Gerhard and I need to talk.

He led Gerhard toward the door to his study. "Son, join me for a brandy."

Gerhard followed his father into the study, brushing a shock of blue-black hair out of his eyes. "Brandy?"

"Yes. It's not every day that one's son receives orders to join the Kaiser's army as an officer candidate. I remember the day I received my summons ..."

Gerhard's mind wandered as his father

4

retold the story he had heard many times before. He straightened the old Spanish masterpiece hanging above a leather armchair so cracked and worn from use that it looked to be the same age as the painting. He stood back and admired the treasured artwork, how it reflected light. Of all the paintings in the house, it was his favourite. It was masculine and powerful. Mars: an inspiration for dedicated warriors.

Gerhard surveyed the room while his father poured the brandy. Everything about the study exuded masculine strength and control. Books referenced by his father filled floor-to-ceiling shelves: books of agriculture, horticulture, and animal husbandry; books of military accounts and strategies; ledgers of supplies, purchases and sales; and books of fiction and non-fiction for personal pleasure, on those rare occasions when time permitted. Michael operated the business of both the estate and his military career from the study, and almost every significant event in the history of the Lange family was, at some point, considered in that study.

Since he had been a small boy, Gerhard had heard stories from his father about adventures of service in the military, and been reminded often that Lange men had served the Kaiser for generations. To a young boy, it was a romantic fantasy. He loved and admired his father: his straight back and commanding presence. He aspired to be just like him one day.

As soon as he and his best friend, Otto Schmidt, were old enough, they had applied to the Prussian military academy. Gerhard had yearned for the day when he would join his father's fellowship as an officer of the Kaiserliche Deutsche Armee. Now, he was a recent graduate of the academy, and the day had finally arrived.

Instead of waiting for an order from the Ersatz Commission, he and his father had agreed that he should volunteer. Of course, Otto and his father had been of the same opinion. The country was electric with the call to fight, and Gerhard and Otto were eager to participate. Plus, by volunteering, they were able to choose their unit of service, which meant they could serve in the same unit in which their fathers had served.

As young officers, they were required to provide their own uniforms, equipment, and rations, and to find their own quarters. Those requirements had worked to their advantage; their uniforms would be well-made, and their equipment and rations of better quality than standard military issue. Before they left the academy, they had been measured for their new uniforms and delivery was expected in the next day or so.

Gerhard's father poured them each a glass of brandy. The clear light of the October afternoon poked through the study window and bounced off the cuts in the crystal glasses, causing the walls to sparkle with small rainbows. Michael handed a glass of the aromatic brandy to his son.

Gerhard's focus shifted when Michael rested a large hand on the back of the old, leather settee. A cameo ring on his third finger reflected the light in the room. *That ring represents the legacy of the Lange family. Grossvater gave it to Vater the day he died,* he mused, admiring the fine detail of the Lange family crest carved into the blue stone. An exact replica of that crest hung over the lintel of the manor's front door.

"I'd like to tell you not to worry about the conflict, son, but the truth is that it could get worse before it gets better. I wish I could go with you when the time comes, but … I'm too old for this campaign. It will be Depot work for me."

Michael's comment jerked Gerhard's attention to the present. "I understand, *Vater.* But you've trained us—me, Otto, and the other boys—every summer since we were small, and that training will keep us safe. Instead of trying to remember what to do, we will respond instinctively." He stood tall and straight, imitating his father's six-foot tower of power, and extended his hand to receive the glass Michael offered.

"I tried," his father said humbly. "Trying to discipline rambunctious boys was challenging. It's up to you now to remember what I've taught you about being a good leader. Bring those boys home safe to their families. We're counting on you."

The leather chair creaked as he lowered himself, appearing resigned to the fate of the young men. Gerhard took the old arm chair opposite Michael, his face solemn.

"I remember what your Uncle Leo told me, not long after I'd enlisted." Michael said. "'Keep your wits about you, boy. It's your wits that'll keep you safe.' He is one man who commands respect—for his accomplishments, and for his commitment to the Kaiser, and, of course, to this country. I've just learnt that he received the Iron Cross. I imagine the Saxon Guard Cavalry has been celebrating his accomplishment. It makes them all look good.

"Apparently," Michael added, "he is to be appointed first secretary to the German Legation at Sofia. Admirable!"

9

Gerhard watched his father lower his eyes, as if reflecting on his long-time friendship.

Michael released an audible sigh and continued. "You remember to keep your wits about you too, son. Stay safe and make us proud."

"I will, Vater." Gerhard raised his glass to meet his father's. Coal black eyes locked in camaraderie with a sense of commonality. "A toast … Uncle Leopold von Hoesch and the Saxon Guard Cavalry."

Together, they sipped their brandy in salute. Gerhard licked his lips and smiled. "Mmm, apples! Crisp and sweet!"

Michael nodded. "This Norman brandy has never disappointed us. It's been a favourite for generations."

"And to the second West Prussian Grenadiers!" Gerhard said, thinking of himself and the immediate future.

"And to King Wilhelm the First Regiment," Michael endorsed. "And may God keep you all safe."

CHAPTER TWO

Later that evening, as Gerhard prepared for bed, he remembered a day a few years past: a cold and snowy February morning, when he and Otto had joined a line to register for the Prussian military academy. Otto had stood behind him, his white-blond hair and rosy face—a sharp contrast to Gerhard's blue-black hair and olive skin—reflecting the frosty morning sun.

Each boy had carried an application form completed with name, address, height, weight, next of kin, medical information, and so on. They had been led to an auditorium and told to take a seat.

Otto and Gerhard sat next to each other on old, wooden chairs set up in orderly rows for the waiting candidates. Their chatter was quiet, yet full of anticipation.

"Lange. Gerhard." The sound of his name startled him when the announcement finally came. He jumped to his feet, scrambling to collect his coat, hat, and form. He had been waiting for the summons, but did not expect the volume of the sergeant's voice.

"Follow me. Right smart."

With a quick, sheepish smile to Otto, Gerhard stepped smartly in time with the sergeant, who led him down a long corridor, at the end of which was one stout, wooden chair.

"Sit here until you're called again."

Gerhard handed him the completed form.

"No, boy. You hold onto that for the doctor. He'll want to see it." The sergeant turned crisply on his heel and stepped back down the corridor the way they had come.

"Lange. Gerhard," another voice snapped, startling Gerhard from his musings a second time.

He jumped to his feet and followed the doctor into the examination room. From down the hall, he heard the muted bellow of, "Schmidt. Otto," and then the doctor's voice again.

"Strip to your underpants. I'll be back in a minute."

The rest of the morning passed quickly. He passed the medical examination and answered all of the questions asked by both the doctor and the enlistment officer who followed. By noon, the application process was complete.

A month later, they had received their invitations to attend the military academy, and in August of that year, their families had waved them good-bye as the train from Liegnitz left the station, carrying them off on the first leg of what was to be a very long journey.

At the academy, Gerhard and Otto had applied themselves competitively, and both had excelled. Just three months ago, they had graduated at the top of their class, Gerhard placing first and Otto third.

Now, in his old room in the family home, Gerhard lay on his back, his right arm bent behind his head. His lips curved upward, drowsy from the brandy. He could feel the apple warmth rise in his throat and blew softly through his nose, enjoying the reminder.

As he drifted off to sleep, it was the vision of a father's face, full of pride, that he saw playing behind his eyelids.

On a Monday morning in October, 1917, just one week following their receipt of the duty notice, Gerhard and Otto met at the District Office, together with eight other young men from the area. All were neatly dressed in their field-grey uniforms, carrying their kits of military paraphernalia, families in tow.

The small group of eager young men huddled together for warmth and assurance, their steaming breath mingling together and creating dewy drops on hair and caps. Anxious with excitement, they teased each other, shifted from one foot to another, and kicked at things unseen. They thoughtlessly straightened their jackets and

14

caps, removed their new leather gloves, and put them on again.

Before he had left the manor that morning, Gerhard had stood on the frost-covered lawn, drinking in one last look of his home. On impulse, he had run back up the stairs and placed his hand on the family crest, which his great-grandfather had mounted over the lintel one day in April of 1865: the day the Lange family had moved into the manor.

He felt the pulse in his hand define the medieval silver helmet and the farmers' coat of arms. He closed his eyes, seeing the red shield broken by the white chevron and three stocks of ripe grain. "I'll come back," he had promised the crest.

A fine mist now hung in the October sky, sparkling like diamonds in the blinding morning light. A skiff of snow had fallen during the night, and the frozen ground crunched under their feet.

Mothers shed tears freely, mopping them with white lace handkerchiefs. Fathers tried to be stoic, but occasionally swiped a damp eye. Younger siblings, bundled against the chill in woollen coats, scarves, and mittens, looked on in awe at their handsome, uniformed brothers.

Gerhard's father had ensured that each young man received a sturdy pair of hobnail boots with horseshoe heels to complete their kits. They had been delivered the day before with a note that read:

Take good care of yourself, and
treat your boots as your best friends.
Replacing them will be impossible.

Boots issued by the military were no longer made in the sturdy manner of previous years. Since South American raw materials had been blockaded as a consequence of the war, access to quality leather had become complicated. However, Michael had used his connections, and soon acquired the necessary material.

The boots made for Gerhard and his friends were fashioned in the military style, embellished with a small sheath on the inside of the right boot in which they could conceal their boot blades. The embellishment was not military issue, and the young men were cautioned not to draw attention to the sheath.

"Others might covet them," Michael cautioned later that day, "especially yours, Otto. Since you're left-handed, I had the sheath put in your left boot."

The others turned their gaze toward Otto, who blushed at the unexpected attention.

Together with their kit, each young man carried orders to meet at the train station in Liegnitz by 1300 that day. From Liegnitz, they would travel to Dresden to join the King Wilhelm the First Regiment. They were given no information about their ultimate destination, and no details of their return. In the throes of war, any suggestion of furlough was vague.

17

The brakes of a military transport truck screeched as it came to a rumbling halt in front of the Ersatz District Office. Inscribed on the driver's door was the same insignia as the envelope Gerhard had opened not so long ago.

"All right boys," a sergeant bellowed as he alighted from the truck, "say good-bye to your families and get on board. Right smart now! We have a train to catch."

To a person, the small group jumped, startled by the boom of the sergeant's voice. Then they laughed together, breaking the tension of their emotional farewells, when they recognized the sergeant as being the same fellow who had greeted them on registration day several years prior.

The sergeant saluted some of the fathers, acknowledging their prior or current service to their country, and walked to the rear of the truck. He lifted a flap and ushered the young men aboard.

Hugs, kisses, and instructions for staying safe followed the young men as they tossed their gear into the truck and climbed in. They each took a seat on one of the wooden benches and tucked their duffle bags between their feet.

Those left behind watched the truck roll away, hastened with the current raised by a multitude of waving hands. As the truck vanished from sight, the families turned away quietly and made their way home, their shadows dissipating into the diamond light.

CHAPTER THREE

The following two years passed quickly for some: not so quickly for those who tromped through mud, snow, rain, and heat; who fought insects, starvation, loneliness, and fear; who saw dismemberment; who smelled the rot of humanity, vomit, and gun powder. It passed not at all for those whose death arrived sooner than expected.

Gerhard's determination to survive was strengthened each time the lifeless form of one of his mates returned home without him. One died during a battle in Flanders, four died during the battle for Verdun, and, in the spring of 1917, one was taken prisoner. Two others sustained injuries at Vimy that resulted in their removal to field hospitals, where they later died.

After Vimy, Gerhard and Otto moved with the Regiment from one bloody battlefield to another, ferociously leading their men into each confrontation. They proved to be the leaders they were trained to be, and their prowess earned them promotions: first to lieutenant and then to captain.

Despite the chaos around them, Gerhard and Otto managed to keep their heads and guide the companies under their command. They had a twin-sense awareness of where the other was, no matter that they might be positioned kilometres apart.

Late in the spring of 1918, their companies fought side-by-side in several battles along the Lys River, the head-count reduced to a mere shadow of their former glory.

At the end of April, they were pinned down by heavy artillery fire. With heads close together discussing strategies, a sniper's bullet hit Otto's left knee, shattering it.

Gerhard grabbed him as he fell and rolled them both toward shelter in a crater created by a mortar that morning.

While Gerhard assessed the damage to Otto's knee, mortars began falling around them again.

Time seemed to stand still. Kneeling next to his unconscious friend, Gerhard tried to staunch the blood flow by applying a tourniquet.

Stray shrapnel from a nearby explosion peppered Gerhard's right side. The percussion sent him flying forward, across Otto's chest. His head smashed into a chunk of mortar debris, and his world went dark.

When the mortar salvo ended a short time later, stretcher-bearers found them where they had fallen, and concluded they were both dead. Their bodies were put onto stretchers and carried unceremoniously to a waiting wagon, where the dead were being loaded.

Two men working together each grabbed an arm and a leg to heft Gerhard's body off the stretcher and into the wagon. Gerhard cried out when uncaring fingers dug into a bloody gash in his arm. The startled bearers almost dropped him.

"Check the other one, while I examine this one." One of them nodded toward Otto. "He may be alive, too."

Fingers pressed into Otto's neck. "I have a weak pulse here," the second bearer said.

Gerhard and Otto were moved to a wagon used to evacuate injured soldiers, and were taken to a nearby field dressing station. An orderly told Gerhard that as soon as their injuries were stabilized, they would be taken from the holding tent to one of the hospitals.

"Then what?" Gerhard asked, struggling to his feet.

"I've heard that any wounded remaining in hospitals when opposing armies take control are being taken away as prisoners," the orderly answered.

Otto stirred as if in response to the orderly's words. "*Nein*! I won't be a prisoner! I must go home!" Otto exclaimed.

"Enough protesting from you, sir," the orderly said as he jabbed a syringe in Otto's shoulder. Otto immediately quieted.

Gerhard swayed.

"Sir," the orderly cautioned, "you really should lie down. You have a nasty gash on

23

your forehead, and you're bleeding from several other injuries."

Gerhard collapsed back onto the stretcher, raising a hand to test the injury to his forehead. He winced, and his hand dropped heavily onto the stretcher.

"I'm going to get some equipment, and see what I can do to clean you two up before the doc comes," the orderly said. "You both look like you've been in the muck for weeks!"

"We have," Gerhard mumbled, lifting his head to scrutinize Otto's injuries. He dropped his head to the cot when he realized the repair was beyond his ability.

As Gerhard rested, awaiting the orderly's return, two events occurred.

Two more orderlies rushed into the tent, carrying a stretcher on which his commanding officer lay groaning. The orderlies dropped the stretcher next to Gerhard's cot and departed briskly.

Gerhard rose to support himself on his elbow. "Sir, how are you injured?" he asked.

The commander rolled his head toward Gerhard, seeming to struggle with recall for a moment. "Ah! Captain Lange! I wondered where you and Captain Schmidt disappeared to. It's not like you to wander off in the midst of a battle. Where's Captain Schmidt?"

"There, sir," Gerhard said, thumbing in the direction of his unconscious friend. No movement came from Otto's cot.

"What's happened to him?"

"Took a sniper shot in the knee. The orderly says he'll never bend it again—if he's lucky." Gerhard shook his head as he gazed upon his friend. "He'll likely lose his leg."

Before the commander could respond, the flap of the tent burst open and a senior surgeon strutted in, bringing with him a gust of chilled wind.

"Colonel," the doctor said as he probed the officer's blood-stained shirt, "where do you hurt?"

The colonel gasped and provided the doctor with details as he breathed through the pain.

"Superficial wounds, sir. I'm certain we can have you patched up and back to your command quickly. Now, what about you two?" the doctor said, turning toward Gerhard.

"I've taken shrapnel here and here," Gerhard said, "but Captain Schmidt has the more serious injury. Can you help him? Save his leg?"

The doctor lifted the blanket, revealing Otto's damaged knee. "This looks nasty," he said, probing the muddy knee.

Otto groaned, but seemed to remain unconscious.

"I don't have time to dwell on this type of injury," the doctor stated. "The way the French are cleaning out hospitals and taking patients as prisoners right now, he'll likely be treated by one of their doctors. My orders are to repair the able-bodied first, then get them out of here and back to the field."

Otto groaned again. "Nein!" he mumbled. "Home!"

Gerhard turned his focus from the doctor to his commander. "We can't leave him to die, or be captured, Colonel!" he pleaded.

The colonel thought for a moment, then reached toward the doctor. "Give me a pen and paper, Doctor."

The doctor withdrew a notepad from his pocket and handed it and a pen to the colonel.

"Here, take this," he said, thrusting the paper toward Gerhard. "If you think you can get Schmidt to a better facility, do it! He's too good a man to lose, and you're no use to us with your injuries, anyway!" The colonel waved his arm.

"Get as far away as you can, as fast as you can," the doctor said. "At the rate the French are advancing, you might have to keep going all the way to Belgium!"

The chaos of battle bled into the field dressing stations. Injured bodies flowed into holding tents, waiting for medical attention. Triaged bodies and the dead were transported elsewhere. There was no time for niceties and social etiquette. Everyone focussed on the body or the task in front of them.

A short while later, Captain Lange staggered out of the holding tent, limping off in search of some way to get Otto to safety: away from the lines and the possibility of capture. It took no little effort on his part to hitch up a bedraggled mule to a small utility cart and urge the mule back to the holding tent.

When he returned, Otto was alone in the tent. He half carried, half dragged Otto's deadweight body from the tent to the cart, stopping twice to allow a wave of nausea to pass.

Ignoring the blood oozing from his own wounds and a blinding headache from the gash on his forehead, Gerhard searched until he found an overlooked medical kit, a heel of stale bread, a few tins of army rations, and a bunch of rubbery carrots. He threw them all in the cart under the seat. He took one last look around the holding tent and found two worn, woollen blankets, which he spread carefully over Otto, tucking their rifles and ammunition next to him.

Satisfied he could do no more, he led the mule into the dark night.

Their journey was a long one. Gerhard sought shelter and rested by day. At night, under bright flares of distant explosions and the glare of flash fires, he limped ahead of the mule and cart. The earth rumbled beneath them with the impact of each explosion.

Travel during the dark had its risks, but travelling during the day left Gerhard feeling uneasy: exposed and vulnerable. Too many wagons, trucks, men, and artillery, all in constant motion. The roads were impassable. Gerhard found movement at night less obstructed.

Before he rested each morning, Gerhard searched until he found fodder and water for the mule, and then tended to Otto's injury, cleaning the wound and re-dressing it. His own wounds were no longer bleeding, although the goose-egg bump on his forehead throbbed, and the shrapnel was irritating, restricting his movement. If not for the injury to his buttock, he would have walked longer, would have found help sooner for Otto. As it was, he was glad for the mule and the load it pulled.

Curious that no one challenges me. No one asks for papers. No one asks about the wagon, the mule, or the body on the cart. No one offers assistance. No one cares! Structure is lost in chaos.

Gerhard needed food and water. As he passed through towns, he found water and filled the canteens. At dusk and dawn, if the mule plodded past cratered farm fields, he searched for overlooked food—vegetables and berries. It helped to have grown up in a farming community. He knew where to look.

Some days, at sunset, he found tart early berries timidly ripening on the tips of sun-exposed branches. He plucked them carefully and wrapped them in a soiled remnant of cloth to share later with Otto.

On other occasions, he found small potatoes—possibly seed potatoes from the year
before—broken carrots—mostly feathered
green tops, but the odd one with a small
carrot growing beneath the soil—and sometimes a cluster of mushrooms. In a barn, he
found dried cabbage leaves and ears of corn
in a pigsty long abandoned by its previous
tenants. He scrounged it all, wishing for a
pot of hot water to cook them in.

Gerhard and Otto ate their food raw,
and sometimes so fast that they promptly
spat it out again. Otto ate little. The pain
and infection made him feverish. Gerhard
forced water down Otto's parched throat
and mopped his brow. His words of encouragement were often lost in Otto's feverish
mind.

The roads were pockmarked with their own
injuries caused by battle and bad weather.
The wagon rocked roughly from side-to-
side and bounced over gouges and ruts. The
gaunt mule dug every step into the drying

mud. Each jostle aggravated Otto's damaged knee, aggravating his agony.

Gerhard encouraged Otto when he was coherent. "Hold on, Otto; we're almost there. Your injuries are your ticket home. You should be there by the fall harvest. Hold on, my brother."

He was grateful when Otto slept, relieved that his friend was beyond pain for a time.

The jostling lessened when they approached towns. Sometimes, Gerhard found small stretches of undamaged road. On those occasions, Otto rested easier.

After five days, he seemed to settle a bit. Gerhard saw, however, that the advancing infection was making Otto delirious. What was left of Otto's knee swelled. The tissue burnt red and crusted with pus seeping from the wound. Gerhard smelled the putrid rot and felt the urgency to find help for his friend.

In towns and German encampments, he made enquiries about medical assistance. The field hospitals were overwhelmed, he was told, with injured and ill soldiers. So close to the battlefront, what few local hospitals existed had no capacity for two more patients, especially for the care that Otto required.

Each time he was turned away, Gerhard wrapped his fingers around the mule's halter and plodded on to the next source of medical aid to which he had been directed. He pressed the mule eastward, deeper into Belgium, toward the border of *Deutschland* and safety.

When exhaustion overcame Gerhard and he could limp no further, he would take respite on the cart's bench. Otherwise, he preferred to walk ahead of the mule and not waste its energy by having to pull the extra weight. The shrapnel in his right buttock and lower back made sitting uncomfortable, and he was grateful that his injuries remained free of infection.

"Surely someone must help us! I can't let Otto die!" Gerhard pleaded, raising his eyes toward the heavens. "Help me help him!"

CHAPTER FOUR

As the sun rose on the morning of the sixth day, Gerhard concluded that Otto would not survive without immediate attention. The odour of infection emanating from the damaged knee was potent. Raw tissue had started to turn black.

Nearing Brussels, he found shelter in an abandoned house and released the mule to graze in the yard behind. He left Otto shivering under a mound of blankets on one of the beds, hid the wagon under debris, and set off in search of medical aid.

A few blocks away, he found a hospital, but was dismayed at the traffic of medical staff, military medics, and injured soldiers shuffling in and out. He watched the pattern of the traffic and soon realized that a change of staff was underway.

Watching the retiring staff dissipate for the day, he noticed a young couple stepping together with locked arms, smiling and chatting easily.

He waited as they walked toward him and, when they turned the corner, he stepped in front of them, his Mauser revolver raised and threatening. Their hands jerked up in surrender and surprise.

"Are you a doctor?" demanded Gerhard.

The young man in a fitted grey-striped suit nodded, waving the black bag he carried in his left hand.

"And you?" he turned the muzzle of the revolver toward the young woman.

She stood unmoving but for the fluttering of the hem of her floral dress. In his angst, Gerhard failed to notice how her straw hat framed her face, its ribbons a corn-flower blue that reflected her eyes.

She responded in German, "I am his cousin. I am a nurse. You are injured. Can we help you?"

Waving the muzzle, Gerhard motioned them to walk ahead of him, guiding them into the house where Otto lay shivering and delirious.

The doctor tossed his hat on a nearby chair and knelt to Otto's aid, placing his bag on the floor next to the bed. "Your friend needs medical attention. Immediately. If he doesn't have that knee removed now, he will be dead before sunrise tomorrow."

"Do it, then," Gerhard insisted.

"We can't do it here," the young woman objected. "It isn't sanitary, and we have no instruments."

"He is not going to the hospital. We will not be taken as prisoners."

"But—"

Placing his hand on her shoulder, the doctor interrupted his cousin's protest. "Nora, he can't be moved. He's too weak. Here, take this." He efficiently wrote a note and handed it to her. "Run back to the hospital and collect the items I've listed. Come back as quickly as you can."

"But ... Pierre."

"Go!"

"Very well," she said, snatching the note and marching out the door.

Gerhard followed her to the door. In the street, she raced back to the hospital, one hand raised to hold her straw hat in place, the blue ribbons fluttering in her wake. When she was out of sight, Gerhard returned to the bedroom.

In his desperation, he felt compelled to trust the two strangers. Time passed slowly for him, as it had when he was in the crater, trying to staunch the flow of Otto's bright red blood.

"I'm sorry," he said to the doctor. "I don't mean to keep you from your home. But my friend was shot a week ago, and I can't let him die." Tears began to spill from Gerhard's eyes. "I couldn't save the others. I must save Otto. I must take him home."

The muzzle of the Mauser drooped as he swiped the tears from his face. He jerked it level again.

"No apology is necessary," the doctor responded, leaning against a wall. "Your

JERENA TOBIASEN

friend would be better off in the hospital, but I understand your concern. Nora will return shortly, and I will do what I can to help him." He pointed to a chair. "Why don't you rest for a moment, Captain? I'll need your help to secure your mate when Nora returns."

"I can't sit. It hurts too much," Gerhard mumbled, peering at the doctor under long, dark lashes. His cheeks pinked with embarrassment.

The doctor turned his gaze from Otto to Gerhard, and only then saw the dried blood on the back of Gerhard's coat and trousers, the rents in the fabric not visible because of the blood caked on the skin beneath.

"Let me have a look at that," he said, pushing the muzzle of the revolver out of the way and walking behind Gerhard. He probed the two lower wounds, and then the third one in Gerhard's arm. Gerhard jerked and winced, but made no sound.

"Shrapnel?" he asked.

Gerhard nodded. "I think the piece that hit my arm sliced straight through.

38

The pieces in my back and arse hurt most. Walking is difficult."

"I noticed your limp earlier. Now I understand why. I can dress your injuries. Neither piece of metal seems to be deeply embedded in the tissue. If you can handle a little more pain and discomfort, I should be able to dig them out before my cousin returns."

Pointing to a nearby chest of drawers, he invited Gerhard to remove his coat, drop his trousers, and lean into the chest for support.

"I'm going to clean the sites, remove the metal, and stitch you up. It won't be pleasant now, but you'll feel better in a few days. Do you think you can tolerate the pain?" he asked.

Gerhard nodded curtly.

"I'll have a look at that gash on your forehead, too. Headaches? Loss of vision?"

"Not so bad now," Gerhard winced in response to the doctor's probing fingers. "Headaches were bad for the first few days. My vision blurred then, too, but both seem to have alleviated."

"What about thought process? Are you feeling a little muddle-headed?"

"In the beginning, I did. Trying to find the things I needed to get Otto away from the fighting was a challenge. I couldn't think straight," Gerhard said.

"And now?" the doctor invited.

"Well ... I guess I'm thinking more clearly, but ... well, I suppose food might help sort that matter. I have three mouths to feed, and haven't been so fortunate to find ... enough," he finished, wondering whether there would ever be enough.

By the time Nora returned with the listed items, Gerhard had fastened his trousers and buttoned his coat, thankful that she had not witnessed his discomfiture.

Together, she and the doctor reassessed Otto's condition, positioned him for treatment, and set about removing his left knee and lower leg. Gerhard held his friend's left leg still, while Nora cradled Otto's head in her hands and spoke reassuringly into his unhearing ear.

The cousins stayed with the two soldiers long enough to satisfy themselves that they had done everything they could to help. They took their leave mid-afternoon and wished the soldiers a safe journey home. Otto's condition was stable, and Gerhard had instructions for his care, including directions to the nearest train station.

Gerhard thanked them both profusely for their kindness and apologized for using his revolver to coerce them. "Your kindness will always be remembered, Doctor ..." Gerhard paused, inviting the doctor to give his surname.

"Depage. Pierre Depage. It was my pleasure, Captain ..." pausing as Gerhard had done, waiting for a name.

"Gerhard Lange," he answered, extending his hand first to the doctor and then to Nora. "Thank you both."

Gerhard inhaled unexpectedly as his fingers folded around the softness of Nora's graceful hand. *Long fingers, like a pianist's,*

41

and her hair falls like a golden waterfall around her shoulders. Her eyes ...

Nora made a small squeaking sound in her throat and gently extracted her hand in that awkward way one does when removing a hand from a distasteful substance. She smiled at him nonetheless.

"Oh! My apologies, *Fraulein*." He dropped his hand, realizing he had held hers overlong. Nora lowered her gaze, blushing, but the smile remained.

Dr. Depage bent to retrieve his medical bag and hat, then placed his hand on Nora's back. "Come along, cousin; we must get home. I'm sure we're being missed, and we don't want anyone to worry."

"Of course!" Gerhard exclaimed, realizing the consequence of his actions.

The doctor placed his hand on Gerhard's arm. "No harm done, friend, but we should get home."

Nora distracted Gerhard from his apology when she placed the straw hat on her head once again.

Cornflower blue, he thought, escorting the young couple to the front of the abandoned house. He waited as they walked briskly to the corner of the intersection, where Nora glanced over her left shoulder. Then they rounded a corner and disappeared.

Gerhard chewed a ration of fresh bread and cheese that Nora had thought to bring with the supplies, his worry for Otto diminishing his appreciation of the fresh food.

He stowed the remainder for later, then he rested on the plank floor next to Otto, keeping watch over him until nightfall.

Otto's groan woke him, leaving him with a memory of pools of cornflower blue and peace—Nora's eyes. *If ever this war ends, I'll find those eyes again*, he promised himself.

The respite and food strengthened Gerhard. He harnessed the mule and loaded the cart with their rifles and ammunition, and the food and medical supplies provided by the Depage cousins.

Otto's fever had dropped. He was coherent when Gerhard explained that his lower left leg had been removed and it was time to move on.

"My boot. Must keep my boot. Your father warned ..." Otto mumbled, struggling with delirium.

Gerhard squeezed Otto's shoulder. "Sorry, brother. We did our best, but the boot didn't make it. Let it go. Vater will understand."

Otto cried out once as Gerhard lifted him to a standing position, wrapping Otto's left arm over his shoulder and holding it fast in his left hand. His right hand snaked around Otto's back and clutched his belt, holding him close.

Otto tried to help using his right leg for support, but quickly became a dead weight when he passed out.

Grateful that his friend was beyond pain for a few minutes, Gerhard dragged Otto the remaining distance to the cart and loaded him onto it as gently as he could.

Otto's face was pale with loss of blood and shock, looking more like the full moon than Gerhard would have liked.

He pulled the blankets gently over Otto to keep him warm, covering his face to block the bright moonlight.

Slipping his fingers through the mule's halter, Gerhard encouraged it to follow him into the night once again, and as they walked, he pondered his next move. The warmth of an evening breeze caressed his cheek. *It must be summer,* Gerhard marvelled, *and I need a bath.* His nose wrinkled in distaste. He was embarrassed to think that Nora had seen him so unkempt.

The train station was on the other side of town. Nora had provided clear directions as she drew, in her neat hand, a map on a scrap of paper taken from Dr. Depage's prescription pad. His ears yearned to hear more of the sweetness that escaped her lips, but the description was brief.

He had no need for a map, but took it as a remembrance. He felt for the pocket that held the map and let his hand rest there for a moment, thinking of Nora and her cornflower blue eyes.

Travel was slow. The streets were narrowed by debris, and the unevenness of the cobblestones jolted the cart. Otto moaned from time to time, but did not wake up. Gerhard was anxious to reach the train station and medical aid while Otto slept.

At the train station, he found personnel from the Wounded Transportation Section who inspected his wounds and Otto's amputation, and agreed that they could be removed to Germany by *Lazarettzug*. The hospital train would take them to the nearest *Reservelazaretten*, a German reserve hospital, for further monitoring and recovery.

"You won't be needing the mule, sir. We'll take care of it."

"Thanks," Gerhard said, tying the reins to a nearby post.

CHAPTER FIVE

Two orderlies moved Otto to a stretcher and carried him through the station with care. Gerhard limped behind, following them to the platform.

"You timed it well, Captain," one of the medics said. "The next *Lazarettzug* is scheduled to depart in twenty minutes."

Steam hissed along the tracks, and a whistle shrieked the train's imminent departure. "We're just finishing the loading. There's space for you both in the last car."

Hours later, Otto and Gerhard were taken to the nearest *Reservelazaretten* for reassessment and intermediate care. Orders were issued for Otto's relocation to a hospital closer to regimental headquarters in Dresden.

"You still have seepage from your wounds, Captain," noted a triage doctor on their arrival, "and you should be examined thoroughly to ensure all of the shrapnel has been removed. It's difficult to determine the extent of your injuries through all that filth!" he said, chuckling. "Once you've bathed, I'll have another look. In the meantime, I'm sending you to Dresden as well. We'll want you healed before you return to active duty."

"Yes, Doctor." Gerhard bashfully acknowledged the suggestion that he bathe, secretly glad that he was being sent to Dresden. *I need a reprieve from this hell!*

"By the way, did a field doctor perform Captain Schmidt's amputation?"

"No," Gerhard responded. "Doctor Pierre Depage performed it. In Brussels."

"Pierre Depage, you say? Son of Doctor Antoine Depage?"

Gerhard shrugged his lack of knowledge. "The name Depage means something to you?"

"Yes, yes. Antoine Depage is one of the best! I have no doubt Pierre Depage was taught well, if he is indeed the son of Doctor

Antoine Depage. Beautiful work, it is. Captain Schmidt is a lucky man. His wounds will heal well, in time. I can assure you"—the doctor emphasized his diagnosis with a nod—"those who've had amputations in the field were not always so lucky."

Before Otto was released from the hospital, he was fitted with crutches, giving him some independence and mobility. Within the week, they had clearance and orders. They would board the next *Lazarettzug* heading east to Dresden, where they would both be reassessed.

At the hospital in Dresden, Otto was detained overnight so that he could be fitted for an artificial limb.

Gerhard took advantage of the delay to report to regimental headquarters. He showed the order written by his commander and requested that he be allowed to return home for his convalescence and a short furlough.

The next day, he returned to the hospital, where he found a much-improved Otto.

When Gerhard entered Otto's room, Otto fluttered a sheet of paper at him. "I have orders to report to the hospital in Liegnitz," he said. "I can convalesce at home while I wait for an artificial limb." He smiled meekly at Gerhard, saying, "We're going home, brother."

The train ride was long, hot and dusty, but at least they were moving homeward. In Dresden, they transferred to another train that took them directly to Liegnitz.

When they finally arrived at the train station from which they had departed some two years earlier, Otto used his new crutches to hobble to a nearby bench, and Gerhard went off to find transport for the final stretch home.

It was quiet in the station. The sun was hinting at its decline in the late summer sky. The only person to be found in the station was the clerk at the ticket window.

"I'm sorry, sir. I'm just closing up," he apologized. "Heading home for dinner. And I'm sure you know it's rare to see a transport of any kind these days," he said, giving "fuel rations" as an excuse. "I do, however, have a bicycle. If you think the two of you can use it, you're welcome to it. It's a short walk home for me, anyway."

"What about the telephone? Perhaps I can call home?" Gerhard asked.

"Again, I'm sorry, sir. The telephone lines have been out for two days. A small forest fire just outside of town took out several poles and broke the line. Supposed to be repaired by tomorrow," the clerk replied, letting his earlier offer dangle.

"Then we'll borrow your bicycle with thanks," Gerhard said, relieved that Otto would not have to walk home on his crutches. "I'll bring it back tomorrow, if that's all right?"

"Take your time," the clerk said. "There's no urgency."

Otto balanced himself on the seat of the rusty, black bicycle, clutching his crutches across his lap to provide counter-weight and keep them clear of the spokes. With the other hand, he kept a firm hold of the belt cinched through Gerhard's trousers.

Gerhard pedalled them out of town, along the country roads toward the lake and home.

It was a lovely evening for a bicycle ride along country lanes, and they joked briefly that it would be better done with a pretty girl on the crossbar. The sun was warm on their backs, the air sweetened by ripening grain. Although evening birds twittered and chased insects recently hatched by the heat of the day, it was quiet; unnervingly quiet, so far away from the battle lines.

Otto broke the silence, startling Gerhard. "Do you remember when we were kids? Riding our bicycles everywhere. Fishing in the estate's lake. Our little sisters, Marie and Emma, trying to keep up with us. It was always Emma's idea to follow us, you know. She was sweet on you then, and still is."

"So you keep telling me," Gerhard said, expressing frustration at Otto's last comment. "If I had a pfennig for every time you've said that over the past fifteen years ..."

"Well, it's true. I think she's been in love with you from the time she could walk! Maybe even longer!" Otto's grin filled his face. "So, are you going to ask her to marry you?"

"Wha—?" Gerhard panted as he pedalled harder up a small rise in the dusty road. "For a guy as thin as you, you sure weigh a lot! Even minus that leg!"

"Emma. Are you going to ask her tonight?" The question hung on a sun passing its zenith.

"No. Not tonight. As soon as I get you billeted, I'm heading home. I need to see my family as much as you need yours."

"There! There it is." Otto pointed his crutches in the direction they travelled. His sudden movement sent the bicycle wobbling, and Gerhard struggled to recover his control.

More softly, almost in awe, Otto sighed. "Home."

Gerhard felt the stiffness drain from his friend's body.

"I never thought I'd see home again.

Danke, Kapitän," he said with sincerity, his eyes glassy with emotion, "for bringing me home."

"Nein. It is I who should be thanking you, for saving me from a lonely journey home." Gerhard responded, checking his emotions under a shaky grin. Of the ten young men who departed the station almost two years ago, only two were returning. *Such a loss, not only to me, but to their families and our community.*

The brown-stuccoed farmhouse trimmed in red brick and white window accents grew into view as Gerhard's legs pumped harder, faster. Before they could speak again, Gerhard was resting the bicycle against the farmhouse and helping his friend dismount onto his crutches.

A black-and-white cat sunning itself on a nearby window ledge rose, stretched, and mewed annoyance at them. Twitching its tail, it jumped into the soft earth below and scooted into a nearby field to be lost from view in a forest of corn stalks.

Otto balanced himself on his crutches, preparing to take the first step. Panting from the exertion, Gerhard leaned toward Otto to help him up two steps to the front door.

"Nein," Otto said harshly. The rigidity of his body conveyed his need for independence. More softly he added, "I need to learn to do this myself. May as well start now. Are you sure you won't come in for a bit?"

"Thanks. No. You go ahead. I'll come by in a couple of days."

"You might want to clean up a bit in the meantime. Maybe a steam bath to soak out the dirt. And shave the whiskers. If you're going to propose to my sister, you won't want to look like a hairy gorilla," Otto said, teasing him.

Gerhard embraced his friend and waited while he hobbled up the steps and turned the doorknob.

"Hello in the house! Anyone home?" Otto shouted. He flashed one last smile at Gerhard as a squeal of voices rose from inside and he clumsily closed the door behind him.

CHAPTER SIX

Gerhard mounted the rusty bicycle once again and pedalled it into the country road. Without the weight of Otto, the bicycle flew over the dusty road and his heart soared above it, knowing that before the sun set on the day he would be embraced by a family he had not seen since his last furlough, almost a year past.

He breathed deeply, appreciating the fragrance of a countryside he had once taken for granted. *Never again.* He closed his eyes against the brightness of the lowering sun. The piercing light created a kaleidoscope of shapes and colours on the inside of his eyelids.

The bicycle suddenly jumped when its front tire hit a stone protruding out of the rut in which it had rolled. Gerhard's attention jarred back to the road, and he laughed at his carelessness. He fought to regain control before his journey diverted to the ditch running alongside the road.

Puffs of dust broke softly in the path of the bicycle's tires. A small rodent darted across his path and into the ditch across the road, followed by the black-and-white cat that he had seen sunning itself on the window ledge.

Ahead, Gerhard spied the standard that marked him home: a square post, two metres tall, painted the bright yellow of the regimental coat of arms. He pedalled faster and took a tight left turn onto the drive that led up to the front of the manor house in which his family had lived for many decades.

He jammed the brakes and the bicycle skidded sideways. He dropped his foot to the gravel for balance and drank in the vision before him, sighing deeply. The white-stuccoed manor house stood nobly before him on its red brick pedestal, crowned by its red-tiled roof. *I'm home.*

Gerhard swung his lanky leg over the saddle and walked the old bicycle the remainder of the way to the front steps. He rested it against the house and pondered what was to come. Slowly, he took the stairs two at a time, pausing between the white pillars that framed the doorway.

Before he opened the heavy oak door, he reached above the lintel and put his hand on the Lange crest, feeling the grooves of the design press into his palm, his pulse defining the shape he knew so well.

"I've come home," he said to it. "I'm safe."

Then, as he had seen Otto do only minutes before, he put his hand on the knob and gently turned it until he heard the snick of the latch releasing. He stepped inside and closed the door quietly.

He stood still and listened, absorbing comforting sounds and smells. He felt the stress of the past months drain from him and searched for something inside that would make him normal again.

From the kitchen, Gerhard heard the voices of his mother and sister as they helped Cook clear away the dinner dishes. Red cabbage, potatoes and …

He sniffed again, dreaming of the possibilities. Beets. Bread. Farmer Schmidt's sausage. How long had it been since he had seen, let alone tasted, such delicacies?

A clink of glass. Liquid flowed, mingled with a low hum of a non-specific tune. He smiled and took the few steps needed to reach the study. His hand on the door, he gently pushed it in as he removed his cap. "Hello, Vater."

Although his voice was soft and low, it was enough to startle Michael Lange, who almost, but not quite, dropped the crystal brandy decanter. Michael spun around to see his son standing in the doorway.

"Gerhard! God be praised!" Michael replaced the decanter and rushed to greet his son. He held him at arm's length, drinking in the sight of the young man and noting the ravages of war on his face. "It's you! You're home!" He pulled his son into an embrace.

Gerhard welcomed his father's arms with the same ferocity.

"*Mutti.* Marie. Our boy has come home!" Michael shouted toward the kitchen. "Let me look at you again," he said, gently pressing his son's shoulders away from him. He blinked rapidly, hoping to recover his emotions before the women arrived. "Looks like you've had a rough go of it!"

Gerhard nodded.

"We haven't heard from you in so long. We were beginning to fear the worst," Michael said, leading Gerhard to the settee. "Sit. Sit. Have brandy with me."

Michael poured two glasses and handed one to Gerhard. Brandy fumes filled Gerhard's senses as the first sip burnt its way down the back of his parched throat.

"Gerhard!" chimed mother and sister as they appeared at the study doorway, their questions and exclamations creating a din of joy.

Gerhard rose to greet them. Each in turn welcomed him with hugs and kisses, reluctant to release him. Embracing each woman, he inhaled deeply the fragrance of home, wishing he could erase the deep worry lines marring their faces.

His mother, Anna, stepped back, reaching up to touch the mark that would scar his forehead and forever remind him of the horrors of war that resided in his brain. "Bend down," she said.

As he responded to her command, she stood on tiptoe to apply the time-honoured balm of a mother's kiss to his wounded pate.

Cook stood behind them, grinning from ear to ear and ringing her hands in her apron. "Welcome home, young master!" She stepped forward in her turn and hugged him briskly. Suddenly embarrassed, she retreated to the kitchen, dashing an errant tear from her cheek.

"Enough from the three of you!" Michael boomed. "I'm sure Gerhard will have much to tell, but first, let him rest." Turning to Gerhard, he suggested, "Finish your brandy, and then you can clean up.

"In the meantime," he said, taking control of the moment, "perhaps you women can find some food for our boy? If we don't get something wholesome into him quickly, his ribs will stick to his backbone."

"Yes, yes. Of course," Anna said. "Marie, come. Set a place at the table. Cook and I will bring some food. Gerhard, we're so glad to have you home." Looking about her, she asked, "Where's your kit? Vater can take it up to your room."

"I have no kit, Mutti. What you see is all I have," he said, dismissing any further discussion on the matter.

"Look Vater!" Gerhard slouched wearily into the black, leather armchair worn with decades of use, raised his legs, and flexed his dusty boots. "I kept my boots, as you ordered. They're a bit worn, but they've carried me a long way." The heels of the well-used boots were worn thin enough to expose the horseshoe shape below, and several hob nails were missing from the soles.

"They're filthy!" Marie exclaimed.

"Ah! Mutti. I apologize." Gerhard said, looking abashed. "I should have removed my boots at the door. Too long in the field, I'm afraid."

"I'll help you." Marie sprinted from behind her mother and bent to pull a boot. Gerhard flexed his foot to help her free it, and she giggled as she fell backward into her father's waiting arms.

She giggled again as her loose, straw-coloured hair flipped forward and covered her face. She handed the boot to her father, brushed her hair from her eyes, and turned back to remove the boot's mate.

Gerhard flexed his feet, great toes protruding from the ends of the worn socks, a contrast to the perfection of the old Spanish painting that hung above him. As he did so, his father examined the well-used boots.

"We'll have these repaired before you report for duty again," Michael said matter-of-factly. "You'll also need new kit, and some better stockings." He raised an eyebrow to the great toes. "I'm glad, at least, that you heeded the warning to keep your wits about you." His look was solemn.

Gerhard lowered his eyes to his lap, remembering the friends he had left behind, and Otto's ruined leg. When he raised his eyes to meet his father's, he nodded. "Yes, Vater. I did my best, but sometimes I wonder whether my best was good enough."

Marie waved her hand in front of her nose. "Phew! I think something else needs attention, too. I'll run you a hot bath, *Bruder*, as soon as you've eaten."

"Thank you, *Schwester*." He dipped his head formally. "I'd appreciate that … very much. It's been a while since I had a soak in hot water."

Gerhard's mother extended her hand to him, beckoning him to follow her into the dining room.

"Mutti, I should change first. I'm too dirty."

"No, Son; sometimes we have to make exceptions, and I think today is one of those occasions." She linked her arm through his and held it tight, walking him into the dining room. Marie helpfully pulled his chair out.

"I feel like royalty!" he said, embarrassed to find himself the centre of attention.

"You are today, Son. Eat now. After your bath, we can visit more, if you're not too tired." Mother, father, and sister each pulled out a chair opposite him.

As Cook set a plate of food in front of him, he surveyed the dining room of his family home. "Nothing's changed," he muttered to himself.

The carved mahogany buffet and hutch stood where they had been since before he was born. Both were laden with porcelain dishes, silverware, and serving dishes inherited from previous generations of the Lange family. The table, large enough to seat sixteen, had been collapsed to host six. Its heavy, carved legs and high-back chairs grounded the room.

I need grounding, he realized.

"I'm sorry, young master," Cook said.

"It is not the meal we would like to serve for you, but we have food rationing."

Gerhard patted her withdrawing hand with reassurance. "It's a meal for a very tired and appreciative monarch," he joked, then solemnly added, "And don't apologize. At least it's cooked! We've had little to eat for months, and what we found was either shrivelled, weather-dried, rotten, or unfit for a dog. This is manna from heaven, Cook!"

Cook clapped her hands together, expressing delight that he appreciated so humble a meal, and returned to the kitchen.

A fork-full of red cabbage reached his lips before he lowered it again, licking his lips and inhaling the buttery aroma.

"I'm sorry," he said to his attending audience, "I am so hungry and have eaten so poorly for a very long time. While I savour this wonderful feast, why don't you tell me what's been happening around here, instead of just staring at me."

The four laughed together, and, as he ate

his meal, they took turns telling him what had happened during his absence.

True to her word, Marie reluctantly excused herself from the table to run a hot bath for Gerhard when Cook brought a plate of sweet biscuits.

"We have no coffee or tea today. Brandy for all, sir?" she asked, deferring to Michael.

"Sherry for me, please, Cook," Anna added to Michael's nod.

"Just a small shot for me. Marie's running my hot bath," Gerhard said as his pushed his plate away. "That meal was the best I've eaten since my last furlough. When was that?"

Before he could calculate, Cook muttered aloud, "Ten months and nine days ago, give or take a few hours," then disappeared into the kitchen with his soiled plate and cutlery.

A few minutes later, she returned with a silver tray of crystal glasses and two decanters, one of a deep-red Spanish sherry, and the other of amber French brandy, all seated on a starched, white lace doily.

Michael poured the liquor and passed glasses to his wife and his son. Gerhard pushed his chair away from the table, far enough to be able to rub his belly with gratitude. He dusted biscuit crumbs from his chin. "Thank you, Cook," he said toasting her meal with his raised glass.

"Pah!" she spat, "wasn't enough for a hungry soldier," and scooted from the room again.

"It was perfect!" Gerhard said, raising his voice loud enough to follow her.

Turning to his parents, he continued. "I've eaten so little for so long. And, I've learnt through experience that it doesn't pay to eat too much or too fast when a belly hasn't had food in it for a while. I have seen many horrible things and heard the stories. Some of the city boys were so hungry that they mixed sawdust in their food to fill their bellies. Sawdust! Can you imagine what that would do to the gut! How desperate they must have been.

"I'm fortunate to have grown up in the country. I scrounged for food. It wasn't always the best, but it was better than sawdust!" Gerhard's calm voice was betrayed by the anger and frustration bubbling through his words.

He stood abruptly. "I should stop now." He made a slight bow toward his parents and excused himself.

Michael and Anna shared owl-like expressions of surprise at Gerhard's abrupt departure.

"War is a nasty business, as you well know, my dear." Michael patted Anna's delicate hand, saying, "I will speak with Gerhard tomorrow and see what I can do to help him."

He leaned toward her and kissed her cheek, then took her hand and escorted her out of the dining room.

CHAPTER SEVEN

"Sis?" Gerhard called when he reached the upper level of the manor house and walked down the carpeted hall.

"In here!" Marie answered from the bathroom.

"Ah. Good. I was afraid I'd be too late, and the water would be cold."

"No. See, the steam still rises from the water." Marie closed the taps and brushed wilting strands of hair off her face as she turned toward Gerhard. "I've left just enough space for you to fill the tub, but not overflow onto the floor. I've even warmed the towels for you." She pointed to a pile of towels on a nearby chair.

"I am so glad you've come home safe," she said, reaching up to caress his furred cheek with the back of her fingers, still damp from testing the water. "I think you know what to do next," she said, teasing him. He smiled his thanks at her and watched her close the door, leaving him alone for the first time since his arrival.

Before he heard the final snick of closure, the door popped open again, and Marie peeked in. "Will we see you downstairs again this evening?"

Gerhard felt a fatigue in his bones. "Do me a favour, sis? Tell them I'm too tired. I'd like to go straight to bed."

"Of course! Sleep well, my brother. We'll see you in the morning," Marie responded before she scooted through the door and hugged him hard. "I'm so glad you've come home," she whispered, then made a hasty departure, leaving her brother in peace.

Gerhard inhaled deeply, clearing his senses. The humidity permeated his clothes as he peeled them off.

In the mirror hanging on the back of the door, he noted his thin reflection. "Scrawny" was the word that came to mind. He was confident that a few weeks of field work and good food would make his body whole again, but he wondered about the rest of him.

Will I ever be truly normal again? Can I return to the front yet again? Perhaps Otto was right. Maybe Emma is the one to help me mend my broken spirit.

He dipped a toe into the water and withdrew it quickly. The heat was a welcome distraction. He tried again, slowly immersing one foot into the water until it burnt up his calf. He shifted his weight into the tub and repeated the same process with his other foot until the burning passed, and he watched small bubbles form and depart from the dark hairs on his legs.

He braced himself, lowering his body into the tub. He knew the next part would not be pleasant. After all, lower extremities were not meant to be boiled. He also knew that once he was seated, the worst would be over.

He felt a shiver run through his body as his skin prickled, adjusting to the extreme temperature. Leaning back, he closed his eyes and let the heat invade his weariness, soothing his body and soul.

Gerhard inhaled the steam once more, trying to detect the scent that filled the room. Opening his eyes, he spied a jar of lavender-coloured bath salts and knew it to be one of Marie's creations.

Marie had a knack for making fragrances from ingredients she sourced near the manor. She found pleasure in experimenting with soaps and candles, even biscuits and cakes. She used roses, rosemary, basil, and thyme. Whatever piqued her curiosity. He knew she enjoyed experimenting.

The bath salts tickled at his body and the lavender made him drowsy. Gerhard closed his eyes again and surrendered to the bath.

His thoughts returned to Emma. *She is pretty, pleasant and capable. Could I make her happy? Would she accept a proposal, if I made one?*

The last time he and Otto had been home on furlough, they had worked in the fields. She had brought them a basket lunch.

They had spread a blanket under a tree near the stream, and shared bread and sausage.

In the months that they had been away fighting, her body had changed, and that day he had noticed. She was still slender and youthful, but she had acquired the graceful curves of a woman.

His thoughts took a side-step, recalling that Marie had changed, too. *She is no longer the little girl I swung in the hallway on the day my orders arrived.*

Reclaiming his thoughts, he remembered the picnic with Emma and Otto under the gnarled sycamore tree by the stream. Emma had set out the food and dishes as if she were the lady of a manor. Otto and Gerhard had said little. While they helped set out the meal, she had filled the silence by telling them how she had prepared it.

Dipping her chin, she retrieved items from the basket, and looked up at him through the chestnut veil of her hair, her hazel eyes shy and uncertain. He had wanted to hook his fingers around that veil and expose her creamy cheek. His fingers had twitched, resisting the impulse.

The water cooled around Gerhard while his memories warmed with visions of Emma. His body began to simmer with desire.

Abruptly, he sat up, smacking the water with the flat of his hands, causing water to splash over the side of the tub.

This is crazy. I have never had an intelligent conversation with her. How could I even think of marriage when I don't know who she is? Desire is not enough! Fool! You'll never know her unless you make the effort. And how will she handle your nightmares? You can't even do that!

He moaned at his stupidity, slapping his forehead for emphasis, and winced painfully from the impact to his healing head wound. He slid under the water trying to clear his mind.

Pools of cornflower blue and peace invaded his musings. *Nora! Oh, God, I must find Nora first! I could never make an offer to Emma so long as I have thoughts of Nora spinning in my head.* His pulse raced recalling their encounter, her soft voice, her confidence, and her unusual blue eyes. He shot upright, out of the cooling water.

Gerhard pulled the plug and let the water drain from the tub. A silty residue collected on the flat of the porcelain. Goosebumps formed on his flesh when he stood to reach for a towel.

He briskly dried himself and resolved to spend more time with Emma. *In the meantime, I'll write to Doctor Depage and enquire about Nora.*

CHAPTER EIGHT

Someone had opened the bedroom window and turned back the covers of Gerhard's bed. The undrawn curtains provided a lacy contrast to the night's blackness. The sound of chirping insects wafted in on the lazy breeze, carrying the fragrance of ripening fields, mowed grass, the honey scent of linden trees in bloom, Marie's roses, and the herb garden.

An irritating buzz stilled by his ear. He smacked the side of his head hard enough to make his ear ring. *Why so hard?* He lowered his hand and scrutinized the flattened mosquito carcass.

Annoyed at its nuisance, he dashed it into the damp towel still wrapped around his waist. He loosened the towel and tossed it unceremoniously onto the floor before falling into his bed.

He laid there, the sound of silence screaming in his ears. He felt lost, out of place. Exasperated, he rolled his head to the left and his body followed, curling into the security of a foetal pose. The power of the hot bath finally overcame him, and he slept.

Until he dreamt of Emma, fresh and natural, of trees and fields and laughter. Laugher changed to moaning and blood, stale air, white gauze, and Nora, then eyes—a pair of eyes, one hazel and one cornflower blue.

"The face is damaged. The head will have to come off. Put him over there, and I'll attend to him shortly." The index finger of a blood-soaked hand holding a saw clogged with bits of pale flesh pointed to an empty table. The table was draped in white cloth and stained with drying blood.

Gerhard felt the strong hands of orderlies holding his arms fast and dragging him toward the table. He looked about the room, realizing it was not really a room. It was a corridor. A dimly-lit hospital corridor.

As the orderlies dragged him toward the table indicated by the doctor's gory hand, they passed several other tables. One had legs, neatly placed side-by-side, some wearing the owner's boot, others naked, pale blue, and lifeless. Otto's mangled knee and lower left leg sat at the end of the row, dressed in Michael's special-order boot.

Another table had rows of arms, some still encircled with a wrist watch, again neatly placed: all pale blue and lifeless.

A hand twitched, displaying its manicured nails and a wedding ring. Another curled into a fist. The table nearest his destination held a row of heads, some wearing helmets, others merely bone, and yet others with flesh and eyeballs dangling, missing ears or hair.

"My eye. Have you seen my eye?" torn lips asked.

Exposed light bulbs dangled overhead, humming with menace.

Gerhard licked his lips, tasting metallic red.

"That's right. Hoist him on the table. One

of you will have to hold his shoulders down tight. You take his head. Hold it firm." The doctor's eyes focussed on Gerhard's neck, and the bloody saw lowered in slow motion.

In terror, Gerhard writhed against the hands that held him firm. "Shush now," the doctor said, "Everything will be all right."

He struggled against his restraints, trying to scream, trying to make them understand. *Don't take my head,* he wanted to scream, but the words would not come.

The blade of the saw poked into tender skin. Gerhard felt the prick and rake of jagged teeth on the exposed flesh of his hyperextended neck. He screamed in a soundless dream-voice.

"Gerhard, Gerhard. Wake up, son! Wake up." Michael urged. He was kneeling at the side of the bed, gently shaking Gerhard's shoulders.

Gerhard's eyes shot open, unseeing. "Nein!" he bellowed, struggling against his father's hands and panting in fear. "Nein! Not my head!"

He sat up abruptly, flailing his arms in defence. Awareness became shock when he realized where he was. "Vater!" He whispered, grasping his father's arms to anchor his emotions.

"Shush now. Everything will be all right." Michael murmured, pulling his son into his arms. "It's all right, son. It's just a dream." Michael's hand caressed the back of Gerhard's head. "It's all right. I have you. It's Vater." Familiar words penetrated Gerhard's fear-filled fog.

With his free hand, Michael rubbed Gerhard's back.

"You used to do this when I was a small boy waking from a nightmare," Gerhard mumbled into his father's chest.

"I did, indeed," Michael said. "Then, you had the dreams of a small boy. Now, you have nightmares no man should have."

Over his shoulder, Michael saw his wife and daughter standing in the doorway, hair dishevelled from sleep, faces contorted in worry. He twitched his head enough for

Anna to understand that they should leave. Anna turned Marie away from the door and closed it. The snick of the latch confirmed the men were alone.

❖

Anna had long since come to terms with unexpected screams interrupting her slumber. Together, she and Michael had shared his horrors and worked through them. When she heard Gerhard's screams, Anna encouraged Michael to respond.

"You were the one he looked up to as a boy. You saved him from his nightmares then. You must go to him now," she said. "If you need me, I'll be right behind you."

They hurried along the hallway to Gerhard's room. Marie joined them at the door, and Anna restrained her when Michael entered the room.

"What is it?" Marie whispered.

Anna wrapped her arm around Marie's shoulder and turned her away from the room. Closing the door, she said, "Gerhard's had a nightmare. Your father knows how to help.

82

Let us leave them. Go back to bed now." She led Marie back to her room and saw her safely into bed, then returned to her own slumber, knowing that her son was in safe hands.

Gerhard inhaled the scent of his father, remembering the comfort he had drawn from that smell as a small boy. He finally pushed away, sobbing and gulping for air. He raised his hand to his neck, fingers probing for injury. His panting slowed. He wanted to let the weight of his fear rest against his father's powerful chest and feel safe. For a moment, at least. Until the nightmare returned.

"Why don't we go down for a brandy," Michael suggested, rising from the side of the bed, rumpling Gerhard's dream-soaked hair as he did so. "We can talk about the preparations for the harvest."

"That's a good idea. Perhaps the brandy will slow my heart." With shaking hands, Gerhard reached for the brown, silk robe he had strewn on the bed earlier.

"Come then," said Michael, leading the way out of the room.

Gerhard followed Michael down the carpeted oak staircase and into the study, where his father poured brandy into two crystal glasses. With the lighting of only one dim lamp, the crystal's life was dead to the eye.

"I'm sorry," Gerhard whispered, accepting the glass his father proffered. "I didn't mean to wake everyone. I suppose my screaming was frightful."

"Better here than on a battlefield," Michael said. "You mustn't worry about the others. They have no idea what you've been through."

Gerhard nodded, watching the dull, amber liquid roll in his glass. "You were always quick to rescue me from my nightmares when I was a child, and you haven't lost your touch." Sheepishly, he grinned, trying to make light of the darkness lodged in his soul.

"Do you want to talk about it?" Michael asked.

"I can't. Not now," Gerhard whispered, as if the sound of his voice might wake the demons again.

"In time then, son. It's important to talk about your dreams. Sharing the horror is a step toward healing," Michael said. "I know. I still have memories of Africa. They never leave."

His eyes rose to the ceiling and he was quiet for a moment, as if he were recalling past struggles with his own demons. "I've learnt to manage mine, and I believe I can help you put your memories in a place where they won't hurt you anymore, if you'd like."

"Thank you, Vater. I was so focussed on my men, and then Otto and getting him home. I need to find me first. I just need a little time."

Gerhard and Michael returned to their beds and slept fitfully for the hours remaining till sunrise. They shared a silent breakfast, interrupted with a brief discussion of work to be done that day.

CHAPTER NINE

"Today will be a hot one," Michael said as they walked toward a blue farm truck. "We'll drive out to the north field. I'm confident that Herr Schmidt will welcome the help."

As they climbed into the truck, Gerhard responded, "Looks like it was a good growing season this year. The harvest will be plentiful."

Michael nodded, assessing the sky as he did so. "It's muggy. See how the clouds are rolling; I wouldn't be surprised if we have a batch of thunder storms this week."

Otto was already in the field supervising the temporary workers, freeing his father to lend a hand with the harvesting. Four more hands were welcomed.

"I hope we get this field in before the rain comes," Farmer Schmidt responded

86

to comments of rain and thunderstorms. "We're almost finished. I'd hate to leave good crops in the ground. People need food. And, of course," he said, grinning, "we can use the income."

After a day of backbreaking labour, Michael and Gerhard returned to the manor more relaxed than when they had set out. They bathed to remove the residue of grit and grain, then joined the women in the dining room for supper. Conversation bantered during the meal, and no one spoke of screams in the night.

The heat of the day lasted into the evening. As night settled in, the first flashes of lightning streaked the blackening sky. Clouds roiled, covering the brightness of the moon, then releasing it again.

After the laborious day in the fields and another of Marie's hot baths, Gerhard readily fell into a deep sleep.

In the early hours of the morning, Gerhard awoke with a start. As he lay still, waiting for his pounding heart to slow, he cracked an eyelid and watched the lace curtains that framed the open window stretch ghostly fingers deep into his room.

The wind picked up, and the curtains thrashed. Lightning flashed and sliced through churning clouds. He heard plops of rain hit the dry road and felt the temperature drop.

Gerhard rolled onto his side and drew the bed covers over his shoulders. As he drifted back to sleep, he was aware of the pinging of rain pellets on the tiled roof and the boom, boom of thunder following close on the heels of crackling lightning.

Cold permeated through the damp in his clothes. Gerhard shivered, chilled to the bone.

They were lying in mud, waiting for the fog to lift, but the fog hung heavy over the entire field. The occasional word drifted clearly on the churning mist, some English, a cry of pain—French—a Deutsch curse. Three men to his left, two to his right. The others were there, but lost in the white weight that pressed down upon them.

High-pitched whistles, flares of blinding light, and the rumbling of the earth beneath them. Screams, pain, silence. Not even a bird twittered. Moaning and crying.

"*Mutti?*

"*Mutti, bist du das?*

"*Mutti, bitte hilf mir.*"

Detached pleas crying for a mother's help. Pleas of the dying.

The fog lifted, teasing visibility, revealing bodies and mangled parts. It lowered again, covering them all in a thick death shroud, sparing them from the vulgarity of war for a few blessed moments.

"Peter! Kirk! Mathias! *Wo seid ihr*? I can't see you. Paul, where are you?" Gerhard peered through the fog, brushing it away without success. A rolling helmet bumped his shoulder, as if in answer to his questions. Impatient, he pushed it away. Paul's empty eyes stared past him. "Paul! Nein!"

The fog shifted again, swirling, lifting,

revealing. *The mud – it's too thick. I can't move. I'm stuck.*

"No! No!" he screamed, "Dead! All Dead!"

⚜

Gerhard writhed in his bed, the sheets drenched in anxious sweat, tangling and restricting his limbs. He swam through mud, searching for his mates.

Michael burst through Gerhard's door for a second night and dropped to his knees at his son's side. "Gerhard!" he snapped, shaking him. "Gerhard! Wake up!" Gerhard flailed his arms, trying to break away, gasping and crying, feeling overwhelming grief.

"Villy!" Gerhard issued one last plaintive cry, and opened his eyes, panting. "Vater! What is it?" his distant voice muttered.

"You were dreaming again."

Gerhard stopped struggling and surrendered to the stability of his father's hands. "Vater! They are all dead. My men, my mates, they are all gone! We ran together like wolf pups when we were children. We pretended

90

to be soldiers in the Kaiser's army. We were just boys!"

Michael's crinkled face wore an expression of understanding.

"But we're no longer those young boys." Gerhard scrubbed his head, trying to find clarity. "They're all dead now, except Otto, and he's crippled. And my head is all messed up," he said, sighing forlornly.

"It's all right, son. You're home. You're safe," Michael murmured again. "Take your time. Let it go."

Gerhard's panting began to subside.

"It's a memory. Your friends are safe now, and no harm will ever come to them again."

Silence settled in the room. Gerhard's calm returned.

"Shall we find that brandy?" Michael asked.

Gerhard nodded and swung his feet to the floor. "I need to wash my face first. I can still see them, dead in the field."

"Yes, of course. Come down when you're ready."

CHAPTER TEN

For the remainder of his furlough, Gerhard and his father worked in the fields, assisting with the fall harvest. Labour was in short supply. Most capable farmhands had enlisted in the war effort and had left long ago. Many women and older children had volunteered to help, including those from nearby towns. Otto assisted where he could, often supervising the townsfolk.

"Looks like Farmer Schmidt will complete the harvest before an early frost can do any damage." Gerhard stood with his hands on his hips, observing the training of volunteers and the results of a day's hard labour.

"Yes," replied Michael. "The volunteers have come each year, and offered what they can, but their time is limited, too. They have their own business to tend, but understand that we must get the crops in, processed, and shipped. The boys at the front need to be fed."

"I, for one, am grateful for their effort. I know what it is to have to fight, hearing the growl of an empty stomach drowned out by mortar fire. We need sustenance—decent food. Hunger plays havoc with mind and body."

"Well, I think we're done here for the day," Michael said, slapping Gerhard on the back affectionately. A plume of dust exploded from his son's shirt. "Let's go investigate what magic Cook has managed for lunch, shall we?"

"I think we'd better wash up first, Vater. She won't appreciate our tracking muck through the house, let alone the dirt under our nails."

"And the straw in your hair! What were you doing in the barn, anyway—wrestling one of the milking cows?"

Gerhard ran his fingers through his hair, looking sheepish. "No, Vater, Emma sur-prised me when I went to fetch the tractor gear. She tried to stuff a handful of straw down the neck of my shirt."

"She's a nice girl, Gerhard. Don't keep her waiting." Michael's voice was deep and encouraging.

"I know, but … I just don't feel I can offer anything good to her. My head is so messed up. Every time I close my eyes, I see … things. Things no one should ever have to see.

"I shouldn't admit this, but I'm glad I don't have to go back to the fighting just now. I don't like the idea of paperwork, though. Hopefully, I can help with training. You know, give the new recruits better survival skills."

"I'll speak to Depot. See if we can't use some of your experiences, as you say, to better prepare the new recruits," Michael suggested.

"Thanks. I worry that folks—Emma—will think me a coward. I wouldn't dare repeat my feelings to anyone but you," Gerhard mumbled.

"Come along. We can talk more after lunch," Michael said. Together, they waved good-bye to Farmer Schmidt and Otto, and set off home.

"I think I'm ready to talk, Vater, if you don't mind listening."

"Good, good. We'll have a drink in the study after we've eaten, shall we?"

A cloud of worry and fear passed over Gerhard's eyes. He nodded agreement, and they walked on in silence.

After lunch, father and son retired to the old study. Michael poured two glasses of brandy and handed one to Gerhard.

"It's a little early," Michael said, chortling, "but I thought some false fortification might be helpful."

Gerhard accepted the glass, indicating his thanks, and took a small sip. He held the amber liquid in his mouth and felt its warmth. Its vapours wafted through his sinuses. Slowly, it sweetened, and he swallowed the mixture of brandy and saliva. He lowered himself into an armchair, feeling the familiarity of the room cocoon him in comfort.

"I don't know where to begin," he said, pausing to collect himself. "We were so naïve. We believed we would win the war in a few months, then come home to tell a story of great adventure. Instead, I come home empty-handed, but for Otto. Oh, God! Otto." He moaned, jamming his fingers through his hair and dropping his face into his hands. "I failed them all."

"Why don't you start at the beginning," Michael said invitingly.

Gerhard sighed and slumped deeper into the leather chair, hair spiked from the finger-combing. He took another sip of the brandy and started from the beginning.

He spoke of bright-eyed, eager young boys who believed they would win the Kaiser's war and return home as heroes. He spoke of the first forays, the first injured, the first death. His words painted pictures of carnage and piercing noise; of chaos, screams and silence; of loss and emptiness; of failure.

"We had no time to stop and mourn, not even to bury our own dead. There were others for that task. We had to keep moving. Such loss of life." He shook his head, eyes hollow, remembering. He sipped again.

"One day the landscape was pristine and tranquil. The next day—pockmarked and mucky with death. Blood was everywhere, body parts—human and animal. Fathers, husbands, sons, brothers, and cousins." His head rolled from side to side, tears traced down the line of his nose to drip from his chin.

"We worried for the ones left behind— our families. We hoped that if we fought hard, maybe someone else would fight just as hard to keep our families safe. We lost sight of the Kaiser's plan and focussed only on the ones we loved. We fought to keep our homes safe. The Kaiser be damned!" Gerhard spat his last words.

✣

Michael sat in the worn chair opposite his son, listening, imagining the words that his son spoke and remembering his own experiences as a young man in Africa: a different battle, but the same sounds and smells, and similar fears. He sipped his brandy and encouraged his son to paint the pictures.

Hours passed. Michael noticed fatigue begin to overtake Gerhard, the fatigue one feels after the release of burdensome emotion. The glasses were empty. Michael raised the decanter, offering the last of the brandy.

Gerhard shook his head, "Nein, danke. What time is it?"

"Four o'clock." Michael answered, looking at the carriage clock on the mantelpiece.

"I'm exhausted, and I'm feeling the effects of a little too much brandy. Would you mind if I rested a bit before Cook calls us for dinner?"

"Not at all. Rest now. You have been very brave to tell your story. Many can't. When you return to Depot, perhaps you will seek help from one more qualified than me. You could set a good example for others, if you're up to it."

"I'll think about it." Gerhard rose from the chair, setting his empty glass next to the decanter. He drew himself to his full height, straightened his shoulders, and saluted his father. "Thank you, sir. Perhaps I might sleep now."

Michael watched his son leave the study, admiring him for his determination to hold his bearing, despite the pain.

"You sleep," he said to his son. "I'll take this watch."

CHAPTER ELEVEN

Gerhard's combined medical leave and furlough was running out. He would have to report to Depot soon, but first he wanted to talk with Otto.

In response to his suggestion that they escape the day's heat the following afternoon, Otto invited him for refreshments in the garden.

"How are you managing, Otto?"

"I suppose I can give you two answers," Otto said. They were sitting on a worn, wooden bench under the shade of the ancient oak tree behind the farmhouse. It was a particularly warm September day, and the heat of the morning left them welcoming the cool shade and the cellar-chilled ale.

Otto took a long draft from the cool bottle. "Aaah! Now that's better." He grinned at Gerhard, the same grin he always had when he was about to tell a story.

"Well … in the first instance, I am happy to be home. Happy to know that I can stay home. I am not expected to report to Depot for months yet: not until the New Year, at least. The artificial limb won't be ready for a few more weeks—they're short on parts and material. And my family is very helpful and understanding. For the most part." He took a swig of the ale.

"I had a bit of a set-to with them a few days after we returned home. They were treating me like an invalid!"

Gerhard raised an eyebrow, expressing his amazement.

"I finally had to tell them, 'Look! This is the way of it. I have one leg. But I'm still normal. I'm capable, and my brain works reasonably well,'" he said, snickering. "'So, don't treat me like anything less.' That seemed to help. They give me space now, and let me fail as I find a new way of doing things."

"Good for you for standing your ground," Gerhard said, then realized his inadvertent pun. "Sorry, I …" Gerhard sheepishly lowered his eyes, embarrassed at his careless words.

Otto grinned, raising his hand to sever his friend's apology before continuing. "Those issues are small. It's the rest that's more of a problem."

Gerhard sat listening.

Otto took another long draft and let the bottle dangle next to his knee. "Do you …? That is … how?" Otto raked his fingers through his white-blond hair and scratched the top of his head while he searched for the desired words. "It's the dreams, you see. Or, rather, the nightmares. I wake up in a cold sweat, screaming. I'm scaring the hell out of my mother and sister!"

He slumped, as if relieved to have finally released the words. "At least Papa understands. And he's been of some help. But. I don't know. Do you think they will ever stop? The nightmares?"

"I don't know, Otto. I have nightmares, too. Cold sweats and screaming are part of it. And we aren't the only ones. Mutti says

Vater still has nightmares, but they've lessened over the years. His nightmares aren't as frequent, and they don't seem to be as detailed. But he still has them."

He sipped his beer. "Vater says talking about it helps, but I wonder. We talked for a long time yesterday afternoon. I even slept for a few hours before dinner—without dreams. But, Mutti told me this morning that Vater had nightmares last night. I'm certain that his dreams were triggered by our discussion in the afternoon."

"Probably," Otto said.

"Vater says that when we return to Depot next week, he is going to investigate whether there's some way to get help for the boys returning. And I'm going to ask whether we can provide preventative training, in addition to the usual stuff taught during boot-camp. Knowing what to expect and how to anticipate the unexpected might go a long way to keeping more recruits alive. Know what I mean?"

"Great ideas! Maybe I can help with

the extra training. They might listen to me when they see what can happen if you don't pay attention," Otto mumbled.

"Don't say that! There is no way you could have known a sniper was so close."

"I know." Otto's mind seemed to wander for a moment. "Don't forget smells! Your father needs to include smells. Don't they bother you?"

"Absolutely! I will tell him. It's amazing how a memory floods into my mind with the most innocent of smells, or a sound, even," Gerhard said.

"I can't go near the shed when father is butchering a pig. The smell and the bits of raw flesh make me gag." Otto continued. "Not that he butchers a lot of pigs, these days. But he did kill one recently in preparation for the harvest. All of the volunteers will be well-fed for their efforts."

"Ha! That's probably why they volunteer," Gerhard said. "They'll be paid with a ration of meat! How is it going, by the way? The harvest celebrations, I mean."

The subject safely changed, the young men talked on. Otto planned to help his father oversee the preparations for the harvest celebration. Everyone from the manor would help, too, except for Gerhard, who would be at Depot.

"If I can get any time off, I'll come back to help."

"Don't worry. We can manage. Just make sure you're back in time for the party." They sat quietly for a moment. A fly buzzed lazily around the mouth of Gerhard's ale bottle.

"Hey! What about Emma? You've been home for weeks now, and you've said nothing to her. You only come to the farm with your father, and you don't spend much time with her. How can you propose, if you don't talk to her?" Otto asked.

Gerhard jumped to his feet, kicking over his empty bottle. It wobbled, then stilled. He stuffed his hands in his pockets and paced impatiently in front of the bench. Head down, searching for words, he said, "Otto, I can't talk to her right now. My head is so messed up. I can't make promises that I can't keep. Do you understand what I mean?"

Otto upended his ale bottle and poured the last drip onto his extended tongue. Dancing between the oak leaves above, sunlight flickered across his tanned face. He blew into the mouth of the bottle, making a long tooting sound, like they had done as boys. He grinned again. "I do. But I'm not certain she will. She's been expecting something."

"Can you help me? Can you say something to her, so she understands my reluctance?" Gerhard asked.

"I don't know, but I'll try. Maybe on your next furlough?" Otto asked hopefully.

"I'm not coming home on my next furlough, so it will be a while." *There! I've said it. Otto will understand that I need time to heal. But, there's something else I need, too. I need to peer into those pools of cornflower blue and peace before I make promises to anyone.*

"Not coming home? But where will you go? There's no place else to go, these days."

"I need to go west for a bit."

"Oh, I get it." Otto said.

Gerhard swung to face Otto with a questioning look. *Does Otto suspect?*

"You want to see if you can go back to the conflict," Otto clarified.

Gerhard hesitated, searching for a response. "Sure. That's exactly it." *Well, I am going west, into chaos, am I not?*

The first days after reporting to Depot reminded Gerhard of his first days at the military school when he was a boy. Time was spent on introductions and orientation, meeting with commanders, and receiving orders.

Some offices and meeting rooms were in the main building, where senior officers and their staff worked. Other offices were lodged in detached buildings. Together with the barns and garages, the buildings formed a wall of discretion around the parade square.

Military vehicles came with messengers, staff, orders, and supplies. Others departed with deployed personnel, officers on missions, and secret dispatches. Depot was a hive of activity at all hours.

Gerhard and Michael were given an opportunity to introduce recommendations for improved physical and mental preparation for those shipped to the front, and for improvements in the debriefing process and psychological assessments following active service and other traumatic experiences while in the service of the Kaiser. Arrangements were made for them to meet with appropriate medical officials to convey their concerns and recommendations.

As soon as the days settled into a routine of sorts, Gerhard dispatched a note of thanks to Dr. Depage, and arranged for it to be delivered to the doctor personally through a network of connections on the *Lazarettzug*. In a firm masculine hand, he wrote:

Dear Doctor Depage,

I hope my greetings find you and your lovely cousin Nora safe and in good health.

I would like to take this opportunity to thank you and Fraulein Nora for your kind efforts to aid Captain Schmidt and myself in a time of need. Captain Schmidt's recovery progresses in a predictable manner, and he awaits an artificial limb. The Captain remains positive and hopeful.

If timing permits, I would welcome an opportunity to visit with you and Fraulein Nora to express, in person, our profound gratitude for your service.

I look forward to meeting with you both once again, under more favourable circumstances, and will remain forever in your debt.

Yours sincerely,
Captain Gerhard Lange

Communication via *Lazarettzug* did not disappoint. In the first week of November,

Gerhard received a response from Dr. Depage, penned in typical medical scrawl.

Dear Captain Lange,

I was delighted to receive your note, and to hear that you and your colleague are mending well.

We live in chaos and grief these days. Constant conflict keeps the wards and surgeries full at all hours of the day and night. Influenza has become an unexpected enemy that takes the young and healthy. It does not discriminate. Those of us who work in the hospitals saw the first cases, and soon after became the victims. I know not why I have been spared thus far, but many of our medical personnel are gone.

It is with a heavy heart that I inform you that our lovely Nora is gone, too. She fought her battle valiantly, but was one of the early victims of this infectious pandemic. I pray that you and your community are spared. It is indeed a nasty business.

I look forward to the day that I might greet you under different circumstances. In the meantime, I recommend that you stay away.

With warm regards,
Pierre Depage, M.D.

Gerhard read the doctor's letter for a third time, unable to grasp the terrible loss. *Nora. Gone. I will never see those cornflower blue eyes again. She's gone before I had the chance to really know her... and love her.*

He sank into the chair behind his desk resting his elbows on it and letting the letter dangle from his fingers. He stared through it, remembering the eyes that had haunted him for months.

When this damn fighting is over, I will find Doctor Depage and we will remember Nora together!

A few days later, Kaiser Wilhelm II abdicated, and shortly after that the Armistice of Compiegne was signed, ending the fighting on the Western Front. It would be a long time before peace was declared. Conflict and chaos continued throughout the country.

Michael retired from the military immediately, and returned home to help rebuild the community.

Gerhard was permanently stationed at Depot, where he fostered the programmes that he and Michael helped implement. He also enrolled in university and studied engineering, which would prove to be an asset to his family as the years passed.

His vow to find Dr. Depage was lost in the business of life that followed.

CHAPTER TWELVE

Gerhard had allowed himself a few days to mourn the loss of Nora. Not Nora herself, but the loss of what might have been. He was clever enough to recognize that continued mourning would amount to nothing. Instead, he considered Otto's constant reminder that Emma was waiting, and determined that he would be wise to focus on building a relationship with her.

For the remainder of the month, Gerhard visited with Emma as often as he could, and quickly surmised that Nora had been a distraction: a dream and nothing more. To his surprise, he realized that he loved Emma; had loved her since before he and Otto had set off to war. By the end of the first week in December, he resolved to speak with his father about a marriage proposal.

One evening, as Cook removed the dinner plates, Gerhard caught his father's eye. "Brandy, Vater?"

"Good idea, son. Mutti, Marie, excuse us." Michael pushed his chair from the polished mahogany table, typically draped in white linen during meals. He folded his napkin and set it neatly on the table in front of him before making a gallant bow to the women.

They giggled at his chivalry, while Marie gathered the folded napkins and returned them to the china cabinet, ready for the next meal.

"Savour your brandy, my dears. The supply is running low," Anna warned. Chortling, she added, "I do hope the war ends before we have none. You may have to resort to water if it doesn't!" To her daughter, she added, "Come, Marie; let's see if we have something to wear for the Christmas festivities. Whatever we find will have to be taken in."

"What is it, son?" Michael poured a small amount of brandy into two crystal glasses.

114

The light in the study was dim: insufficient to cast rainbows through the crystal.

"Sir?" Gerhard accepted the glass his father held out to him. Out of uniform, his father was still formidable. His belly clenched with eagerness.

"You never suggest a brandy after dinner. You have something on your mind."

Gerhard sipped the brandy, hoping it would warm his throat. It suddenly felt tight. "Yes," he croaked, half-choking. He cleared his throat and began again. "Yes. I wanted to speak with you about Emma."

"Emma Schmidt, I presume," Michael said with a twinkle in his eye.

Gerhard nodded. "I ... That is ... I, uh, I would like to ask Farmer Schmidt for permission to marry her, but I wanted your advice first."

"I see ... and is Emma aware of your interest? Your intent?"

"Uh, I believe so. I mean ... maybe not in so many words. But ... well. I've been spending time with her, and Otto seems to think we would be a good match. And she seems to like spending time with me."

"Otto thinks it's a good match? I'm glad to hear it! Have you doubts?" Michael sipped his brandy and held it in his mouth, as if to savour the warmth and the delicate aroma.

"No, Vater, not at all! I want to propose. I, well, I thought it would be helpful to have your advice before I asked her. I'm worried about my nightmares and how they might affect her. And, I'd like your blessing for the marriage, of course."

"Gerhard, this is a small community. If we lived in one of the cities, your choice of young women would be plentiful, but I'm not necessarily convinced that the selection would be so agreeable. I know the family well, and our families have worked side-by-side in common purpose for decades.

"Emma is a lovely young woman," Michael said, "and I've seen how her eyes follow you. That girl has time for no one else. Ask. And your mother and I will welcome her as a new daughter.

"As for the nightmares, if every man returning from war abstained from marriage because of nightmares, the country we all fought to save would disappear," Michael said. "I'm certain that Emma is aware of nightmares caused by the horrors of war. Talk with her about them, and help her understand her role in your healing. I'm sure that the Schmidts have had discussions similar to ours."

"I will Vater, thank you."

Michael raised his glass toward his son. "A toast, then, to a safe future without war; a future of prosperity, good health, and a bountiful family!"

Each man drank the last mouthful of brandy. Gerhard felt the warmth of it bloom and trickle down his gullet.

The next morning, Gerhard set off in search of Farmer Schmidt, who received him in the farmhouse study. As Gerhard had hoped, Farmer Schmidt was enthusiastic and agreeable to his proposal. He excused himself from the parlour and went off to find Emma, leaving Gerhard to wait alone.

Emma entered the study moments later. "I was in the garden with Mama, pulling winter vegetables," she said, as if an apology was warranted. "Papa said you were here and asked to see me?" Her last words were more of a question than a statement.

Gerhard took her hand. It was cool and soft. Soil was embedded under her nails, and she tried to withdraw her hand.

"My hands, they are dirty," she stammered. "I should have washed before I came, but ... well. It sounded important." She tried to hide her hands under her apron, but Gerhard grabbed the one that had just escaped his grip.

"No. Please. It, it doesn't matter." *This isn't going how I thought it would*. Flustered, he held Emma's hand firmly, searching her eyes for any sign of understanding.

She tugged at her hand. When it did not come free, she waited.

When she raised her eyes to meet his, as if to question his actions, he blurted, "Willyoumarryme?"

The rushed question hung in the silence of the room for a brief moment.

"Uh. I mean ..." he said.

Before he could recover from his discomfiture and try again, Emma stepped toward him, wrapping her arms around his neck. "Of course I'll marry you, Gerhard Lange! Heaven knows I've waited long enough for you to ask! Kiss me quick, before the others show up."

"Truly?" he asked in disbelief. *That was easier than I expected!*

She gave an eager nod, her face turned up to him. Hazel eyes—not cornflower blue—glassy with tears. Her flushed cheeks, fair skin, pink lips—slightly parted—all indicated her willingness, and an awareness crept into his foggy brain.

Of their own accord, his arms embraced her, his body awakening in response to his caress of the curves he admired. He kissed her then, first a chaste kiss on her forehead.

She closed her eyes and waited. Then one on each smooth cheek. She leaned toward him and opened her hazel eyes.

He found her mouth, soft and willing, and vowed never to think of cornflower blue again.

Moments later, they were interrupted by a firm knock on the open door, accompanied by the sound of Herr Schmidt clearing his throat.

Otto and his parents stood in the doorway, grinning. Otto wobbled as he struggled to find balance on his crutches. Behind them were Marie and his parents. Marie jumped up and down, trying to see over Otto's shoulder.

The young couple flushed at being caught in a heated embrace.

"Pardon me, sir." Gerhard took a side-step to put space between him and Emma, but kept his hand resting possessively on the small of her back. *Another curve to be appreciated.*

"We shall have a toast!" Farmer Schmidt declared. "To the marriage of two very fine young people. Two well-matched young people, if I say so myself!"

As he spoke, he poured eight glasses of a sweet Spanish sherry and passed them about the room.

Together, the two families raised their glasses to Herr Schmidt's next words. "May you always find happiness. May your troubles be evasive. And"—he grinned mischievously—"may you bless our families with a multitude of grandchildren!"

Gerhard and Emma blushed amid cheers of well-wishes and congratulations.

Given the chaos in the community and the overall shortage of goods, the families decided to take advantage of the Christmas celebrations. Emma and her mother joined Marie and Anna, and together they worked diligently to fashion wedding clothes and organize their men and the nuptials.

Gerhard and Emma were married Friday, December 20th, in the Year of our Lord 1918.

Anna and Marie assembled a group of townsfolk willing to help with the rejuvenation of some of the unused rooms in the Lange manor, converting them into a suite where the newlyweds could live until they were ready to live on their own.

The weeks through Christmas were a happy time for many, especially the Lange and Schmidt families, lending promise for a better future.

CHAPTER THIRTEEN

Life on the Lange estate and neighbouring farms became routine—a new routine—as the misery of war wound down and the country worked to recover from its losses. When Gerhard was finally discharged from the Regiment, he joined his father in the business of running the estate.

He and Emma built a house on a corner of the estate, so that they could be close to the manor and the farmhouse.

The first of a new generation of Langes arrived toward the end of 1919, and two more were added in subsequent years.

Together, the Lange and Schmidt families persevered. They overcame war, pandemic disease, poor economy, and questionable markets. Each year was a year of healing and growing for both families and the community in which they lived.

⚜

Liegnitz reinstated its annual fall fair, an event that it had hosted until the outbreak of the Great War.

During the fall fair of 1920, Otto met a Dutch sea captain who was in town visiting kin. Otto was manning the Schmidt sausage display, and business was brisk. The sea captain kept his distance, observing the popularity of and demand for Schmidt sausages.

When the din died down, the captain approached the display and caught Otto's eye.

"How may I help you, sir? A taste of Schmidt's famous sausage?" Otto's grin of confidence stretched from ear to ear. He was in his element.

"I wouldn't mind a taste," the sea captain responded. "Injured in the war, were you?"

"Sniper got my knee," Otto said, slicing random sausages for the sampling. "You?"

"My home is in the Netherlands. We tried to stay out of the conflict," the captain shared.

Otto nodded his acknowledgement.

"I've been watching your table. You do a brisk business. Nothing seems to slow you down, either." He reached for the wedge of waxy paper Otto offered and tasted a piece of sausage. "Mmm. Jägerwurst," he said. "Delicious!"

"My family is always amazed, but I don't let the lack of a lower limb stop me. It is the sum of my parts that makes me whole." Otto continued to answer the sea captain's previous question. "Here. Try this one. This is the sausage that everyone clamours for."

As he accepted another small slice, the sea captain said, "Zabar Anker, by the way. I sail out of Amsterdam twice a year. I'm in Liegnitz to visit my cousin, Alexi Puchinski. Perhaps you know him?" He extended a hand toward Otto.

"Alexi! I know him well. The Grand Hotel is one of our biggest commercial customers," Otto said. "I'm Otto. Schmidt," he added, pointing to the sign behind him. "So ... what do you think of our special sausage?"

125

"This is by far the best sausage I have ever tasted," Zabar said. "What is your secret ingredient?"

"Special ingredients, plural," Otto said, a twinkle of mischief in his eye. "But they're not for the telling. My mother would have my head, and I have no intention of parting with another part of my anatomy!"

"It matters not to me," Zabar said. "What matters is the taste and the demand. As I mentioned ... I was watching your table. Your family's business is sausage. My family runs an import and export business ... *Oyster Pearl Imports*."

He paused, searching for the best words. "Would you be interested in a little off-shore business?"

"Pardon me?"

"Would you consider exporting your sausages to Amsterdam? I think together our families could make some good money." Zabar gave Otto an inviting grin. "My brother Konstantin also travels to Germany twice a year. That amounts to one shipment

126

every three months, if you can handle it.
We're always looking for import goods."

"You want to import our sausages? To
Amsterdam?" Otto asked in amazement.

Zabar nodded.

"Well, I'll be …"

He studied Zabar for a moment longer.
"Your suggestion certainly has merit, but
it also raises a lot of questions. Why don't
you stop by the farm tomorrow? I'd like my
parents and my wife to be involved in the
discussion. We're not set up for export, but
that doesn't mean we'd decline. Just need to
think things through."

"Certainly," Zabar answered.

The men exchanged personal information and shook hands. "I'm having dinner
with Cousin Alexi this evening. I hope he
has enough sausage on hand to meet my
hunger! Until tomorrow."

Zabar disappeared into the throng of
fairgoers.

Otto's eyes followed him until the sea captain disappeared from his view. He scratched

his fingers through his silvering blond hair, a look of wonderment on his face.

⚜

The following day, Captain Zabar Anker arrived at the farmhouse mid-morning. As Otto had promised, he had invited his parents and his wife, Hildegard, to join them.

While Otto made introductions, they were interrupted by a light rap on the study door. "Gerhard! Right on time. Come in. I am just introducing Captain Anker to the family.

"I hope you don't mind, Captain, but I invited our neighbour, Gerhard Lange, to join our discussion. Our families work closely together, and I thought it would be important for him to be involved."

"Not at all," Zabar responded. "My brother, Konstantin, and I work together as well. I regret only that he is not here, but I am confident that, in time, you will meet him."

Once they were seated, Otto's wife passed around cups of coffee and the meeting began. They discussed how the two businesses could work together for a profitable result, and a few hours later were satisfied with their arrangements.

Hildegard appeared to sense that the meeting would run into the lunch hour and excused herself. With her usual efficiency, she arranged for a hardy luncheon to be prepared.

By the time the meeting concluded, a meal showcasing some of the goods proposed for export to Amsterdam had been laid out on the dining room table. Captain Anker was encouraged to sample it all.

As the meal concluded, Zabar rubbed his belly and savoured a mouthful of ale before he said, "That was a most delicious meal, *Frau* Schmidt. My compliments!"

Hildegard beamed at him.

"I understand now why your husband was so busy at the fair yesterday. The sausage especially was outstanding."

"Thank you, Captain," Hildegard said, her voice full of pride. "I personally oversee the making of the sausage!"

"And she is very particular ... I insist!" Otto's mother affirmed. "It is my recipe, after all."

"Marvellous, indeed!" Zabar said, taking pleasure in acknowledging the tasty meal.

As they spoke, Otto's father poured glasses of Spanish sherry and handed them around the table. "To a long and profitable relationship!" he said, raising his glass.

"Hear, hear!" the others responded.

CHAPTER FOURTEEN

Foraging for mushrooms in the fall was a family tradition that reached far back to the days when Gerhard's family had first settled in southern Silesia, and it was one of the first traditions to be reinstated at the end of the Great War.

The city of Liegnitz had hosted a mushroom hunt annually until the outbreak of the war. The contest was the high point of every fall fair held to celebrate the harvest, and when the fair was reinstated in 1920, so too was the contest.

At the end of the first day of the fair, when most folks had had their fill of rides and games, of sausage-eating contests and tables of best baked goods and preserves, of livestock shows and horse races, they gathered together to hear who had won the ribbon for the Fairest Fungus.

The Fairest Fungus ribbon was a curiosity. The winner received neither prize money nor any special privilege—simply the honour of being known as the best mushroom hunter of the year. The winner was draped with a banner of blue, taffeta ribbon, on which was written *Extraordinary Hunter of the Fairest Fungus* and the year of the contest.

Gerhard slid out of bed the morning before the 1928 Fair was to start, and donned woollen stockings and trousers against the chill of the room.

Under the warm comforter that covered their bed, Emma stretched, cat-like. "Is it time already?"

"Only if you want to collect prize-winning fungus specimens," Gerhard replied. "I'll organize the pull-cart. You get the children ready."

As he buttoned his shirt, he leaned over the bed and kissed her hungrily.

"Or perhaps we should just forget—"

"Although your suggestion is very tempting," Emma purred, "you'd better go. We don't want to disappoint the children."

"Later, then …" he said, giving her a lustful grin before closing the bedroom door. His tuneless whistle disappeared down the hallway.

The previous year, Gerhard had extended the garden shed to twice its size, and dug the floor of the extension deeper by a metre and a half, creating a cellar that would remain cool throughout the year.

The cellar had a high ceiling, sharing its roof laterally with the garden shed. From the outside, the shed looked abnormally long, but the deception was not obvious without entering the building.

Inside, a gradual ramp sloped from the shed to the centre of the cellar, allowing hand-carts of produce to be rolled down into it. Shelves lining the cellar were slowly starting to fill with preserves, dried fruit, and winter roots. Soon, the shelves would be burdened with the bounty of another promising harvest.

By the time Gerhard had collected the necessary baskets and tools required for fungus hunting, loaded them onto the cart, and tugged it to the back door, a fire had been lit in the kitchen and smoke wafted above the chimney. His family had risen.

"Where have you been, Papa?" his youngest asked in her tinny voice. "You weren't here when I woke." Gerda's large, round eyes peered up at him under questioning, straw-coloured brows.

"I've been organizing the cart for our mushroom hunt," he said, hoisting her into his arms. He nuzzled her head of morning hair and inhaled the sweet scent of his only daughter. Gerda squealed with delight when his whiskers tickled her neck.

"Here's your coffee," Emma said, placing a steaming cup on the table, "and some bread and cheese."

Gerhard set Gerda down, then kissed his wife's cheek.

"Children, hurry with your breakfast," Emma said. "If we don't leave soon, others will have picked the best fungi."

The children finished the last bites of their breakfast and raced to see who could be first dressed and waiting at the back door. Worn boots were pulled on over heavy socks, woollen coats were buttoned up, and hats were pulled snug on their heads.

Ten minutes later, each child assembled at the door, waiting for their father to announce their departure.

Emma pulled on her leather boots and buttoned her coat. She handed out mittens to the boys, giving each of them a stern look that told them that the mittens were to be worn.

The cook helped Gerda struggle into her mittens before putting on her coat. A long strand of wool, stitched into the cuff of each mitten, was threaded through the sleeves of her coat. Once Gerda's coat was on, the mittens might come off her hands, but she would not lose them.

"Time to go! Ready?" Gerhard asked, his hand on the doorknob.

"Ready!" his eager family chimed.

He held the door wide while his children filed into the yard. As his wife approached the doorway, he made a small bow of mischief.

"The twinkle in your eye tells me you're up to something," Emma said suspiciously. "What is it?"

"Nothing," Gerhard said, the tips of his ears turning pink.

"I know how competitive you are, Gerhard Lange," Emma whispered, slapping his arm playfully.

"Is no one else coming?" he asked, changing the subject. "Vater, Mutti, your parents?"

"No," Emma answered. "They prefer to stay home today. They're all recovering from a cold."

⚜

"Let's head this way," Gerhard said, tromping into the woods, pulling the hand cart behind him. "I found a glade a while back, and I've been monitoring it. I think we might have some success there."

One of the Lange family staples was *Laetiporus Sulphureous*, affectionately known as "chicken of the woods." New fungi were moist and rubbery, but the orange and yellow tubular filaments soon faded, becoming chalk-like and pungent; not unlike some people Gerhard knew.

"Chicken of the woods," he told his family, "prefer wounded oak trees. They send their spores into the moist decay beneath the fractured wood. Early last spring, I noticed that one of the trees had been hit by lightning, right at the major fork of its trunk. Since then, the heavier piece has fallen away. The last time I passed this way, fungi were growing nicely in the wound."

Twenty minutes later, the young family stepped into the glade and stood in awe. The colony of chicken of the woods fungi had flourished.

"*Mein Gott*! Look at that," he said.

"I've never seen such a colony," Emma affirmed. "And, look around, children. I'm seeing quite an assortment of mushrooms to fill our baskets. It appears that the tall trees here provide an excellent environment for mushroom growth."

Gerhard handed a basket and mushroom spatula to each of the boys and his wife.

"Where's mine, Papa?" Gerda asked, jumping up and down with impatience.

"Here," Gerhard said, handing her the smallest basket. "Go with your mother. She's the best mushroom hunter. Boys, don't go further than you can hear us talking."

"Yes, Papa," they said together and headed into the brush.

"What are you going to do?" Emma asked, holding her hand out to Gerda.

"I'm going to stay right here. That tree," he said, pointing at the injured oak, "is about to part company with some brackets."

Gerhard placed his wicker basket at the base of the oak tree, removed his jacket, and reached for his spatula. Setting to work, he gently tickled brackets from the tree, marvelling at how easily they came away. *It's as if they've been waiting for me!*

One of the brackets was bigger than anything he had ever seen. As it peeled away from the tree trunk, Gerhard's heart began to race. *Mein Gott, this could be the one that wins the prize!*

Adrenaline pumped through his veins as he braced himself to take the weight of it. His hands shook, betraying his excitement. *I'm glad I kept the largest of the baskets for myself. It will easily hold this bracket. Perhaps even a few more.*

When the basket was full, Gerhard gently tugged a piece of cotton fabric from inside the basket until he had enough of it free to cover the contents. He bent his knees, gingerly embraced the basket, and slowly rose, feeling his body protest against the weight. As he manoeuvred the sizable basket, he waddled toward the cart. *Mein Gott, if I were a betting man, I'd say this monster weighs close to forty kilograms! I've heard they can reach that weight, but would never have believed it possible. Until now!*

Soon, Emma and the children returned with brimming baskets of their own.

"I didn't bother looking for chicken of the woods," Emma said. "I expect that you collected enough for all of us. Gerda and I found some lovely chanterelles."

"We didn't either," said Paul, Gerhard's eldest son. "We thought we'd have a better chance of winning with these." He held up his basket filled with pig mushrooms, and Arthur proudly displayed the stone mushrooms in his.

"Clever boys," Emma responded. Her sons grinned at her praise.

"I'm glad I brought the cart," Gerhard said. "There's no way I could carry my collection, and you all have full baskets, too. Boys, help me organize it. You may have to lend a hand to get this thing moving."

When they returned home, Emma took Gerda into the house. "Boys, help your father store the mushrooms," she said. "When you come in, the midday meal will be on the table."

The boys helped Gerhard manoeuvre the cart into the cellar and gently place the bursting baskets on a special shelf built for just such treasures. Each basket was labeled with the name of the collector, just in case the fungi in it happened to be the winning collection. Tomorrow would be the day of telling.

A walk in the forest, fresh air, the anticipation of a fall fair, and the possibility of winning a prize was enough to exhaust everyone, including Gerhard. They all slept soundly that night, each with their own dream of winning the prize for best mushroom.

The following morning was a cacophony of sound and activity as everyone prepared for a day at the fair. Gerhard hitched a plough horse to a flatbed wagon. He had divided the deck into two portions. Under the driver's bench, he safely stashed the baskets, including a large picnic basket packed by the cook with sufficient food and necessities for the day's outing.

An assortment of blankets and other articles that might be needed throughout the day—hats, shawl, mittens, and coats to keep them comfortable—held the baskets secure. At this time of year, the sun set earlier, bringing with it a damp chill. The blankets could be used for the picnic, and later to make soft beds for exhausted children on the ride home. The chill did not concern Gerhard. Emma would be snuggled next to him, after all.

Time passed unnoticed by the Lange family. They were happily distracted by chatter, filled with anticipation and speculation.

Presently, the wagon full of family and fungi approached the gates of the 1928 Fall Fair. It was mid-morning, and the fair was well underway. Emma and the children planned to wander through the alley of travelling entertainers. She and Paul wanted to have their fortunes told, while the two younger ones hoped for mystery and magic.

Gerhard grasped Emma's waist with familiarity and helped her hop to the ground. The boys jumped down on their own, forgetting to help Gerda.

"Papa, catch me!" Gerda hollered, jumping off the wagon bed. Gerhard turned sharply from Emma and caught his daughter mid-air.

"Careful, my small one," he warned, setting her safely on her feet and straightening her coat and hat. "Next time, be certain that I'm watching. I almost missed you. You could have been hurt."

"Yes, Papa," she said, a look of petulance on her face.

Gerhard climbed back into the wagon and watched for a moment as Emma shepherded her brood safely down the alley.

"Have fun," he said. "I'll find you later." He waved them good-bye and flicked the reins.

The wagon rolled on, following its horse to the fungus drop and weigh-in: a huge drive-through tent made by raising two tents with door flaps evenly matched side-by-side. By placing the tents so, drivers could roll their carts into the first tent to deposit their secret fungus collections, then roll through the dividing drop curtain to the next tent where other cargo—fresh vegetables, baked goods, preserves, crafts, and the like—could be deposited. From there, the goods would be distributed in small hand carts, hauled by volunteers, to other parts of the fair.

The deposit, weighing, and storage of the fungus collections was an interesting process, taken very seriously by all who participated in the competition, and even by those who did not. Everyone, to a person, religiously respected the process.

Many waited in line, mostly men and a few women with horses, wagons, fungi, and other goods, for their turn in the secret tent. They called competitive remarks to one another, each bragging about their winning entry.

Finally, Gerhard was motioned forward. He flicked the reins, and the horse leaned into the pull. The curtain closed behind the wagon and an officious-looking marshal approached him. "What goods have you today, sir?" he asked.

"Oh, you know: the usual children's collections. My wife found some nice brackets worth looking at," he offered, but he said nothing of his own basket, the last one to be drawn out and weighed.

Gerhard held his excitement in check as each basket was gently weighed, first in aggregate after noting the name of each fungus collected, then, after ascertaining the largest single piece, its weight and type. Each basket was labeled with the contestant's name and placed reverently on shelving built for the competition.

Gerhard looked around him, noting the several constables posted strategically to ensure that no tampering would occur during the competition. The air was pungent with the fragrance of earthy fruit, kept humid by the weight of the tent fabric and its closed curtains. Only one lantern was permitted to cast light for the marshal's task.

CHAPTER FIFTEEN

Entertainment alley thrummed with activity: travelling musicians, singers, actors, and readers. The smell of fall and aromatic foods filled the air—roasting meats, quick breads, and sweets.

"Where shall we go first?" Emma asked.

"Candy?" Arthur, her youngest son, asked with a hopeful grin.

"It's a little early for candy," she said, guiding her children toward a group of musicians dressed in colourful costumes and playing lively music. A crowd had gathered to listen. She and Paul stood the small children in front of them, and they clapped their hands in time with the beat.

When Gerda and Arthur began fidgeting, Emma moved them along.

"Paul," Emma addressed her nine-year-old son, "you said you wanted to have your fortune told."

"Yes, Mutti," Paul replied with enthusiasm. "Look over there. The wagon with the gold paint. That lady doesn't appear to be occupied."

Holding Gerda's hand, she guided her sons toward the wagon. "Hello," she said to the woman as they approached. "We're the Lange family, and some of us have come for a reading."

"And who will have a reading?" the woman asked.

"My son Paul and I will, please," Emma answered. "You go first, Paul. When it's my turn, you can watch your sister and brother."

Paul dipped his head, acknowledging his mother's instructions.

"I am Rosalee, Master Paul," the woman said, inviting him up the stairs and into the wagon.

The boy followed Rosalee into her reading wagon, marvelling at the bright colours of her clothing and the copper disks sewn into her skirt. They tinkled like music as she moved.

Rosalee closed the door and directed Paul to a chair, then filled the dark interior of the wagon by lighting candles and incense.

Very mystical, Paul thought, watching her prepare.

Rosalee sat opposite him. A table covered with a red-and-white checkered cloth stood between them. In the centre of the table rested a crystal ball mounted on a golden base. To Paul's left sat a square of black cloth, something bulging beneath it.

Rosalee lifted the crystal ball and its base, and placed it on the table to his right, covering it with the black fabric. She retrieved the stack of tarot cards that lay exposed and shuffled them. She gazed at Paul with sincerity. He relaxed, resting his hands on his knees.

"Have you any concerns today, young sir? Any questions for the cards?"

Rosalee fanned the cards on the table before her and the reading began. Sometimes she exposed a card, sometimes she dealt them. She invited him to ask questions, and when he did, she asked him to choose cards. She then placed his choice on the table and interpreted the answers.

"I see you come from a powerful lineage," Rosalee remarked at one point. "You will be an inspiring leader in a conflict to come, and a hero to your people one day; but before you are called a hero, you will see much danger: much death and horror. You must take great care, or you, yourself, will die."

"Shall we ask the crystal ball if there is more in store for you?" she said cheerily, as if her ominous prediction had never been made.

Before Paul could answer, she folded the cards and returned them to their original location, covering them with the black cloth. Rosalee placed the crystal ball between them again and sat quietly for several moments, her focus on the crystal ball. Paul looked about him, contemplating the interior of the wagon and Rosalee's warning.

"Ah!" Rosalee lifted her head and smiled, her dark eyes shining in the candle light. "I see that you will have three children and the youngest – a son – will have great adventures." She frowned. "But, alas, love will break his heart."

"Does it say why?" he asked.

Rosalee shook her head.

"Curious," Rosalee muttered to herself, "eyes like melted dark chocolate."

"Pardon me?" Paul asked, leaning toward her.

"Do you know anyone with eyes the colour of melted dark chocolate?" Rosalee demanded. Puzzlement and fear appeared to shadow her face.

"Aside from you, no," he answered. "Will I?"

"That is not for me to say," she said abruptly, before adding, "The reading is over for today, young master. The crystal has gone silent."

"But, what about those brown eyes?" he insisted.

"I can only say that they will play a significant role in the future of your family. What that role might be, I cannot say. But you must take care!"

Paul was shaken by her words. His thoughts clogged with churning questions.

"The reading is over," Rosalee said firmly, rising from her chair and indicating Paul's way to the door.

Paul left his payment on the table and thanked Rosalee for the reading. Outside, he hailed his mother for her turn, and wandered into the alley with his siblings in tow.

"Watch for your father," Emma hollered as she ascended the ornately-carved stairs painted red and gold. "And don't wander out of sight. I need to be able to find you when I'm done."

Paul acknowledged her instructions and allowed the banter and curiosity of his siblings to lead him along the alley while he contemplated the curious predictions of the fortune-teller.

CHAPTER SIXTEEN

W hen the baskets of mushrooms collected by his wife and children had been processed, Gerhard took a deep breath and reached into the wagon again, bracing himself for the weight of the last basket. He could feel beads of excitement trickle down his spine.

Although the tent was warm and humid, and the shirts of the men within were stained with great marks of moisture, Gerhard knew that his was steeped with adrenaline. The winning kind.

"Ho! That looks like a heavy one," the marshal said. "You there ... come and lend a hand."

In response to his bark, one of the constables approached. Between the three men, the basket was gently shifted from wagon to table. As Gerhard slowly peeled back the cotton cover, the others gasped.

"I'll need some help," he said. "It was all I could do to get this monster into the basket without breaking it."

Each man cautiously slid his fingers in and under the fungus bracket.

"Easy; we don't want to break it," the marshal said. "On three: one, two, three!"

The three men braced themselves and lifted the awkward giant onto the scale. The pan of the scale fell sharply, and each man reached to steady it before it hit hard on the table.

"Phew!" said the constable. "That was close."

"It wouldn't be promising," the marshal agreed as he stretched his back, "for my future as marshal of the Fairest Fungus competition if this prize smashed."

Gerhard knew that every man in that tent was sworn to secrecy. Nothing could be said of the specimens until the unveiling later that afternoon. They all stood with eyes bugged, mouths agape. Those on guard dared to step a little closer, as if to assure their eyes that what they saw was indeed real, then quickly returned to their posts.

The marshal weighed the specimen, recording the weight and type. "It appears that all of the specimens in this basket are the same," he said.

"That's correct," Gerhard said. "The old tree was covered with it."

"What tree is that?" the marshal asked.

"There's a little glade at the back of our property," he said with a glint in his eye. "Last spring an ancient oak was hit by lightning ..."

"... creating a perfect spore field," the marshal completed the sentence, shaking his head in wonder.

"Indeed," Gerhard said.

"Well then, Herr Lange, if that's all you've got for us, you'd best be on your way. There are other folks outside waiting to have their monsters weighed, too." The marshal smirked. "It may be a waste of time to process the rest, but I have a responsibility to see it done."

As with the others, the monster fungus was covered and stowed until the great reveal.

Gerhard flicked the reins again, and the wagon jumped to life behind the steady horse. The curtains parted, allowing a breath of fresh air into the humid mushroom tent. The wagon moved forward into the next tent, where Gerhard deposited some contest entries—Cook's preserves and Otto's famous sausages.

Customarily, Otto and his wife, Hildegard, would have brought the sausages themselves, but Hildegard's mother was ailing, and they had gone off earlier in the week to care for her.

Having deposited all of the contest entries, Gerhard drove the wagon to a field set aside as a wagon drop. He unhitched the horse and turned it loose into a fenced pasture, where other horses lounged and grazed on late sweet grass and hay.

On foot, carrying the picnic basket and some blankets, Gerhard sought out his wife and children. It was time for lunch.

✤

Gerhard found his family watching an ancient game called "kubb." Kubb was rarely played except at exhibitions and fairs, and the faces of onlookers, including his wife and children, were filled with curiosity.

"Papa, watch them play," Paul said enthusiastically. "It's similar to a game of horseshoes."

The other children were just as excited to see him, and told him of their adventures amongst the entertainers. Emma slipped her hand around his arm and leaned into him.

"Missed you," she whispered. "How did it go with the weigh-in?"

Gerhard cast a soft smile at her. "The usual. You had some nice pieces that could give folks a run for their money."

"And yours?"

"We'll see," he said, his mischievous smile telling more than he did. He squeezed his arm against his chest, pressing her small hand into him.

She squeezed back and smiled coquettishly.

"Let's have lunch," Gerhard encouraged, and marched his family off to the picnic area. They found a shady spot, and while the children helped Gerhard spread a blanket, Emma opened the basket prepared by the cook.

Gerhard watched her covertly, remembering the first time she had opened a picnic basket for him and Otto more than ten years past. *She is still as graceful as she was that day.*

Emma broke through his musings. "The cook has prepared a lovely basket for us. Come children. Find a spot on the blanket, and I'll pass you something to eat."

They eagerly ate their lunch, their hunger piqued by the fresh air. Afterward, Gerhard and Emma tidied up the leftovers, then savoured a few minutes enjoying each other's company and catching up on fair gossip.

The younger children frolicked with their friends. Like a magnet, Paul migrated to a group of boys his own age and bantered with them. Gerhard noted the sun's movement across the sky and checked his pocket watch.

"The fungus judging will take place in an hour," he remarked to Emma before calling the children back. They packed up the remnants of their lunch, returned it to the wagon, and wandered off to enjoy the fair, heading in the general direction of the fungus-judging tent.

"Make sure you find us for the contest results," Gerhard reminded Paul.

In response, Paul snapped to attention and saluted his father, something he had done out of respect since he was three years old. Gerhard recalled one day six years in the past, when his company marched on parade and Paul imitated them.

Before Gerhard could shift his focus, Paul appeared at his side.

"Don't you want to stay with your mates?" he asked.

"No. I'd rather walk with you," Paul said. "Besides, we're all heading to hear the results of the mushroom contest, anyway."

JERENA TOBIASEN

"Are you enjoying the fair? See anything interesting?" Gerhard asked.

"Yes, Papa. I've seen many interesting things. Impressive livestock—especially the race horses. The entertainers were amazing, too."

"What's your favourite?"

"I have two, actually," Paul said. "One man swallowed a sword! Can you imagine?"

Gerhard rumpled his son's ebony hair.

"And the other, a fortune-teller, was very … curious." Paul softened his words as he spoke of the fortune-teller.

"Why curious?"

Paul looked up at his father, seeming to search for words. He breathed deeply and straightened to his full height. "She told me about my future. It was a little exciting, and a little scary."

"You know that she is just an entertainer," Gerhard said, trying to assure him. "What she told you isn't true,"

"But it has to be, Papa. She told me that I would grow up to be just like you. That

160

another war would come. And ... and ... that my son would have a great adventure. And a broken heart." He brightened, smiling at his father. "At least I know that I will survive the war!" Abruptly, his smile disappeared.

"What is it, Paul?" *We don't need another war. We haven't recovered from the last one. God help us.*

"She said something else that made no sense. She stared at me for several minutes, saying nothing, then shook her head as if in disbelief. Then she asked whether I knew anyone with eyes the colour of melted dark chocolate. I told her I didn't. When I pressed her for more information, she said that someone with that eye colour would play a significant role in the future of my family, and that I should take care!"

"That is indeed curious, son."

"Can you think of anyone with eyes like that?"

"Hmm, I'll need to think more on the matter," Gerhard responded, feeling the

161

small hairs on the back of his neck prickle. *I'm not inclined to believe the predictions of a fortune-teller, but, since there are threads of possibility in what she says, I must pay attention.*

They arrived early at the fungus-judging tent and found a fine spot near the entrance. Others started gathering around them. The air was electric with expectation.

Precisely on the hour, the curtains of the fungus-judging tent were raised, revealing table upon table of remarkable fungus specimens of many types. On one such table, the judging table strategically placed at the front of the tent, sat the winning specimens, each held in a basket of equal size, covered with a remnant of the same blue-checkered fabric, intending to hold the suspense a little longer.

A gong sounded nearby, and a herald announced, in formal delivery, that the contest results were about to be announced. The crowd, bubbling with anticipation, waited patiently.

The marshal, now wearing a bowtie and black jacket with gold buttons, stepped forward.

Everyone clapped. Gerhard drew in a deep breath to still himself and swallowed hard: a little too hard. Emma flashed a knowing grin.

"Exciting, isn't it?" he said, gesturing that they should pay attention.

Most of the marshal's announcements passed in a blur—best specimen this type, best specimen that type. Emma proudly accepted a ribbon for the prettiest collection of chanterelles and beamed with pride as she returned to Gerhard's side from the judge's podium. Finally, all of the baskets had been revealed but one.

Nervous anticipation was getting the better of Gerhard. He shoved his hands deep into his pockets, hunching his shoulders and taking a deep breath. Beads of sweat pearled slowly down his spine again. *Get a grip, Lange. It's only a mushroom contest.*

"You're vibrating," Emma said to her competitive husband.

"Ladies and gentlemen." The marshal called everyone's attention to the stage. The murmuring crowd settled. "We have come to the last basket. The ribbon for the contents of this basket will go to the person who brought the fairest fungus to the fair today."

He paused, as if waiting for his comment to sink in. "As a reminder, the fairest fungus must have all of the attributes that have so far been awarded piecemeal: firm and fresh, meaty texture, proper colour, size, and, if appropriate, weight. In other words, a beauty to look at, but it must also have the taste to go with it. This beauty"—the marshal hovered his hand lightly over the last covered basket—"meets all conditions and then some."

He cast his gaze over the crowd before proceeding. "As you know, weight is the least important attribute. Some of the lovely pieces we viewed earlier have little to no weight at all. In this case, however, weight does matter, because the species is a heavy-weighted one."

One more pause followed for effect. The marshal enjoyed creating suspense.

"I have had the privilege of inspecting and weighing many entries today, but, by far, none comes close to what's in this basket. In fact"—the marshal caressed the checked cover—"I have never, ever, seen such a specimen as this in all the years that I've been judging, and that, my friends, has been a long time. And many mushrooms."

Gerda tugged at Gerhard's jacket and raised her arms. In one smooth movement, he raised her high and sat her astride his shoulders, holding fast to her legs. She placed her tiny hands under his chin to anchor herself.

"To win the ribbon for the *Extraordinary Hunter of the Fairest Fungus 1928*," the marshal went on, "this specimen must also be in one piece. The constables and I have inspected it thoroughly to ensure no trickery. The only things we found alien to it, but not holding it together ..."

Once again, the marshal's eyes panned the crowd. They waited. Gerhard felt the knot in his belly squeeze.

"The only thing we found," the marshal began again, "was the odd worm. Extra protein, that's all. Besides, everyone knows that the quickest way to identify a crop of mushrooms is the presence of worms!"

The crowd rippled in giggles and guffaws.

"Makes great worm jerky!" someone bellowed.

The crowd erupted in cheers and laughter. The tension broke.

The marshal grinned and waited for the crowd to quiet again. He reached for the checkered covering that lay over the basket. Gently, he teased back the cover, as he had seen it done earlier, to reveal the monster bracket of chicken of the woods. As he continued to remove the cover, the crowd stood in stunned silence. There was no basket. The bracket stood alone.

"The bracket," the marshal shouted to break the hush of amazement, "weighed in at forty-five kilos!"

The crowd erupted with awe.

Gerhard slowly released the breath he had not realized that he held. A smile crept from a corner of his mouth and twitched into first a grin, and then a toothy smile as the marshal called out his name. He slid Gerda from his shoulders and handed her to Emma.

Arthur bounced with glee. "Oh Papa! You won! Hurrah for Papa!"

"Hurrah for Papa!" Gerda said in her small voice.

Emma placed her hand lovingly on his muscled forearm and squeezed. "Go get your ribbon, Master Hunter," she whispered on a husky breath.

And that is exactly what the Extraordinary Mushroom Hunter of 1928 did.

CHAPTER SEVENTEEN

T wice a year, Gerhard and his eldest son Paul took a load of farm goods—canned fruits and vegetables, jams, cheese, and, of course, Schmidt's sausages—to the dock in Schinawa, timing their delivery with the arrival of the coastal freighter operated by Konstantin Anker. Otto preferred that his two deliveries coincide with Zabar Anker's arrival.

The trading relationship established with Oyster Pearl Imports in 1920 had proven to be a lucrative business, especially the Schmidt sausages, which were in high demand in Amsterdam.

In late October of 1934, Gerhard was surprised to have almost missed the freighter. On the morning that he and Paul arrived at the Schinawa dock, Konstantin appeared anxious. Commands to his crew were terse.

Konstantin nodded toward them as they approached, inviting Gerhard and Paul to board the ship.

"What is it, my friend? Are you in a hurry?" asked Gerhard, extending his hand in friendship. "It's not like you to bark at your crew."

"Unfortunately, I am pressed for time this trip." Konstantin accepted Gerhard's hand and gave his right arm a friendly jab. "We aren't going south as usual. Instead, we are returning north tomorrow morning, so I have the crew working double-time to ensure our cargo is sorted and stowed safely. I can't tell you how pleased I am that you arrived as you have. I would hate to return to Amsterdam without Schmidt's famous sausage. The distributors would tan me alive!"

The men shared a laugh.

"You must promise never to tell Schmidt how desired his sausage is. He would increase the price, and I'd never be able to afford it!"

"I won't. My brother-in-law's head is fat enough with the demand of our local customers! He raises the price for them, but I insist that the price for you be kept reasonable," Gerhard said.

"Paul, my boy! You've grown since last year. You're turning into a fine young man. Here." Konstantin greeted Paul and tossed him a coin. "You have time for a treat. Off you go, while your father and I do some business."

In a still-fluctuating adolescent voice, Paul thanked Konstantin for the coin, looked for his father's permission to leave, then disappeared off the dock, heading for town.

"Have you any lace with you, Konstantin? The women are screaming for it!"

"I set aside a few bundles, and some other items that you might like to see. Come below."

⚜

Konstantin and Gerhard stood on the deck, watching Paul meander along the road from town. Gerhard checked his pocket watch, noting that it was past noon. If they departed soon, he and Paul would arrive home in time for the evening meal.

"Paul!" Gerhard waved to his son to hasten his step, and the young man jogged toward them, almost colliding with a dilapidated cart that had drawn to a halt on the roadway near the dock.

At sight of the cart, Konstantin tipped his cap to Gerhard. "Excuse me; this fellow will need directions." He nodded toward the cart.

Gerhard watched Konstantin march up the ramp to the dock and steady Paul as the two passed midway. While Konstantin rumpled the boy's ebony hair, Gerhard heard him say, "Look like your father, you do! You'll have the girls chasing you soon." In response, Paul blushed, then paused to watch Konstantin approach the cart.

Paul hurried onboard. "Papa, did you see the driver of the cart?" he asked. "He could be a twin to Captain Konstantin, except that he has darker hair."

They watched Konstantin greet each of the folks from the cart with an affectionate embrace, then direct the tallest fellow toward a nearby stable. Turning to the smaller ones, Konstantin gestured for them to follow him onboard.

"Permit me to conduct introductions," Konstantin said. "Gerhard, may I introduce my cousin-in-law, Rosalee Kota, and her daughter, Punita?" Turning to his guests, he introduced Gerhard and Paul.

Gerhard saw Paul's face shifted from curiosity to astonishment as he watched Punita remove her straw hat and loosen her long, dark hair. It rippled and fell like a glossy waterfall over her shoulders and down her back. The smudges of dirt on her nose and cheeks failed to dampen her beauty—high cheekbones, full, red lips, and lashes long and black.

But for the rope belt tied neatly at her slender waist, the over-large ratty clothes she wore hid her tiny frame and what lay beneath.

Her gaze held Paul's for a moment before she blushed and looked away.

"Paul!" Gerhard snapped, interrupting his son's stare, then he turned to Konstantin with a quizzical look.

"My cousin has been travelling through the countryside, which, as you can well appreciate, is not safe right now. They thought it best to use the disguise."

Turning to Rosalee, he indicated that she and Punita should go below-deck. "I'll be along presently," he told them.

"Well, we must be off," Gerhard said. "We'll leave you to your business. Paul ..." He turned his head, indicating that Paul should precede him up the ramp. Paul said good-bye to Konstantin and headed toward the road.

Sotto-voice, Gerhard said, "Konstantin, I won't ask what business it is, but I caution you to take great care. Life is too uncertain these days. Your journey on the river may be in danger."

"Thank you, my friend. I'll heed your warning. Safe journey to you."

"And to you, Konstantin. Fair winds and following seas till we meet again." They shook hands affectionately before Gerhard scooted up the ramp, following Paul.

On the dock, Gerhard put his arm around Paul and turned him away from the ship with idle chatter about hurrying home for dinner.

"Papa, what was that about? Why were those women dressed as farmers?" Paul asked.

"You heard Konstantin. It's risky business travelling about the countryside these days."

"She was very beautiful, wasn't she, Papa?"

"Hmm?" Although he had implied that Konstantin's business was not his, Gerhard contemplated the possibilities regardless, and missed Paul's question.

"The girl. She was very beautiful. Was she not?"

"Indeed, son. Both women were remarkably beautiful." *And their eyes were dark*

174

brown, Gerhard recalled, *like melted chocolate.*

"I know that woman, Papa. The one Captain Konstantin called Rosalee."

"Oh?" Gerhard replied, his attention returning abruptly to Paul's remarks.

"She's the one who told my future. The one who talked about 'eyes of dark chocolate'! I still don't know what she meant, but the girl … her eyes were like dark chocolate, weren't they? Did you see them?" His words were excited, almost breathless.

How could I miss them! "Remind me what Rosalee said to you, if you remember?"

"Of course!" Paul said. "I'll never forget!" As they walked toward the truck, Paul retold the story of his encounter with Rosalee at the 1928 Fall Fair in Liegnitz.

"Ah, yes! I remember now," Gerhard said. "Although I don't believe in the predictions of fortune-tellers, I am inclined to pay closer attention to your future, especially if another war breaks out." *And how those interesting eyes might be involved.*

CHAPTER EIGHTEEN

T he sun was low in the sky by the time the truck rolled into the yard behind the estate. A crimson glow lit the yard. At that hour, it was often busy with farmhands ending work for the day and rushing home to their dinner. On this particular day, men still milled about in small groups, speaking in quiet voices.

"I wonder why they're still here," Paul said as they disembarked from the truck.

A young man broke away from the group, removing his hat as he approached them. "Sir. We're very sorry, sir. We only just heard when we came to put the vehicles away."

"Heard what, son?" Gerhard looked at him and the others in puzzlement. "We've only just returned from Schinawa ourselves. What's happened?"

One of the older farmhands approached.

"Heinz, be off home now," he said in clipped words and shooed the boy away. "Sir, you'd best get yourselves into the house. It's the old master. You'll have some sad news, I'm afraid."

Gerhard nodded, and he and Paul hurried toward the manor.

The house was cold. Aromas of the evening meal should have greeted them, but there was nothing welcoming about their entry. Every room was dark. "Where is Cook? She hasn't made the meal. There's not even a light in the kitchen." Paul said.

"Shhh!" Gerhard cocked his head. "They're in the parlour." Leading the way, he snapped on light switches as he passed.

The parlour door was open. Marie and Anna sat together on the worn settee, Marie's hands wrapped around her mother's. With a free hand, Anna dabbed the corner of her eye with a handkerchief. Emma and Cook stood behind the settee, leaning on one another.

"What is it?" Gerhard said, bursting into the room.

The women looked at him, then beyond him, and he turned. He had not seen the doctor standing just inside the doorway. He turned back to Anna. "Mutti?"

"It's your father, Gerhard. He's had a heart attack. Doctor Lennhoff was just telling us that his heart is quite damaged, and that he won't live much longer. I think he's been waiting for you. He keeps asking …"

Gerhard turned fully to the doctor. "May I see him, then?"

"Yes, of course. He's in his room. I'll accompany you up and fill you in as we go."

Gerhard led the way up to his father's room and listened as the doctor described the severity of the heart attack. "I've decided to leave him here, and have arranged for a nurse to be with him 'round the clock. Transporting him to the hospital would only exacerbate his condition."

"How long?"

"Any time now. At the most, a few days."

"But how? He was fine when we left this morning."

"Your father has had a heart condition for many years. Medication has helped delay the inevitable. As you know, he is a strong, determined man, and he refused to heed my advice," the doctor said.

They stopped at the top of the stairs outside the room that Michael and Anna shared. No sound came from within.

"Your father will do as he's always done," Dr. Lennhoff said. "He will die as he has lived. In his own way."

"Thank you, Doctor. I will have some time alone with him, if you don't mind."

"Of course," Dr. Lennhoff nodded and headed down the stairs, returning to the parlour.

Gerhard made a soft knock on the bedroom door and entered without bidding.

Michael appeared to be sleeping, but opened his eyes when the floorboard creaked under Gerhard's foot. "Damn board. Should have fixed that years ago," Michael said as Gerhard tried to settle himself on his mother's dainty armchair, recently covered with a cream-coloured fabric and lavender irises.

Perched on the edge, he leaned forward and took his father's hand. "Vater, what is this about your heart? You've never said anything to us."

"I didn't want to worry your mother." Michael's words were soft and breathy. "My will is in order. You'll inherit everything, of course. And you'll take care of my Anna. Promise me that."

"Of course, Vater. But, must we speak of such things now?" He rubbed the old scar on his forehead. It had begun to throb as the doctor described his father's condition.

Since his injury during the Great War, the familiar throb returned whenever he experienced stress. His counsellor had told him that the throb would disappear in time; that it was a psychological symptom, connected to his sense of responsibility for saving the men lost or injured during the War.

"Yes. It is time," Michael gasped. "I have lived a good life … most of the time. And I've always tried to do what was right. I have loved one woman. And I think I've loved her well. You. Marie. The children. They are my wealth. My joy."

Michael coughed. Shifted his weight. "Some water, please."

Gerhard took the glass of water from the bedside table. Bubbles escaped from the clear sides and popped at the surface. He lifted Michael gently and put the glass to dried lips.

Michael took a sip, one sip, and lowered his head to the pillow, visibly exhausted from his effort. Gerhard choked back his emotions.

"You and me, we have seen the worst of life. But we have also seen the best. Family. Family is what is important. It is our duty to keep our family safe."

He coughed again, and Gerhard reached for the water.

Michael's hand flopped in dismissal. "Nein. We have seen the unrest brewing hereabouts. I am worried for their safety. Sometime soon, you must take them away from here. They will resist, but you must be steadfast. Too much turmoil. Too much conflict." Michael tried to sit up. He became agitated as he spoke.

Gerhard placed his hand on his father's shoulder. "Rest, Vater. I can come back. We can speak more of this later."

"Nein. It must be … said. There won't be … a later." His words were choppy with effort. The room was quiet. Michael closed his eyes.

Thinking him asleep, Gerhard started to rise.

Michael's hand reached out to stop him. "Sit … a little longer … please. I think safety … will be … in the city. Not Liegnitz. Not Berlin. Bavaria. Yes! *Nürnberg*, perhaps. Or *München*. Maybe something smaller. Need to get away … from Silesia."

"Vater. Can we not talk about this tomorrow? You will be stronger tomorrow."

"No, son. No tomorrow … for me."

They talked awhile longer, until Michael had said what he needed to say.

With one last sharp movement, he tugged the blue cameo ring from his finger and enclosed it in Gerhard's hand. "Yours now," he whispered huskily.

Gerhard stared at his fist and felt the warmth of the ring he held. A lump of emotion knotted in his throat.

"Need to see Paul," Michael said. "He is … the last … then … I can die … in peace."

A hasty effort was made by the women to open some of the rooms, so the family could sleep close through the night. Cook made simple food for those who were hungry and helped put the children to bed. Each adult and Paul took a turn keeping watch with Michael.

Early in the morning, Gerhard watched as a nurse checked his pulse and respiration. Michael's breathing was laboured. His body struggled for each wheezy breath. His lungs gurgled with fluid. She tugged the cover loose from the end of his bed and placed her hands on his feet, then his legs.

"It won't be long now, sir. His extremities are cold. His heart is failing."

Gerhard took his father's hand. "Vater?"

"He can't hear you now, sir. He's travelling." She stayed with him, sitting quietly in a corner of the room. The only sound was Michael's death breaths.

Half an hour later, the gurgling stopped. The nurse straightened the covers on the bed and left the two men alone. Gerhard hunched over the hand that still clasped his father's and wept.

✥

Liegnitz, Silesia
29 October 1934
PRIVATE

Dear Uncle Leo,
It is with a heavy heart that I write to tell you that my beloved father died yesterday. On his death bed, he insisted that I write to you. You know Vater. Nothing, not

even his own death bed, is going to stand in the way of what he thinks is important.

He wanted you to know what a profound influence you have been in his life and mine. Your influence in our respective military careers made us stronger, better soldiers. We are devoted to this country, as you are.

Vater sends his wishes of support and encouragement in the work you do on behalf of Germany. He bids you, stay the course.

You were in his last thoughts.

With admiration and appreciation,
Your loving nephew
Gerhard Lange

London
15 November 1934

Dear Nephew,
I am deeply saddened at your news. I shall miss your father's presence. He was a

steadfast friend. The world will be a lesser place without him.

Stay the course, my boy, and keep your wits about you.

Your loving uncle,
Leo

CHAPTER NINETEEN

Toward the end of November, Gerhard received a telephone call from his friend Alexi Puchinski. Alexi owned and operated the Grand Hotel in Liegnitz. He asked Gerhard to stop by the hotel the next time he drove into town.

"I have plans to be in town tomorrow," Gerhard replied. "I'll stop by then: say, ten o'clock?"

The following day, the hotel receptionist rapped on the office door and opened it to admit Gerhard.

"Inge," Alexi said to his secretary, "would you please arrange for coffee to be sent in? Then perhaps you can help at the front desk for a while. Yes?"

"Certainly, sir."

"Welcome, Gerhard, and thanks for coming." Alexi invited Gerhard to sit on a blood-red leather armchair and sat in an

JERENA TOBIASEN

identical chair opposite him. "I need to discuss a delicate matter with you," he said.

Alexi leaned forward, resting his arms on his knees as he spoke. "Six years ago, my cousin's daughter came to live with us." Alexi rubbed his shaking hands together. "I use the term 'cousin' loosely. We share the same great-grandfather. Nicolai travels a lot, and we all felt that his daughter would receive a better education if she lived with Stefan and me until she finished school.

"As you know, Stefan graduated last term, and is now in the youth military serving his one-year of obligatory service. My cousin was in town for the fall fair last month, and his daughter is now travelling with him once again. However, before they left, Stefan and Punita were betrothed. They'll be married next—"

"Punita? Do you mean that pretty young woman I've seen in town with Stefan?"

"Yes. She is very pretty, indeed. Even if I say so myself," Alexi said proudly.

"Wait!" Gerhard said, knuckling his

188

chin in contemplation. "Your cousin's wife. Her name wouldn't be Rose ... Rosemary ... Rosina ... Rosa—"

"Rosalee. Yes. Have you met her?"

"As a matter of fact, I have. Paul and I took a load of goods to Schinawa recently and met up with Konstantin Anker." Gerhard puzzled further, the small hairs on the back of his neck prickling. "Konstantin introduced us to two very attractive women. I think he said the mother was Rosalee and the daughter was Punita."

And they both have dark brown eyes. I wonder whether they might be the women linked to Paul's future. Paul said Rosalee's behaviour was abrupt after she noted the eyes. She must have seen something!

"Yes, yes. That would be them," Alexi said. "I received a message just yesterday that they travelled with Konstantin to Amsterdam. They must have sailed shortly after you met them." Alexi shook his head in wonder. "The world is so small, is it not?"

"Indeed," Gerhard agreed. "Does your telephone call yesterday have something to do with Rosalee and Punita?"

"Yes and no," Alexi said. "It's more to do with Nicolai, Rosalee's husband. He was to sail with Konstantin as well, but for some reason he was detained."

A light rap sounded at the office door before it opened slowly and a cart was wheeled in, pushed by a young man from the kitchen. "Pardon me, sir. I understand you wished coffee?"

"Yes, Benjamin. Please bring it in. I'll serve. Inge will let you know when we're finished."

Benjamin pushed the cart into the room and excused himself.

Alexi rose from his chair and poured a cup of coffee for Gerhard.

"Go on," Gerhard urged. "I'm listening ..."

Alexi poured himself a cup of the steaming coffee, stirred in a lump of sugar, and resumed his seat.

"Nicolai had some business with one of the farmers just outside of Schinawa. As I understand it, the morning the ship was to leave, he had gone out to the farm and was expected to return by mid-morning. He didn't arrive. Konstantin sent some of the crew to make enquiries.

"Apparently, there was a rousting that morning. Some Jewish families were taken away in trucks. Nicolai was stopped outside the town gate and forced into one of those trucks. I've been unable to find out anything that will tell me why he was picked up or where he was taken."

Alexi sipped his coffee, then hung his head. "Gerhard, I don't want to impose, but I am concerned for my cousin," he said. His dark eyes seemed to will Gerhard to understand. "Do you have any idea where he might have been taken?"

"No, my friend, I don't."

"Would it be possible for you to make enquiries?" Alexi begged.

"Of course," Gerhard said, rising to

set his empty cup and saucer on the cart. "Write down the full name of your cousin and any other details you can think of. Height, weight, colouring, etcetera. I'll see what I can find."

Alexi went to his desk and scribbled the information on a sheet of paper. "His name is Nicolai Kota. He resembles Konstantin remarkably. Except his hair is a little darker. Konstantin and I have a Roma heritage. Nicolai is the true wanderer, though." He handed the paper to Gerhard.

"He looks like Konstantin, you say?" Gerhard pondered Alexi's words. "I think I saw him the day we met Rosalee. I remember Paul commenting on the resemblance, noting that Nicolai's hair was darker as well."

As an afterthought, he said, "Is he the one who raced that purebred called *Bang* at the Fair?"

"*Bang* was his horse, yes," Nicolai reflected, "but he will have sold his horses by now. He would have had to raise money to start a new life in Amsterdam. Such a shame. Nicolai loved that horse."

Gerhard saluted Alexi with the piece of paper, promising to make enquiries. "I'll get back to you as quick as I can, but it may take some time," he warned, shaking Alexi's hand and taking his leave.

With his hand on the doorknob, Gerhard turned abruptly. "Tell me," he said. "Your cousin's wife, Rosalee ... she is a fortune-teller, I believe."

"That's correct." Alexi smiled. "Did she read for you?"

"No, no." Gerhard chuckled, staring at a spot on the carpet. "But she did read for Paul. I don't really believe in that stuff, but, given what she said to Paul ..."

"If Rosalee told Paul something of his future," Alexi said, placing his hand on Gerhard's shoulder and gazing at him with sincerity, "you can believe it! She has a gift, and I've never known her to be wrong."

"Then, I will keep my eye on Paul," Gerhard said. "Rosalee's predictions were quite ominous. I will also do my best to find your cousin. I have no concern for Rosalee's safety, if she is with Konstantin, but I can't promise you the same for Nicolai. Good-bye, my friend." Gerhard opened the door and walked along the hallway toward the hotel lobby.

A burning sensation bloomed in his chest. *Alexi and Konstantin are true and loyal friends. I hope I can find their cousin. I don't want to disappoint them.*

Several days later, Gerhard kissed his wife good-bye and drove the Rohr west. "If I'm going to find a missing Roma, I can do it better from the offices in Dresden," he said to Emma that morning while they ate their breakfast.

The weather was cold and crisp, and a skiff of snow blanketed the ground. The tires on the 1928 Rohr handled the icy roads well, and within four hours Gerhard was parking in front of military headquarters. He spent the day speaking with officers

194

and making telephone calls. As the light of day faded, he phoned home.

"Emma, my dear, I'm off to Bavaria! I'm sorry you won't be able to keep me company, but I must go directly there. I think time is critical. I promise I will take you there soon. We'll have the honeymoon we've never had!"

The drive to Dachau in Upper Bavaria took him three chilly days. *One day, it would be nice to have a car that could be warmed up on the inside. Heated seats. Ah, that would be wonderful!*

He breathed heavily into his gloved hands, trying to warm them for a moment, then tightened the muffler around his neck.

As the Rohr approached the gates to the Dachau holding camp, a guard stepped out of a small office in the wall. Gerhard stopped his car next to the guard and rolled down the window.

"How may I help you, sir?"

Gerhard handed the guard his credentials. The guard scanned the papers and snapped to attention. "I'll just open the gates for you, Major," he said, before jogging toward the great gate, unlocking it and pushing one side open. As the Rohr rolled past the guard, he saluted and pointed Gerhard in the direction of the administrative offices.

Gerhard rolled the Rohr to a stop outside the entrance of a three-story, white-brick building. Unfolding his stiff legs, he stretched to his full height and surveyed the compound. Hundreds of skeletal men clothed in striped uniforms worked like automatons.

This is outrageous! Disgust and compassion rose in his gorge.

Inside the administrative building, he cleared his throat and knocked on a wooden countertop. He had not worn his uniform, and no one paid him any attention.

"Pardon me," he said in a loud, clear voice. "I'm looking for the commander of this camp."

Three office workers turned their eyes in his direction. Before anything further was

196

said, a chair in an adjoining room grated on the wooden floor and heavy footsteps carried the commander into the front office.

"I am Inspector General of this camp. Theodor Eicke," he said. "Who are you?"

"Retired Major Gerhard Lange, formerly of the Regiment of King Wilhelm the First," Gerhard said, showing his papers.

"How may I help you, sir?"

"I am enquiring after an individual," he said. "A cousin of a friend of mine." Gerhard assessed Eicke, not liking what he saw. "The individual goes by the name of Nicolai Kota. I understand that he was detained outside of Schinawa, perhaps a month or so ago. I believe he was brought here, and I'm wondering whether you can confirm the information I've been given."

"And who gave you this information, sir?" Eicke asked.

"As I mentioned"—Gerhard continued to scrutinize Eicke—"a friend of mine told me that his cousin was missing, and asked whether I might help. I've asked about, and it became more of a word here and a word there. Nothing particularly concrete. I've driven from Liegnitz trying to track Herr Kota's journey and thought that—since I'm in the area—I'd ask here. Have you any record that might indicate whether he's passed through the gates of this camp?"

Gerhard watched the eyes of his opponent for clues of deception. *Aha! My intuition has not betrayed me. Shadows of evil move in this man's eyes.*

"Kota, you say. Hmm. Let me check." Eicke turned toward the staff. "Bring me the register," he growled. Turning to Gerhard, he asked, "You said within the past month or so?"

Gerhard nodded.

"The register for the last quarter," Eicke elaborated to his staff.

The appropriate register was deposited on the counter between the two men. Eicke opened it and scanned the names of entries since September.

Well into the list, he prodded a page and looked up. "Kota, you said. Nicolai Kota?"

"That's correct."

"This entry shows that Nicolai Kota, a Jew from Schinawa, was brought into the camp in early November. He had a broken right hand and a broken right rib," Eicke said.

"Mein Gott!" Gerhard spat, glaring at Eicke. "Your record is mistaken. He's not a Jew. Herr Kota is a renowned German horse trainer. His skills are invaluable. I demand his immediate release."

"Can't do that, sir." Eicke glared back.

"And why not?" Gerhard stood to his full height, holding Eicke's glare.

"Because he's dead."

"What! How?"

"We had an outbreak of epidemic typhus. Still do," Eicke said. "It's almost under control, but Kota was one of the first to die."

Gerhard tried to contain his rage. "And his body? Where can I find it? I'd like to at least take it back with me for a decent burial."

"Can't do that either," Eicke grunted.

"Why not?"

"The bodies of anyone who died from typhus have been burnt to reduce contamination."

"And his possessions?" Gerhard asked.

"Says here"—Eicke ran his finger across the page—"that he had none. They seldom do. They usually come in here with only the clothes on their back. No papers, no money, no possessions."

Eicke snapped the register closed. "Will that be all, sir? Any other missing bodies you'd like to enquire after?" Eicke said in a bullying tone.

"No," Gerhard said, deflated. "That is all."

⚜

Outside, Gerhard's narrowed eyes scanned the camp again, seeing in more detail the misery of its occupants. *This place is hopeless! I must speak to someone about Eicke and these deplorable conditions. These poor folks! Surely, Herr Hitler didn't intend this. This is 1934 Germany, for God's sake!*

Icy flakes of snow swirled around him. He wrapped the muffler tight around his neck and pulled his cap over his ears, then stuffed his hands into his leather gloves and slid onto the icy leather seat. He jabbed the key into the ignition, and the Rohr sprang to life.

On the return drive to Liegnitz, he toyed with words, trying to find the kindest way to tell Alexi what had happened to his cousin. He thought of Rosalee and her daughter, and how devastated they would be to receive the news.

When his mind was sorted, he contemplated the conditions at Dachau and what might be done to improve them. *First, I must find someone who will listen. If I encounter any more men like Eicke, I doubt I'll get very far, if at all!*

CHAPTER TWENTY

Gerhard and Emma dropped Paul at the Liegnitz train station at the end of August, 1935. They waited with the other parents who were also there to see their young men off to the military academy.

"It's hard to imagine that it was twenty-one years ago when we all stood here to see you and Otto and the others off," Emma said.

"Yes, well, several of us are missing now. And, I doubt that anything in the coming conflict will resemble what happened twenty years ago," Gerhard said with sadness, reflecting on that long-ago day. He reached out to his son. "Paul! The train is coming. Let us say good-bye before the sergeant calls you together."

"Stop fidgeting," Emma said as she fussed over her son. "Let me adjust your collar and strap. There now. That's better."

"Mutti," Paul snapped. Embarrassed by her ministrations, he shrugged his shoulder from her grasp. "How will I ever learn to keep myself neat without your hawk-like eyes to sort me out?" A glint of affection betrayed his stern glare.

"It will take an entire military academy to replace me!" she retorted. "Let me look at you. Every bit as handsome as your old father, I dare say. What do you think, husband?"

"Beauty is in the eye of the beholder, my dear." Gerhard kissed the top of Emma's head and admired the young man before him. "He'll do."

The sergeant walked up behind Paul and snapped a tidy salute for Gerhard.

In reflex, Gerhard returned the salute. "No need for that, Sergeant. I've been a civilian for some time now."

"Yes, sir. But, with respect, your service to our country is always worthy of acknowledgement."

"You're away then?" Gerhard asked.

"Yes, sir. I'm about to assemble the boys and have them board. Seems not so long ago that I was assembling your generation. Perhaps it's time for me to consider retirement, too." He sighed and continued. "But, then what would I do with myself?"

Before Gerhard could think of a smart response, a warning toot sounded from the train. Turning toward it, the sergeant blew a loud whistle and issued a command for the young men to assemble. He winked at Gerhard and departed.

Heading toward the platform, the sergeant bellowed, "Snap to it!" and the young men began to assemble in front of him. When they quieted, he gave them instructions for boarding and ushered them down the tunnel toward the platform. Families followed.

Paul stepped away from his comrades as they clambered aboard the train, brought himself to attention, and saluted his father. Gerhard snapped a salute in response, releasing Paul to join his troop.

With one hand on the rail and a foot on the lower step, Paul turned again to his parents. "See you soon," he said and disappeared into the passenger car.

Gerhard and Emma waited until the train had begun to roll and Paul's waving arm could no longer be seen.

"God help him," Gerhard said, feeling a sense of foreboding. He wrapped his arm around Emma's shoulder, giving her an affectionate squeeze, and guided her out of the station.

They stood for a moment outside the station, letting the warmth of the sun penetrate their skin. Inside the station, the stones kept the air cold and damp. As if on cue, they each tugged the brim of their hats lower, to shade their eyes from the smile of the noonday sun.

Gerhard stuck out his elbow, inviting Emma to take hold. "Care for a drive to Bavaria, my dear?"

"That sounds lovely." She took his arm and leaned into him as they walked to the

205

car. More like two youths in love than a couple married for sixteen years.

⚜

Gerhard and Emma enjoyed the drive from Liegnitz to Bavaria. They spent several weeks visiting various small towns like tourists and driving through the countryside to gain a sense of the surrounding farming communities. It was mid-September, and the trees were beginning to change their coats of green for gold and orange.

Well into the second week, they hired an agent and visited manufacturing plants and farming industries. They even took time to look at houses in the smaller cities, and overall viewed their time away as the honeymoon they had never had.

Driving home, they reviewed where they had been and what they had seen.

"What do you think, *Liebling*? Have you seen anything of interest?" asked Emma.

"I have, indeed. I like the idea of an industry related to farming. It's easier to evaluate what you already know. Father suggested that we invest our money first. We can relocate in time, if and when the need arises. We have enough equity to purchase any one of the farms or manufacturing plants. All we need to do now is decide which option is best for us. Mutti should be part of our discussions."

"I agree."

"What about you, Emma? Did you see anything appealing?"

"As a matter of fact, I did." Emma clapped her hands with pleasure, her blue kid gloves making a soft thud.

She straightened in the seat beside him and smoothed the hem of her skirt. She had bought a new suit in Nurnberg—brown tweed—and a creamy silk blouse that tied in a bow at her neck. The rich creaminess accentuated her hazel eyes.

Emma flexed her crossed ankles, admiring her two-toned spectator shoes. The movement distracted Gerhard's gaze from the road, and the car jerked off the pavement momentarily before he corrected its direction.

"Stop thinking about my hat!" she warned.

"I wasn't thinking about your hat!" he defended before his mind wandered again.

"How you found kid gloves and shoes of the same shade of blue is beyond me," he had remarked when she had modelled her new outfit earlier that morning. "And your hat! Now that is a work of art. The way it pulls together all of the colours in your outfit."

He grinned as he walked around her, eyeing her slim figure. "I particularly like the way it frames your face."

"In fact," he said, continuing to ogle her, "the entire outfit is most ... tantalizing, my darling! And when you put on that hat"— he leaned toward her—"I can't keep my lips off yours!" He seized her swiftly, his kiss leaving her gasping for air when he finally released her.

All during breakfast and while they loaded the car, Emma had shamelessly taunted him with her hat. By the time they were on the road, her lips were bruised and swollen, making them, in his opinion, even more desirable.

A grin played over his lips when he glanced at her.

"Do you want to hear my thoughts?" she said, interrupting his musings.

"Hmm?" His attention returned to the road. "Your thoughts? Oh! Certainly," he said, remembering that he had asked a question. "Please. Tell me what appeals to you. I know what appeals to me." He winked at her.

"You are impossible!" She laughed, slapping his arm playfully. "Keep your eyes on the road, or we'll end up in the ditch, you letch!"

He reached to grab her arm, but she swatted it away, insisting that he watch the road.

"In all seriousness." She continued. "I liked the houses. I especially liked the red brick one in Bayreuth. The gardens were lovely, and so many rooms. The way it stretched wide and open on each floor. It even had three toilets! Just imagine … no waiting!"

"Indeed! A little different from what we have now, I dare say," Gerhard said, snickering.

"Yes. We could even convert some of the rooms into a suite for your mother. I think she'd like that."

"Well, let's not lose sight of that house, then. I'll follow up with the agent once we've discussed everything with Mutti."

"Gerhard?" She looked at him, her face sincere. "I have so enjoyed these past weeks alone with you. I feel that I love you even more. Yet, how that could be, I can't say."

He reached across and took her hand, raising it to his lips. "I understand exactly how you feel, Liebling," he said before dropping her hand and taking control of the wheel as the vehicle once again veered, the right front tire dipping off the pavement and raising a small dust plume. "Emma, you are such a distraction!"

"It's a good thing that we're almost home! Look! There's the standard!" She pointed.

CHAPTER TWENTY-ONE

In the year that followed, Gerhard, Emma, and Anna planned their great migration. They agreed that their initial investment would involve farming. Their intention was to relocate not just themselves, but anyone employed on the estate as well. They bought a dairy business on the condition that the vendor would continue to operate it for at least three years. Six months later, they added a business that repaired farm equipment.

"Was that the bell, my dear?" Gerhard asked as Emma entered the kitchen from the hallway.

He removed his muddy boots just outside the door and stepped into the kitchen. "That rain has made a nasty mess of everything," he prattled, leaving his question dangling while he shook plops of water from his hat and jacket onto the doorstep before hanging them on a hook just inside the door.

He shut the door and padded into the warm kitchen in his stocking feet, rubbing his hands to dry them.

Cook stirred a pot of soup, steam rising as it burbled. Short wisps of silver-grey hair escaped her tidy bun, forming tiny, damp curls on her forehead.

He leaned over the pot and sniffed. "Beef and vegetables. Mmm! My favourite." He smiled dreamily at her.

"Off with you," she said. "Everything is your favourite!" She flipped a dish towel at him, then reached for the oven door to remove a tray of biscuits.

Cook, whose real name was Henny Braumburg, had been a member of the Lange household since before Gerhard went to war. Her husband had died in that war, and she had no children or extended family. The Lange family had adopted her and offered her rooms of her own off the kitchen. They also offered her employment for as long as she chose to stay with them.

When Michael died, Gerhard and Emma

had moved their family into the manor, where Cook had remained in service. The cook whom they had employed to that point had conveniently been called away on a family matter, and soon after she advised that she would not be returning.

Paul and his siblings had started calling Henny '*Tante* Cook' and the name had stuck. Gerhard could not imagine another cook in the manor's kitchen.

He turned toward Emma, who continued to stand in the kitchen doorway, twisting an envelope between her fingers as if she were trying to decipher the contents without opening it.

His earlier question forgotten, he asked, "Who's the letter from?"

"Hmm? Oh! It's not a letter, really. I mean. Yes. You did hear the door. It's a telegram. For you. From London," Emma answered both questions.

Gerhard took the envelope and tore it open. The note typed on telegraph paper read:

11 April 1936 stop Sir stop With regret
stop Leopold Gustav Alexander von
Hoesch German Ambassador to the Court
of St James died 10 April 1936 stop Office
of Dr von Hoesch stop

Gerhard reached for a nearby chair and dropped into it, handing the telegram to Emma as he sat. "That's it then. First Vater, now Uncle Leo. What a tragic loss to us all."

"Yes, it marks the end of an era, doesn't it?" Emma said sadly.

"Indeed. I have a sense that we should begin preparations to leave for Bayreuth. Depending on how our investments play out, and how Herr Hitler manages the country, we should be well on our way within the next few years."

In the following months, they began to organize their future, and took time to speak privately with each employee, offering them the opportunity to relocate to the new farm or business. Some chose to take the offer. Others preferred to stay with the estate, where they had lived and worked for generations.

Late one July afternoon three years later, the Bayreuth property agent telephoned Gerhard. "I have good news for you. The house in Bayreuth is available. Are you still interested?"

Emma and Gerhard left for Bayreuth the following morning to look at the house one more time. As they stood in the foyer of the great empty house, Gerhard declared, "We'll buy it!"

"Would you not like to see the rest of the house first?" the agent asked.

"We'll certainly take another tour," Gerhard responded, watching the dreamy expression on Emma's face. "Regardless, we'll buy it."

"I thought you might say that," the agent responded. "I have the papers here. Shall we tour first, or would you prefer to sign ..."

When Gerhard turned to defer to Emma, he noted that she was already ascending the wide oak staircase that led to the second floor. "Looks like my wife wishes a tour first," he said. He turned from the agent and took the stairs two at a time to catch up.

"Fine," the agent said, scrambling behind them. "Upstairs, you'll find …"

❖

"The businesses are operating well. You have your house, and the timing couldn't be better." Gerhard summarized on the way home. "If we work it right, we should be able to move into the new house before Christmas, and the workers can follow when they're ready."

"I'm happy that Paul will be home at the end of August. He won't have to report for duty until January. He will be able to help with the move and settle into the new house before he reports," Emma said. "I wish Otto would come with us. He could run the farm."

"He knows, Emma, but he prefers to stay in Liegnitz for now. He will oversee the running of the estate, as well. Should things become difficult, he is prepared to drop everything. As I do, he feels a responsibility to the land and the farmhands."

"Well," Emma said, "I'm glad Tante Cook is coming. She and Mutti have been together so long, I can't imagine one without the other."

"I'm not worried about them. I'm worried about your parents, though."

"But they're obstinate. They will not give up their land and their home easily," Emma lamented.

During the days that followed, the manor was a beehive of activity. Emma supervised the overall packing, keeping an inventory of the furniture and other household items that would be packed and shipped to Bayreuth. The children worked with Anna to ensure personal items were packed. Tante Cook oversaw the packing of her kitchen.

Gerhard gave instructions to the farmhands, who would travel to Bavaria in the New Year. He also met with Otto, Farmer

Schmidt, and the remaining farmhands to discuss management of the estate in his absence.

The day following Paul's return from the academy, Otto arrived at the door of Gerhard's study soon after the midday meal.

"Otto, why are you here in the middle of the day?" Gerhard said, teasing him. "It's not like you to quit before the cows are in the barn."

Otto's face was difficult to read, lacking his usual grin.

"Come in, sit." Gerhard lifted the decanter. "Brandy?" He began pouring into crystal glasses. Sun through the window cast rainbows through the cut glass and onto the walls.

"Your room sparkles this time of year," Otto said. "I will miss that. And the brandy, of course."

He sipped the brandy blissfully, stretching his long right leg to rest atop his prosthetic left, crossing his ankles. Then he tipped his glass to Gerhard in a toast. "I have news that can't wait. I've just returned from *Oppeln*. While I waited for Zabar Anker to arrive with his ship, I spoke with a few locals. Word is that trouble is coming. I suggest that you get out as quickly as you can. Send the old ladies off today, if they'll go. They can take the children."

"Why? What have you heard?"

"All the nonsense in Poland. No one knows who they are anymore. The Russians want one half of the country, and, of course, Deutschland wants the other half. Anyone caught in the middle is at risk."

"Yes, we've heard that on the wireless. I had hoped that we would have more time." Gerhard paced across the room, turned, and paced back. "Will you come with us?"

"No. Not yet. I think we'll be safe for now. Farmers haven't been upgraded to gentry yet, so we don't pose the threat that you folks do. Hilde and I will stay and run the farm and the estate as long as we can."

"What about your parents? Can you convince them to come with us?"

"If I can, I'll have them ready to travel with the old ladies."

"Who are you calling old ladies, Otto Schmidt?" Anna's voice preceded her entry from the hallway. She smiled as she stepped into the room, extending her arms in greeting. Otto gave her a warm hug, lifting her off the floor.

"Take care you don't off-balance the both of us, you burly farmer! Old ladies break easily, you know."

"I beg your pardon, Anna. No offence," Otto said in response to her jest. "I was just telling Gerhard of the news from Oppeln. I strongly suggest that you and Tante Cook take the children and go on ahead. Today, if you can."

"Well. It could be a bit tricky, but, if one of the farmhands can drive us, I think we can be ready to leave after dinner."

"Make it a quick dinner," Otto suggested, "and pack extra food for the *Kinder*. They never stop eating, those ones."

"I'll arrange for two vehicles," Gerhard

said, planning aloud. "One of the trucks for your cases and whatever other small things you might need. You and the children can ride in the Rohr. You might have a tight fit, but it's better than sending you off in all of the trucks and leaving the farm without a vehicle for several days."

"I'm going to ask my folks to go with you," Otto added. "But. Well, you know how stubborn they can be."

"Give me a minute, Otto. Let me speak with Cook and Emma, and I'll walk back to the farmhouse with you. Let's see how persuasive the two of us can be."

While they waited for Anna, Gerhard and Otto exchanged last-minute transportation concerns.

"Let's go," Anna said, pulling on her sweater. "Sounds like we have no time to waste."

Leaving the manor by the front steps, Anna said to Gerhard, "Make sure the roof of the Rohr is up. It will be too windy and cold driving at night with it down. If the weather turns too warm tomorrow, we can always put it down during one of the rest stops."

✤

As the blushing sun dissolved into the ripening field, a bright blue farm truck and a cream-coloured Rohr with the blue soft-top still up pulled away from the manor, laden with grandparents, children, and luggage. Anna and the two drivers had travel instructions that would see them safely to Bayreuth.

"As soon as everything is arranged here, Emma, Paul, and I will follow." Gerhard told his mother.

The vehicles rolled down the drive and onto the road. A cloud of dust chased them as they disappeared into the dusk.

✤

The following days took on an urgent schedule of their own. Hasty breakfasts. Cold lunches. Small dinners. In between, they packed, wrapped, organized, and sorted, until all of their goods were loaded onto farm trucks and sent on to the house in Bayreuth.

In the meantime, the blue truck and the Rohr returned from Bayreuth, with confirmation that the old folks and children had been settled in the new house. The weather held, too: the usual rain for that time of year stood at bay against the continuing warm weather.

While the dry weather made it easier for vehicles to travel on the highway, it also made it easier for the German air force to hit their Polish targets, and for the military to move transports and equipment on the ground. Roads were congested with a mêlée of traffic. Fortunately, the vehicles from the Lange estate were headed in the opposite direction.

Emma, Gerhard, and Paul spent their last night in Silesia at the farmhouse with Otto and his wife, Hildegard. The meal was humble by comparison to Cook's feasts, but delicious nonetheless, and they shared one last glass of brandy before retiring for the night. Gerhard had kept back two bottles for just that occasion.

Early the next morning, they shared a hasty breakfast and packed the last of their personal items.

While Emma and Paul waited in the Rohr, Gerhard took one last photograph of the manor, and hugged Otto as only two long-time friends might. "Take care, my friend, and don't stay too long."

"I won't," Otto replied, steadying himself on the driveway so he could wave good-bye.

"I won't let him," Hildegard chimed in.

Gerhard put the Rohr in gear and let it roll to the end of the drive. He hollered one last time, "Don't stay too long!" before turning onto the side road.

The gears groaned as Gerhard shifted again and the car accelerated, dust swirling around the cream rims of the tires. With the promise of another warm day, the roof was down, allowing its occupants to wave good-bye. A convoy of loaded farm trucks followed.

Otto and Hildegard waved wildly until the Rohr disappeared beyond their sight.

Once they were settled in Bayreuth, Gerhard contacted the farm manager he had engaged to operate the *Neue*-farm—the name they used to distinguish it from the Schmidt farm—until Otto was available.

He assured Gerhard that the farmhouse was empty, and that Herr and Frau Schmidt could move into it whenever they chose. "I'd be happy to work with them as long as you have need of me," he assured Gerhard. "I've been living in the guesthouse, and am comfortable to continue doing so."

In the weeks following, the farmhouse was organized for Otto's parents. They were quick to take up residence, and found the working relationship with the farm manager quite agreeable.

CHAPTER TWENTY-TWO

Gerhard's imminent concern for the relocation was petrol. He had heard about shortages near sites of conflict, and hoped that his vehicles would be able to reach Bayreuth and return to Silesia without difficulty. He hoped to return the trucks quickly, with a surplus of petrol, to see the harvest reaped.

Otto needed the farmhands to help him manage the harvest. A bountiful harvest was expected, requiring all available help. Once the harvest was in, the families of those farmhands who chose to relocate would migrate to Bavaria.

The new year isn't so far away, Gerhard mused. *With it will come a change from sleepy country life to busy city life and the industry of Bavaria. And, God help us all, another war. And I hope that the Polish business will be settled before Paul is required to report for duty.*

Before the threat of conflict had become a common topic, Paul and Gerhard had spent many hours discussing Paul's career choices: he preferred that his son follow in his footsteps and study engineering at the university in Bayreuth. Paul had expressed a desire to enter the priesthood from a young age, and would not be swayed.

As he contemplated the past and the current conditions in Germany, Gerhard's stomach clenched with anxiety and fear.

He had tried to speak with his former superiors about the conditions in Dachau and warn them about the risks of other camps being built, but the discussion ended in a shouting match, with him on the losing end. The superiors scoffed at his concerns and refused to believe his description of the Dachau camp. Herr Hitler would not allow such conditions, they argued.

He felt helpless, and worried for any souls incarcerated in Hitler's camps.

❖

Early in January 1940, the post brought orders for Paul to report for duty. Unlike the day Gerhard received his orders in 1914, no celebration followed. Instead, Gerhard erupted in anger when he read the paper Paul handed him.

He looked to be certain the study door was closed, then bellowed, "*Verdammte* Nazis! I won't have it!" He paced, shaking the orders wildly. "I won't have my son put his life in jeopardy for that pissant corporal and his thugs!

"Deutschland is bound by the Treaty of Versailles. Hitler continues to defy the terms and puts the entire country at risk. Someone needs to stand up to his government. His tyranny."

Gerhard slammed his fist on his desk, dropping the paper as if it was poisoned. "Goddamn Nazis!" he cursed again.

"Papa, keep your voice down," Paul hissed, resting a cautionary hand briefly on Gerhard's shoulder. "I like to think that the new cook is loyal to the family, but we can never know for certain."

"It's bad enough that he puts the *Wehrmacht* at risk with this Polish conflict," Gerhard continued in a lower, but still angry, voice. "It won't be long before Britain and France act against us, too. They declared war months ago. We're just waiting for the other shoe to drop." He sighed deeply.

"And what about the priesthood?" He waved the orders at Paul. "Damn them all to hell!" He pounded his fist again, rattling everything on the desk.

"Gerhard, please," Emma said, trying to diffuse his anger. "Keep your voice down! Cursing isn't going to solve anything. Besides, the children might hear."

Agitated, Gerhard grabbed the brandy decanter and poured three glasses, then thrust two toward Emma and Paul. "This is so wrong in so many ways. I'm not satisfied. Before Paul reports for duty, I'm going to the Depot myself. I want more information."

Paul took a sip of the brandy as he listened to his father's rant. The apple fumes bloomed in his throat, choking him. He flushed, trying to stifle an urge to cough.

"Son! Are you all right?" Gerhard asked, catching sight of his son's distress.

Paul nodded, unable to speak.

"Brandy is for sipping, son. I forgot it's your first time." Gerhard rubbed Paul's back, trying to soothe him. "Take another sip and hold it for a moment, then swallow slowly. That should settle your throat." Paul did as instructed, and his convulsing throat calmed.

"Better?"

"Yes, Papa," he squeaked. His throat continued to spasm, and he coughed again. "Papa, I agree with you. I don't like Hitler's reasoning. I think he's using us to do his dirty work and feed his greed. Plus, he's playing the people. They think he's wonderful because he's promising employment for everyone, yet I've seen no evidence of jobs for the masses."

Paul jabbed his fingers through his cropped hair, creating ebony spikes. "Have you ever noticed his eyes? They seem shifty to me, as if he has no soul."

Paul sighed audibly. "Besides, military enlistment goes against all of my principles. Do you think I can convince the recruiting office that I'm better suited to be a military chaplain?" he asked. "May I go with you to Depot to put my own ideas forward?"

"Of course. We'll go first thing in the morning."

Changing subjects, Gerhard added, "While we're at it, we'll have your boots made. I can't tell you how important good boots are. My father knew. He had a pair made for me and my schoolmates. We can have a look at other items you'll need in your kit, too. Herr Hitler doesn't provide much, I can tell you that! And nothing is of any quality."

Sotto-voice, he added, "The worthless *Arschloch*!"

"Gerhard!" Emma snapped. "It's counter-productive to be calling the leader of our beloved country an asshole, even if he is a toxic influence."

"Pardon me, my dear," he said, having the good sense to show his remorse.

⚜

"I should have known, Emma," Gerhard sighed the following evening. "It was a waste of time. Just as my pleas about the detention camps were."

He leaned against the kitchen counter, arms crossed over his chest, and described the meeting with the Depot officers. "If we were in Silesia, my seniority might have had some influence. They have little knowledge of me at the Würzburg Depot, only my records from Dresden. The military is different now. There's no respect for status or experience. Those young pups are power-hungry, just like their Chancellor."

"Papa tried to explain the family's military history," Paul interrupted, "and my preference to be a chaplain. They would have none of it. They told me that, if I refused to follow orders and fight for

Hitler's principles, my entire family would be sent to a camp, and all of our assets would be seized to help fund his cause. I'm sorry, Mama, I had no choice …"

Gerhard placed a hand on his son's shoulder. "You tried, Paul. And we are all grateful for your decision."

"Grateful for his decision!" Emma exclaimed. "How can you suggest that our assets are worth our son's life?"

Emma paced across the kitchen. "No! I won't have it! Neither of you will go! Let them take everything. I don't care! I want my family safe, and if that means spending time in a work camp, so be it. At least we'll all be together."

"Emma, my dear," Gerhard said, racing to her side and taking her in his arms. "We wouldn't be together. Men and women are separated, and the conditions in those camps—remember, I've seen Dachau—are very poor: food is paltry, and disease is rampant. Think of the old ladies and the children. You don't want them to suffer."

"Papa is right, Mama. This is something I need to do. For my family," Paul insisted.

"But … what is to happen to Paul?" Emma wailed. She pushed away from Gerhard and stood alone, twisting her hands.

"Paul is to report for duty as ordered," Gerhard explained. "He will start as a junior officer. At least they acknowledged his training and our family's long service to this country so far as enlistment is concerned. The priesthood will have to wait. All we can do now is prepare Paul for whatever he might encounter. Psychologically, that is. He has been well-trained for combat and command; it is hard to prepare for the horror. No matter how much training, reality still takes a soldier by surprise."

"We also arranged for my kit and ordered my boots," Paul added. "They'll be ready before I report."

"The only good news we have in all of this is that the Wehrmacht won't take the Rohr," Gerhard said, making a repugnant face. "They've determined it to be useless for military purposes because its wheel base is too long!"

"Well, that is good news," Emma lamented. "The old ones can continue to use it to get around. So long as we have fuel, that is."

She tapped her fingernail on her teeth, thinking. "What more can we do for you, Paul?" Emma asked. "Shall we have a family party on the eve of your departure? The children would like that."

"Don't worry about me, Mama," Paul responded. "I don't need a party to celebrate something I find repugnant."

"Emma, my dear." Gerhard took her hands in his and kissed them. "I know you're worried. And for good cause. It's not usual, but if it will distract you to organize a party, go ahead. Perhaps the children can help too, hmm?"

He took Emma in his arms and held her, trying to absorb some of her anxiety. *But how can anyone absorb a mother's worry?* he wondered.

235

✤

"Damn them all to hell!" Gerhard yelled the words as he read the orders.

"What is it, Gerhard? Did I hear the bell?" Emma flew down the oak staircase in response to her husband's words.

"Yes," he barked, waving the paper to express his outrage. "Not one, but two! I can't believe the audacity!"

"Please. Gerhard. Calm yourself and come into the study, where we can talk privately."

She took his arm and led him across the hall, closing the door behind them. "Now. What is it?"

His anger blinded him to the deep grains of the oak that panelled the study, the worn leather of the chairs and settee, and the stained glass in the windows. He focussed on the old Spanish painting—his favourite, first hung in the manor in Silesia by his great-grandfather in 1870—before he continued. "It seems that Hitler is not satisfied with one Lange. He wants us both!"

"Oh, nein." Emma's knees buckled, and she sank into the edge of the settee. "This is a dream. A bad dream. What can we do? Gerhard, you can't go," she pleaded. "You mustn't!"

"I must. And you know it, my dear."

"But what about your nightmares? You worked so hard to overcome them. In fact, you haven't had them for years," she said, expressing her worry. "Lately ... they're coming back, aren't they? You've called out in your sleep several times in the past few nights. Your sleep is restless. And you're irritable."

"Emma, I am so sorry to put you through all of that again. I've tried to protect you from it." He stopped pacing and stood before her. "I haven't done a good job of it, have I?"

Emma had been holding her head in her hands. She looked up at him. "Will you see battle, do you think?" Her question was quiet with concern.

"No. I'll start with the rank of Major. As I was when I retired in '24," he said. "I am to oversee recruitment and training. I've also offered to organize post-battle care for returning troops."

She stood again, wrapping her arms around his waist, resting her head on his chest. "*Das ist gut*," she murmured into his shirt. "If anything can be good about this nonsense."

CHAPTER TWENTY-THREE

Gerhard reported for duty several weeks later.

"Paul," Gerhard had told Emma, "has been sent to Norway. We may not see him before the end of summer."

At the end of June, however, Paul arrived home. His brother and sister danced around him, cheering as his mother gave him a hearty embrace. She felt him stiffen and wince.

"You've changed," she said, brushing a shock of blue-black hair from his forehead, watching a cloud of pain pass through his charcoal eyes. 'Charcoal eyes, just like your father's,' she had told him as soon as the new-born-blue had faded, and many times since.

"You must have grown! Look at you!" She walked around him, assessing the changes. "A fine soldier you are. Your father will be so proud."

Uncomfortable with Emma's fussing,

Paul acknowledged his siblings, giving a hug to his sister, Gerda, and exercising a little rough play with his brother, Arthur.

"How's the boxing going, Arthur?" Then he fired a second question over his shoulder at his mother. "When do you expect Papa home?"

Arthur answered first, in a spiky voice that betrayed his puberty. "I won the championship this year!"

Paul threw a few false punches in Arthur's direction, air-boxing with him.

"Papa's away for a few days. But, he'll be home to see you before you leave again." Emma stood with hands on her hips, observing his playfulness. "What's wrong with your arm?"

"Nothing."

"What's wrong with your arm, Paul?" she asked in her mother-voice.

Arthur and Gerda stilled, looking first to their mother, then to their brother.

"Have you a glass of brandy for a weary soldier, Mama?"

Emma caught his deflection. "Yes, of course. Come into the study." She led the way.

"You two"—she turned to Gerda and Arthur—"go tell Cook that we'll have another mouth for dinner. A very hungry mouth, from the looks of it." She eyed Paul to determine how much more food would be required, knowing supplies were not plentiful.

Paul closed the study door, muffling the boisterous noise racing to the kitchen. He turned to Emma.

Once again, she stood with hands on hips. "I'm waiting."

"I know that look, Mama. No point putting it off. I was shot."

"When? What happened?"

"Well." He poured himself a glass of brandy, and held up the decanter, inviting his mother to take a glass.

"Yes, please," she answered. "It's not every day your eldest child gets shot! I need something to soften this news."

He passed a glass of the amber relief to his mother and continued. "As to when ..." he said, turning his gaze from the Spanish painting of Mars to face his mother, "the end of March."

He rolled the brandy around the glass, airing it, then took a sip.

"Shall we sit?" Emma said, lowering herself onto the settee and sinking into the worn cushion. She waited patiently, as if knowing that Paul was deliberately delaying the telling of his news.

He shrugged, sipped, and continued again. "We were ordered to Norway on a reconnaissance mission. At one point, we were pinned down and took some fire. Actually, it was a bit of luck for the other side. One of the shots hit a stone wall behind us. Debris ricocheted. Caught me in the shoulder; did a bit of damage to the bone. Passed through my arm. Broke a bone here, too." He massaged his arm where the ache persisted.

"I bet I'll be the only soldier in the entire war to disclose that I was shot by a stone wall!" he said, stifling a snort, hoping he had minimized her fussing. "More brandy?" he asked, up-ending his glass and pouring another.

"In March, you say. Why didn't you come home earlier?"

"I was extracted, shall we say, to a field hospital. Had some surgery to repair the bone damage, then spent some time getting my arm and shoulder working again. I needed to be certain that my men were healing, too, before I left, and that added further delay."

He sipped the brandy again, savouring it. "As soon as I had mobility in my arm and shoulder, I was given leave. We all were. Those of us who are able-bodied have been ordered east in three weeks."

"East! Nein! Not east."

"Unfortunately, yes. I hope it's a slow road east. But don't repeat that to the *Führer der Nation*." He made a face of distaste. "We're supposed to be enthusiastic and feel honoured to be in his service."

Emma folded her hands in her lap, unable to hide the concern etched across her face.

"Hitler continues to promise jobs for everyone and a better economy," Paul said, shaking his head. "People love him for it. But, I was right ... all I see are his false promises and his prejudice. The Brown Shirts single out anyone who doesn't toe the line. They instil fear and brutalize those who protest. Hitler says one thing and does another," he spat.

"Paul ..." Emma began.

"We're fighting another damned war— and for what! All I ever wanted was to be a priest. After this, I won't be worthy." He wound down his diatribe of frustration and disappointment and finished by saying, "I'm constantly reminding myself to hold my tongue. Wouldn't help my cause if my men heard me spewing off about that *Dummkopf*. They don't necessarily agree with my opinions."

⚜

A few days later, the Lange family enjoyed a

special meal prepared by Cook in honour of the two returning soldiers. Tante Cook and Anna supervised the new cook's preparations to ensure that their fighting boys would have their favourite, traditional dishes.

Tante Cook continued to prepare simple meals for herself and Anna, but when it came to preparing meals for the family, a younger cook had been engaged following the move to Bayreuth. Tante Cook shared a suite with Anna upstairs, and they kept each other company.

"That was delicious, ladies," Gerhard said, rising from the dining table, bowing formally to Tante Cook and his mother. "Would you mind if Paul and I excuse ourselves? We have things to discuss."

The women shooed them from the dining room and helped with the clearing of the dishes.

"May I come too, Papa?" Arthur asked.

"Not tonight, son. Paul and I have military business to review. Don't you have homework?"

"Yes, sir." Arthur took a boxing pose with Paul and punched the air in front of him. "I was hoping to defer the in-e-vit-able." Arthur exaggerated his pronunciation mischievously.

"Evading homework is not a way to succeed in life. Off you go."

"Yes, sir." Arthur snapped to attention, saluted his father and brother, and darted up the old oak staircase to his room.

⚜

Paul closed the door. Gerhard poured the brandy.

"I hear congratulations are in order, Lieutenant. Or should I say, Captain." Gerhard smiled at his son, holding a glass of brandy out to him.

"Sir?" Paul accepted a proffered crystal glass.

"Word's filtered down to our humble Depot. I understand your heroics in Norway have earned you the Iron Cross! Congratulations. It takes a lot of guts to stand up to overwhelming opposition, to take crippling gunfire, and still get your men out safely."

Gerhard inhaled brandy fumes before raising his glass to his lips. "I'm proud of you, Paul. I hate this war and everything it stands for. And I'm proud of you for conducting yourself as the leader I always knew you would be." His forehead had begun to throb, and he absent-mindedly massaged the old battle wound as he spoke.

"Thanks, Papa. Coming from a military family certainly makes a difference. All that horsing around that we did when we were young. The war games you instigated in the fields. The boot-camp training and military tutoring we had at the academy—it all kicked in."

He walked over to the old painting of Mars, the warrior god, and straightened it with his free hand. "The military training is invaluable, of course. But you, grandfather, and Uncle Otto. Your early influence helped make my responses intuitive. And Great Uncle Leo's words kept me focussed. 'Keep your wits' became my mantra."

He studied his glass of brandy. "We were

out-numbered. I drew on everything I knew to get us out of that spot. It was tricky. Some of us were injured, yes. But none of the injuries were fatal or incapacitating. At least, not for long." He flexed his injured arm and shoulder.

"Did you tell your mother?"

"Nein. I didn't want to worry her. She worries enough already. I just told her that we were under fire and debris ricocheted off a rock wall. She doesn't need to know the rest."

"I agree. We'll leave it at that," Gerhard said. "I understand that you and your men have had some additional training."

"Yes. After Trondheim, I approached my commander and asked whether we might hone our marksmanship. I felt we could have defended ourselves better if we'd had specific training before going in. We are all now certified as sharpshooters, but half of us will serve as spotters, and we'll work in teams of two—one spotter and one sniper."

"When do you leave for the east?"

"I have three weeks to get my arm working again. I think I'll visit with Uncle Otto for a bit. Do you mind? I need to practise my shooting, too, and I know I can do that out in one of the fields without being questioned. We were reminded constantly during the training that the only way to be the best was to practise. I intend to be the best. I don't want to be in another position where the safety of my men is compromised. I can't call on you for advice when I'm trapped. And I certainly can't look to grandfather or old Uncle Leo."

"I'm sure Otto will appreciate all the help he can get. He's lost a lot of the farmhands to the conflict. The Jewish fellow who used to do our bookwork disappeared without a word. He may have relocated with his family or been caught in a round-up. Some of the Polish folks are still there; others have joined the Russians, or gone underground. All of the German hands capable of fighting are serving in the military now."

CHAPTER TWENTY-FOUR

Paul reunited with his men three weeks later. They were based in Breslau, but their orders kept them scouting north and south and, when necessary, defending the German position from counterattacks by the Red Army. Fighting was fierce wherever they were assigned.

They also carried out raids to intercept Russian intelligence, and interpreted dispatches before sending the information further up the line. They set up sniper nests and rotated stations frequently to avoid predictability.

Paul often volunteered to take the night shift, allowing most of his men to rest. With dark, though, came the greatest risk. He and his spotter had to remain vigilant—ensuring they were adequately camouflaged, and that their rifle barrels and other gear did not reflect the moonlight. Lighting no fires, they stared into a black void for long hours at a time, watching for the slightest movement, always aware that it was just as easy to be seen as it was to see. Stakeout time passed slowly, especially when the weather was foul with heavy rain or snow and biting cold.

In time, his platoon became renowned amongst the division for their night work along the front.

One bitterly cold night, Paul and his spotter, Werner Friedrich, were embedded in a pit at the edge of a forested area. The pit was lined with decayed foliage collected from the forest floor.

Once they were entrenched, they had piled more decay on top of themselves, which served to better hide and insulate them in their beds of frozen earth.

Paul was grateful for the winter field uniforms, including woollen overcoats, which were issued at the beginning of October. Unlike the Great War, troops no longer relied on their families to provide well-made uniforms. The standard-issue garments were made from a mixture of wool and rayon, which ensured that their uniforms had endurance, and maintained a high thermal efficiency. They were also comfortable and easy to move in.

Paul had no care about the political reasoning behind the design: that traditional features and trims were retained to improve morale and cultivate unit spirit. He cared only that his men were warm and capable of performing their duties when required.

Although the standard-issue uniform included a toque, Paul had his men replace theirs with a balaclava that could cover their face and reduce reflection. Paul was glad for his balaclava. It kept warmth around his face and minimized the likelihood of his frosty breath revealing his location.

Before them lay the no-man's-land of a harvested hay field. Another grove of trees edged the east side of the field.

Clothed as they were in military camouflage, Paul and Werner blended in to the winter foliage. Small branches were bound with wire to the barrels of their Karabiner 98Ks, telescopic sights, and binoculars.

Paul felt an involuntary shiver of dread run through his body. *1941! How much longer will this war business go on? How did a candidate for the priesthood become a killing machine? Focus, fool! You can't afford to let your mind wander.*

After hours of stillness in their shared pit, even the sheepskin lining in his boots and mittens could not keep the cold at bay. The flexibility of his finger joints had lessened, his toes were numb, and his muscles felt par-frozen.

Paul had given an order that, when the ability to make an accurate shot was compromised by stiff fingers, shivering, or simply a sense of frozen brain, he expected the shooter to identify the need to stand down. A precise shot was difficult enough to make, but waiting to take a shot with exposed hands and a freezing rifle compromised that precision. *I'm going to have to call for a stand-down soon.*

Moonlight reflected off the thin layer of frost blanketing the field.

"I'm glad we have nature's cover to help keep us warm," Werner whispered, a cloud of icy breath escaping from below his binoculars. Paul withheld his response, knowing the risk Werner took with his words.

I'll have to remind him later to take care of when and how he speaks.

In the instant that it took for Paul to form his thought, he heard the tell-tale whistle, followed by a deep and deadly thud. A fine spray of crimson droplets erupted in slow motion from the gaping hole, ringed in blackened flesh, between Werner's frosted eyebrows.

Paul was momentarily distracted by a recollection of the birthday cake presented to his sister on her eighth birthday. Its white icing had been covered with red sprinkles.

Paul's movement was miniscule, shifting only his eyes to witness the shot, before his mind screamed, *Duck*!

Two more bullets whistled in his

direction, the first thudding into the trunk of a sapling directly behind Werner's lifeless body. The second skimmed across the brim of his helmet, even before he could distance himself from the line of fire and collapse deeper into the pit for cover. The percussion of bullet against helmet gave him an instant headache, which amplified when his head crashed into the nest wall as he fell backward.

Werner lay beside him, unmoving, braced as he had been before his life escaped him. The binoculars remained as they had been positioned, on the earthen wall at Werner's nose.

Before the second bullet found its lodging, Paul had heard more familiar whistles from nests to his left and right, where other members of his squad had settled. Seconds later, a Russian voice echoed from across the field.

"Mama?" he cried.

Silence followed. Except for the crawling of time, nothing moved.

Paul tried to still his racing heart. Adren-aline pulsed through his body, and he fought to overcome its control. *I can't sight with shaking hands,* his mind screamed.

He took several deep breaths, releasing them into his mitted hand. When he felt his heart slow, and control return to his limbs, he raised the barrel of the Karabiner 98K slowly, until it rested on the lip of the pit. He was well aware that any movement put him at risk of being spotted by a Russian sniper.

Paul settled the weight of the rifle butt and placed his finger on the trigger while he sighted the trees on the opposite side of the field. False dawn was approaching. Soon, the dark would hide no one.

He found a target, high in a fir tree, and focussed. Squeezing the trigger slightly in preparation, he took a deep breath, steadied his body for a count of three, then squeezed the trigger home.

Through the sight, he watched the bul-let's trajectory until a faint, crimson spray confirmed the accuracy of his shot and the shadow of his opponent slumped against the tree trunk. A moment later, the target's rifle fell through the branches. Once again, silence followed; time crawled and nothing else moved.

When Paul was confident that the immediate threat had passed, he gave the command to withdraw, before the light of dawn put his men at greater risk. He alone remained in his pit, scanning the far side of the field for danger. When he heard the quiet shuffle of his men assembling behind him, he began his own withdrawal.

Paul reached for the rifles and other gear that he and Werner had brought into their pit and shoved them toward his feet. Feeling one of his men tug them away, he scrambled backward, grabbed Werner's ankles, and pulled the spotter clear. With Werner hoisted over his shoulder, he lumbered to the fall-back position, signalling for his men to return to base.

It's time for someone else to assume the German control of that field. We've done

*our part this nasty night. I'm tired. My soul
feels empty.*

Seeing Werner's body slung over their
captain's shoulder, the other squad members remained quiet and contemplative,
giving Paul an opportunity to reflect on the
early morning events.

*For the first time since I was dragged
into this wicked war, I've lost a man! How
do I tell his family? I'm relieved to be out of
that damn pit and heading back base. But,
God help me, a man died on my watch!
I need to get Werner's body back to base
before it freezes solid.*

When they had retreated deeper into
the forest, Paul gave the leader of the relief
squad a status report and passed command
of the field to him. In the meantime, his
men secured transportation back to the city
for all of them, including Werner's body.

When Paul and his men returned to
camp, he directed some of them to take
Werner's body to the makeshift morgue
while he went in search of a field hospital.

His head had been pounding since Werner had been killed, such that he wondered how he was able to make his last shot. He needed something more than a brandy to end the pain.

He entered a field hospital tent and hailed a medic as he removed his helmet and balaclava.

"Let me have a look at that," the medic said, approaching him. "That's a wicked bump. What happened?"

Paul raised his hand to his forehead and felt the bump for the first time, then looked at his helmet. At the crease above the brim of the helmet was a narrow gouge about three centimetres long, exposing shiny steel beneath.

"No wonder I have a headache!" Paul said, and proceeded to tell the medic what had happened earlier. "The percussion of the bullet when it grazed my helmet was obviously greater than I realized. It had to have banged the helmet hard into my head to create this lump!"

The medic concluded his examination of the welt and applied a small bandage to the broken skin. "There's not much I can do about the bump, but I'll give you something for the pain," he said. "You're lucky not to have died with your spotter, sir. Any other injuries you like me to look at?"

Paul shook his head. "If only there was a way for you to mend my spotter's injury," he said quietly.

Werner's body, his men confirmed later, was to be transported out within twenty-four hours. Paul told his men to stand down for the rest of the night. "Go have a beer and remember a good man," he said, sadness filling his voice. "I have a letter to write."

Paul returned to his quarters. He slumped into a wooden chair in front of his make-shift desk and struggled to compose the letter of condolence that would accompany Werner on his last leave home. *October 12, 1941,* he wrote, addressing the correspondence to Herr and Frau Friedrich. *It is with sincere regret that I write to advise …*

Paul dropped his pen and pressed the heels of his hands into his eyes, intuitively trying to suppress the tears that threatened to flow. Memories of the day's early hours filled his mind and tore at his heart.

This may be the first condolence letter I write, but I doubt it will be the last.

His wounded forehead throbbed, reminding him to be grateful that the bullet only clipped his helmet. He shuddered and reclaimed his focus. *It is with sincere regret that I write to advise*, he read. His pen found its place on the coarse paper and continued its task.

Paul was injured twice more the following year—a stray bullet lodged in his left side, the brunt of its impact absorbed by his ammunition belt; and shrapnel that pierced his right thigh, lodging deep into a muscle. Both injuries required minor surgery and some stitches, and a few days' medical leave that ended when bleeding and risk of infection had passed.

During the many months that followed, Paul continued to lead his men, scouting the Eastern Front and engaging in random skirmishes. He had been forced to write two more letters to loved ones of men whose lives ended early. After each such occasion, he assembled his men and discussed the consequence of those deaths.

"Not only are we forced to fill the vacant positions," he scolded them, "but we must train those men and learn to trust them." He concluded his lecture with a reminder that he did not appreciate having to write letters to accompany bodies home, and that he expected his men to not only take care of themselves, but of each other.

"I don't want to be writing another letter," he said firmly. He paused, glaring into the assembly. "No one's family should have to receive a regrets letter from me. Understood?"

"Aye, Captain," the assembled men mumbled en masse.

"Good! Dismissed."

CHAPTER TWENTY-FIVE

In August, 1944, Hitler declared that the city of Breslau would be his fortress, and it was to be defended vigorously. As Paul and his men were already stationed in the area, he was invited to speak to arriving forces and assist with the coordination of a defence plan. At the same time, he was grateful that he and his platoon were not to be party to the round-ups and impromptu executions organized by the generals.

Early one morning in November, as his platoon returned to Breslau from a night foray, they came upon a group of six school girls who were walking down the middle of a road.

He motioned for his men to take cover in the trees before the girls could see them. As he watched the girls, he realized that something was amiss.

"Franz," he whispered to the spotter who had replaced Werner, "use your glasses. What do you see?"

Franz Keitel was quiet while he peered through his field glasses, studying the young girls. As he spoke, his ire increased. "The girls look to range in age from six years to fifteen years—school girls."

He looked at Paul briefly, then returned to his binoculars. "They are clearly not dressed for this time of year. They should be wearing coats and boots. See how their clothing is rumpled and torn? And look! They're filthy, covered in … Why, it's blood! Sir, they've been harmed!"

He lowered his binoculars and looked wide-eyed at Paul. "Commander, is it possible that they have been violated?"

Paul grabbed the field glasses and examined the girls himself. He immediately thought of his younger sister, Gerda, and imagined her in a similar situation. "*Gott im Himmel*! I've heard rumours, but … they're just girls! They must have been caught up in some skirmish.

"Tell the men to circle them, but keep their distance," Paul whispered. "Ensure no danger: to them or us. Report back when the area is secure."

When Paul had the all-clear, he crept with stealth through the bushes until he was ahead of the girls. He removed his weapons, helmet, and overcoat.

"Cover me," he said, whispering his command to the soldiers within hearing.

In shirt sleeves, with arms extended in the air from his sides at shoulder level, he stepped from the trees and walked slowly along the road into the girls' line of vision.

The first girl to see him shrieked and ran to another, older girl, hiding her face in the girl's shoulder. The girls quickly huddled together behind the eldest. Some shook, others cried. One stopped in her tracks and did not move.

"Hello," Paul said in a gentle voice. "Do you speak German?"

The oldest girl nodded yes.

"I'm a German officer," he said trying to assure them. "My name is Captain Paul

Lange. Can you tell me what has happened to you? Why you are so close to the fighting?"

The oldest girl looked up from comforting a small one. "We are from Brieggen," she said. "The Russians came to our school two days ago. They took the boys and men away in trucks. The girls were assembled in the auditorium with the women."

The girl's lower lip quivered, and tears traced down her dust-streaked cheeks. "They started with the teachers, then the older girls." She covered her face and sobbed.

Paul reached out to reassure her.

Collectively, the girls took two steps away from him and huddled closer together.

"Please," he urged, dropping to one knee to bring himself within eye-level of most of the girls, "don't be frightened. Let us help you."

The girls' heads jerked up. They had been solely focussed on Paul; it was not until he said "us" that they looked around them and saw the other men. The youngest one screamed.

"What is your name?" Paul asked over the din, trying to maintain eye contact with the oldest girl.

"Nayda," the oldest girl said, hugging the others to her.

"Nayda, we are German soldiers. We are here to protect you." He paused, searching for a way to win their trust. "Let us get you somewhere safe."

Nayda reflected for a moment. "Do you have water? Food? We have had nothing to eat or drink."

"Franz! Collect the canteens and any food the men have," he ordered over his shoulder. A shuffling sound filled the space behind the trees.

The girls tightened their huddle as Franz mingled among the men, collecting what he could and carrying it back to the edge of the forest behind Paul. "I'm here, sir. What shall I do with it?"

"Nayda," Paul said, holding her focus, "if it's all right with you, Franz and I will bring the food and water and put it right there." He pointed to a spot near the edge of the forest, midway between himself and the huddle. "Then we'll step away, so you can take what you like. Is that acceptable?"

Nayda nodded, and Paul helped Franz relocate the food and water.

Nayda looked about the huddle and selected two of the older girls, giving them instructions to retrieve the bundles of food and water.

Paul ordered the men to stand down, but remain alert while they waited for the girls to eat.

"May I suggest," Paul interrupted their consumption, hoping his smile would reassure them, "that you not eat or drink too much or too fast. Learn from an old soldier's experience; it's hard on an empty belly to receive too much food or drink too quickly. If you eat too fast, you will only throw it up again."

With the last of his words, one of the younger girls retched. Nayda issued words of caution, and the girls slowed their eating.

"Save some for later," Paul encouraged.

When Paul saw that the girls were finished eating, he said, "We should be going soon. It's not safe for any of us to be here. It's too open."

Nayda acknowledged his concern.

"We are on our way back to Breslau. Will you come with us?"

Nayda spread her arms to encompass the girls, like a hen mothering her chicks. They whispered amongst themselves for several minutes before she responded.

"The Russian ..." Nayda began timidly, then straightened herself. "The Russians ... they took turns violating every teacher and every girl in that auditorium. Even the little ones."

Forlornly, Nayda reached for the smallest girls, who had begun to whimper, and hugged them to her. The other girls looked at their feet, no longer comfortable looking anywhere else.

"When they finished, they beat the teachers. Some of them died. Then they took the rest, one by one, to the end of the hall and put a bullet in their head. They made us watch. Blood was everywhere."

Nayda paused, licked her lips, and sipped from a canteen. "I-I was to be next. But one of the soldiers came—an officer, I think. He said something to the others a-and they left. When the other soldiers were gone, the officer lifted his machine gun and started shooting. Somehow, we few survived."

The men in the trees waited quietly, listening to Nayda's words, gasping with shock. Some angrily kicked the ground at their feet.

"We waited until it was quiet outside. Then we walked together out of the school. We went to our homes, but no one was there."

Nayda wrapped her arms across her chest and began rubbing them, as if to warm herself. "We didn't ... couldn't think, not even to take coats or food. We just started walking."

Her words were hollow, void of emotion. She looked at the other girls. The older ones nodded for her to continue.

"We will go with you," she said. "I think

… I think … we should see a doctor. The little ones especially."

Paul rose slowly from his seat in the road and dusted his trousers. Franz stepped to the edge of the road with some of the men's jackets.

"Please," he said, holding them up to the girls.

The two older girls took the jackets, returned to the huddle, and passed them to the others.

"Nayda, we must be off. We are too exposed here. Can all of you walk? Does anyone need help?"

"We can walk for now," she said, taking the hands of the two smallest girls. "Come on girls; let's show these men that we can be soldiers, too!"

Each girl raised her head and stood more erect. They walked in pairs, holding hands, one older and one younger.

Slowly, the men fell into formation on either side of the road, with the girls walking in their midst.

"Move out!" Paul ordered, and the march began.

They had not walked far when a small farm vehicle came rumbling toward them.

"Private Scholtz went ahead in search of transport," Franz said quietly in answer to Paul's quirked eyebrow.

Paul raised his arm, a command for his men to halt. "Nayda," he called quietly, "there is a cloister a few minutes up the road. Will you and the girls climb aboard?" He swept his arm toward the vehicle. "You can ride the rest of the way. It will be warmer for you, and faster for us. The nuns will take care of you, and I'll arrange for a doctor to see to your injuries."

Nayda consulted with the girls. "All right," she said, "but we want you to come with us."

Paul looked at his men, then back to Nayda. "We'll accompany you until you're safe inside the convent. Then we must be off."

She nodded.

"Come," he extended his hand to them, offering to help them up.

Ignoring his offer, Nayda lifted the smaller ones, then helped the older ones jump up. She allowed Paul to assist only her.

The vehicle rumbled back the way it had come, with Paul's men jogging along either side near the forest edge.

When Paul returned to Breslau with his men, he reported to the commander, filling him in on the work his men had conducted the night before, and describing the encounter with the young school girls.

"Go back out tonight," the commander ordered. "Investigate. If you encounter any trouble and can handle it, do so. If you need reinforcements, let me know."

That night, Paul's platoon set out for Brieggen. Cloud cover hid them from the moon's shine.

In the false dawn of the next morning, they reconnoitered the town, discovering evidence that corroborated the girls' story.

They found the executed bodies of the town's women, old and young, and small children in the nave of a local church. But for infants and very young boys, all had been raped and shot. Bodies of elderly men were found in a heap in the narthex, all executed with one shot in the centre of their brow.

Paul's platoon scouted the town and surrounding area, looking for tracks. Once they discovered the direction taken by the "Reds," Paul sent two spotters back to Breslau with a report and a request for reinforcements. He led his men out of town, following the Russians who had taken the missing men and boys of Brieggen.

When the last of his men had cleared the town, Paul said a prayer, crossed himself, and set fire to the school and the church. A kilometre beyond Brieggen, he caught up with his men.

While they waited for him to catch his breath, they watched black plumes of smoke, slashed by licking red flames, billow over the skyline of the town. Moments later, as small bits of ash began to fall on them, Paul gave a signal to move out.

By noon, the spotters and another platoon caught up with them, thereby doubling their manpower. Together, the angry soldiers pressed eastward, searching for the Red Russians who had ruined the town of Brieggen.

Before darkness set again, two scouts who had been sent ahead rejoined the search party and reported to Paul that they had tracked the Russians to the next town.

"The Reds have set up camp outside the town, but don't seem to be in a hurry to harm the townsfolk," one scout remarked.

"Good! We'll catch them unawares," he said. "Pass the word to stand down for twenty minutes. Eat, sleep. Do whatever you need to be fresh when I give the order to move."

Twenty minutes later, Paul gave the anticipated order. Cloud cover camouflaged their movement, giving them stealth and an element of surprise.

By early morning, they were engaged in a quiet skirmish with the unsuspecting Russians troopers.

During the mêlée, Paul trapped a junior

Russian officer who had sought shelter in a church near the outskirts of the town. They exchanged gunfire. A bullet pierced Paul's upper left arm, not far from the injury he had sustained in the Trondheim battle, before he silenced his opponent.

When the fighting subsided, Franz applied a temporary treatment to Paul's arm that would enable him to return to Breslau before having to seek medical attention.

As the sun rose, Paul called for an inventory. "Bring me survivors," he said, "and find me the men from Brieggen!"

"Captain Lange." A sergeant, unknown to Paul, saluted as he approached a while later. "You wish information about the men from Brieggen, and the survivors."

Paul returned the salute. "If you have it …"

"Sir, we were unable to find the men from Brieggen. We interviewed the townsfolk and searched the area, but we found no evidence of them being here. One of the Russians, before he died, said that the captives were at the front of the line, and this camp here"—the sergeant turned to view the bloodied landscape—"was the rear. The others are at least another day, if not two, ahead."

The sergeant paused, allowing Paul the opportunity to question him further. When Paul said nothing, the sergeant added, "Sir, given the direction we've been travelling, I'd say they're well into Poland by now."

"Thank you, Sergeant," Paul said, dismissing him before bellowing into the camp. "Shoes!"

Moments later, Private Joachim "Shoes" Lothar appeared at Paul's side.

"Sir?" he said.

"Shoes, round up the officers again. Tell them that we need to revise our plan."

Shoes saluted smartly and disappeared.

Two days later, the soldiers who had set out to find the Brieggen men returned to Breslau empty-handed. No prisoners accompanied them, and, although some of his men had been injured, to Paul's great relief none had been killed.

CHAPTER TWENTY-SIX

Word had trickled down from high command that the battle for Breslau was heating up. If the first campaign of 1945 was to be as intense as predicted, Paul wanted his men fresh. Leave was hard to come by, but a word in the battle commander's ear won Paul's men a two-day stand-down. A furlough was not possible, the commander told him. "We need to have every man prepared by the 20th," he said.

When Paul explained his concern for an aunt and uncle who owned a farm in Liegnitz, the commander agreed that Paul could borrow a car from the motor pool on two conditions: he must return with fresh provisions, since he was visiting a farm, and he must be back in Breslau no later than January 19th, battle-ready. He could leave at the end of the week.

Paul saluted his acknowledgement and

departed the office quickly, before the commander changed his mind.

⚜

Paul leaned against the brick wall of the old church located at the edge of the city's market square, contemplating the journey to Liegnitz. He drew on the cheap cigarette that dangled between his thumb and forefinger and attempted to create smoke rings as he exhaled.

He had begun smoking after the battle in Trondheim. It helped pass the time while he and his men recovered. Now the habit helped pass the time between missions.

The evening was cold and still. Crystals of ice floated to their death under the light of a full moon in a cloudless sky. His smoke rings floated briefly then dissipated into the crystal dark.

A young woman, scarf wrapped around her ears and hat pulled down snugly, hastened toward him, the heels of her boots clacking on the cobblestones.

He straightened, dropped the cigarette,

and ground it out with the ball of his boot.
Damn things, he chastised himself, *don't
know why I bother. They're nasty.* He
released the last smoke from his lungs as
she approached, aiming it away from the
woman with a turn of his lips.

"Good evening, Captain," she said in
greeting before stopping directly in front of
him. She wrung her gloved hands.

She's nervous, he observed. *She needn't
be. She's German.*

"Fraulein." He touched the tip of his
helmet. The chinstrap dangled carelessly.
He was off-duty and had not bothered to
fasten it. "You shouldn't be out this late.
If you have accommodation nearby, I can
escort you."

"Uh, yes. I live nearby. And I can find my
own way home, thank you." Her frosted
reply morphed into crystals and hovered
between them. She looked down at her
hands, searching for words. "I'm just wondering whether civilians are still safe here?"

"Let me walk you home." He indicated

for her to take the lead. "We can talk along the way."

"Thank you," she said. "I noticed the light catch the medal at your throat. I suppose I can feel safe with a soldier wearing a Knight's Cross!"

He acknowledged her comment with a tip of his helmet, but said no more.

Her name was Ilse-Renata Chemiker, she told him. The laboratory in which she worked was not far from the church. At the lab, she assisted with formula development, including special greases and oils for the axles and wheels of military vehicles and a formula for a unique detergent. Originally developed by a local soap manufacturer to remove grease spots from clothing, her colleagues had discovered that the formula could be adapted to eliminate grease trails that followed fired torpedoes.

Her employer, a "White Russian" named Prow Kobelev, was concerned that it was time to leave the city. Rumours were circulating that the Red Russians were getting close. Not only was he concerned for his employees—especially Ilse-Renata—but he was concerned for himself. His family lived in Dresden, but they were originally from Russia. His political views were at odds with the communists.

The walk to her home took less than fifteen minutes. Paul knew the answer to her earlier question about civilian safety, but, selfishly, he wanted to see Ilse-Renata again, and contrived a distraction. "Let me make enquiries. I'll let you know tomorrow. Do you often walk past the church on your way home?" he asked.

"Not always. I'm sure I would have seen you before if I did. But, I can pass that way again tomorrow if it will help."

"No need," he said. "I can find you at the laboratory tomorrow afternoon, if you'd like company walking home again?"

She had ascended two steps toward the front door of her home and halted. The added height allowed her to look directly into his eyes. She smiled demurely.

"Unless ..." The word hung while he contemplated what next to say. Searching for a way to delay her departure.

"Unless?" she asked, her eyes wide with curiosity.

Her voice rings like a church bell, true and clear. I could listen to her speak forever.

"I don't suppose you'd be free to have dinner with me tomorrow evening? I know a great little restaurant." He turned to point in its general direction.

"I really shouldn't," she said. "I don't know you." She twisted her gloved hands again.

"Hey! I'm the guy with the Knight's Cross. Remember?" he teased. "It's my job to protect the citizens of Deutschland. Especially the very pretty ones." He flashed her a toothy, white grin.

Her laughter chimed like perfect notes of tiny bells. "Well. All right. Since you put it that way."

"You will?" he asked, not expecting her to agree, and found himself at a loss for words. "Wonderful! Um, what time do you get off work?" he asked.

"Five o'clock. Is that too early for you?" Her words were rushed, anxious.

"N-no! Five o'clock is perfect!" He fought to contain his excitement. "I'll meet you outside the laboratory at five o'clock tomorrow, then."

"All right," she said, her voice soft and sincere. "I'll see you then."

Paul waited for her to climb the remaining two steps and open the door. She switched on the light when she stepped inside and turned toward the stairway again. "Good night," her silhouette said as it slowly closed the door.

"Good night," he said, waiting for the thud of the closing door to sever the connection. *I must be crazy. I don't know her, and I'm falling all over her like a fool! And we're in the middle of a war, for God's sake!*

He jammed his hands in his jacket pockets and set off toward the barracks, whistling a tuneless melody. *If this war ever ends, I'm going to marry that girl!*

⚜

Dinner the following evening was awkward, but friendly. Each felt drawn to the other, but neither had much experience socializing with the opposite sex.

She was born in Neisse, Ilse-Renata told him, but had completed her studies in Dresden at the beginning of the war. She was eighteen when she graduated and considered herself lucky to find a position at the laboratory straight away. She also found accommodation in the home of the president of the technical institute. Since she had moved to Breslau two years previous, the president had driven her to and from the laboratory every day.

"Last week, he and his family left for Heidelberg, where they'll stay until the conflict ends. Now I stay alone in that big house, but I'm not afraid!" she exclaimed. A tinge of defiance appeared in a flush on her cheeks.

285

In answer to her question the prior evening, Paul told her that the city was safe.

"Herr Hitler has determined Breslau to be his fortress. It is well protected. You need not worry," he assured her.

Avoiding any further military discussion, he told her of his upcoming leave and that he had decided to visit his aunt and uncle in Liegnitz.

"How lucky you are," Ilse-Renata said. "I wish I had someone to visit once in a while. I'm here alone now, except for my colleagues."

"Why don't you come with me," he suggested, without forethought. "I mean ... my aunt and uncle have a huge house, and I know you'd be welcome," he blurted.

"Oh!" she said, blushing at the unexpected invitation.

"You don't have to ..." he said, trying to recover his offer.

"Oh no! I mean ..." she wrung her hands together under the table. "It's just ... well ... I don't really know you, and ..."

"I understand," he said, feeling deflated, then brightened. "I know! Why don't we have dinner together tomorrow evening, and the evening after that? In fact, let's have dinner every evening this week, so you can get to know me better. Then you can say yes!"

Pleased with his idea, he smacked the table to cement it, and gave her another toothy grin.

"Well … I suppose," she said thoughtfully. "It couldn't hurt. And … and … if I don't feel comfortable by then. Well, I simply won't go!" she said, grinning back at him. "After all, that gives us almost a week to get to know each other."

"Would you care for a sweet and coffee?" interrupted the waiter.

Ilse-Renata blushed again. "Yes, please. That is. If you would," she asked, deferring to Paul, peering at him through a dark fringe of lashes.

"Ah. Yes! Coffee and cake would be excellent!" he declared. "The evening is still young. We have time."

"Ration books, please," the waiter asked. He snipped stamps from the appropriate food groups and returned their books before serving their coffee and cake. "Just a reminder folks—this is the artificial coffee. We're out of the real stuff."

"Oh, that's fine," Ilse-Renata said. "I quite like the way it's made with the fruit. So long as the water is pure, it tastes wonderful! And, I know you use only the best water!"

Each subsequent evening, they concluded their meal with coffee and cake, much to Ilse-Renata's pleasure.

On the eve of his departure, as Paul walked Ilse-Renata to her door, he asked, "Well, have you decided? Will you come with me tomorrow to visit my aunt and uncle?"

"I will," she said confidently before jogging up the four stairs to the front door. "Good night."

"Good night," he said, and turned to wind his way back to the barracks, whistling a tuneless melody. He did not remember the walk back, such was his joy.

CHAPTER TWENTY-SEVEN

The following morning, Paul secured a car from the motor pool and drove to the house where Ilse-Renata boarded. She opened the door when he knocked.

In the light of the morning and without the hat that always covered her hair and shadowed her face, he hesitated. He knew from the previous evenings that she was a small woman; the top of her head did not reach his shoulders. What was hidden beneath the shadow of her hat was the beauty that shaped her face. Creamy complexion, with pale, pink cheeks and three small freckles on the tip of her nose. Dark blonde hair, almost brown. *Hazel eyes like Mama's.*

"Good morning, Captain! Right on time. I'll just grab my coat and hat."

"You're packed, then?"

"Yes," she said tugging on her coat. "My case is just there."

"That's it? That's all you have?"

"Yes; I only have a few things." Ilse-Renata fit a grey, felt hat over her braids and fastened it in place with a pearl hatpin.

"Do you have your papers?" he asked.

She held them up in response to his question.

Paul picked up her suitcase and jogged down the four steps. He stowed the suitcase in the boot of the black military vehicle and returned to open the passenger door for Ilse-Renata. In that time, she had locked the door to the house and appeared at his side as the door opened.

They settled into the car and Paul prepared for the journey to Liegnitz, easing it away from the curb and heading toward the blockade that would see them into the countryside of southern Silesia.

Movement of military transports, blockades, constant requests to produce papers, and civilians fleeing west slowed their journey. Paul's Knight's Cross helped move matters along at each blockade, but could do nothing

290

about the volume of vehicle and pedestrian traffic that inhibited their progress.

They chatted easily about her work and the farm. Paul steered any conversation about military matters to safer topics.

"I don't know about you," he said as they neared the farm, "but I'm starving. Are you hungry?"

In response to his question, Ilse-Renata's stomach emitted a loud gurgle. Ilse snapped her mitted hands to her belly, giggling in surprise.

"I'll take that as a yes," he said, grinning. "Uncle Otto is usually good for a bit of sausage, at the very least."

She looked away from him, in the direction of the not-yet-visible destination of Uncle Otto's farm. Beside her, Paul straightened in his seat, holding the wheel secure, and hummed contentedly.

Paul turned right, off the paved road and onto a rutted dirt lane. Patches of snow lay scattered in the fields, deeper in the ploughed furrows. Puddles formed by sun-warmed snow were framed in a crust of ice. The tires crunched in the frozen ruts and the car bounced awkwardly, their heads bobbing in response.

"Not far now," Paul stated. "My uncle's farm is just ahead on the left."

Paul raised his arm in quick salute as he drove past the standard that marked him home—a square post, two metres tall and painted the bright yellow of his grandfather's regimental coat of arms.

"What was that about? The salute?"

"Oh. Nothing. Just being silly." The salute was a knee-jerk reaction, which Paul regretted as soon as he had done it. He did not know Ilse-Renata well enough to tell her everything about himself and his family. *Need-to-know basis.*

"There it is." Paul pointed to the gated entrance of Uncle Otto's farm, always open during the day. He slowed the car and took an easy left into the yard, allowing the car to roll close to the old, brick farmhouse.

"If you don't mind waiting a moment,"

he said, stepping on the clutch and the brake
before putting the car into neutral and killing the engine. "I'll try to locate Uncle Otto
and let him know we're here." He yanked
the hand-brake and lit from the car.

Paul walked around to the back of the
house, knocked on the door, and stepped
into the kitchen. It was midday, and
familiar aromas permeated the warm air,
releasing childhood memories fondly held
in his heart of hearts.

A middle-aged woman scooted through
the doorway opposite where it led from the
hallway. Startled, she dropped the platter
she was carrying on the tiled floor.

"What's happened, Hilde?" hollered
Otto, following behind her.

Paul heard the thump of his uncle's
familiar gait on the tiled floor, and recalled
the story that Otto and his father rarely
told of how Otto lost his lower leg during
the Great War. The prosthetic limb that
replaced his loss landed heavily each time
he stepped on the artificial foot.

Before Hildegard could collect herself, Otto spied Paul standing at the outside door. With delight, he moved past Hildegard with arms outstretched.

"Paul, my boy! This is a wonderful surprise. Isn't it, Hilde?"

Paul walked into his uncle's embrace and mumbled apologies to Hildegard while Otto slapped him heartily on the back.

"No worries, Paul, none at all. You've actually saved us the need of a decision."

"Sir?"

"Hildegard and I were just debating whether the platter was worth packing. Looks like it's made up our minds for us!"

"One less dish to pack," Hildegard replied, dusting her hands together. "Besides, it was a wedding gift from my mother's second cousin's uncle. I never liked it. Perhaps now I do!"

Smiling, Hildegard bent to pick up the shards and discarded them.

"Paul, what brings you here?" Otto asked.

"I have a few days' leave and thought I'd

visit with you two. The fighting is getting closer, and I worry about you, being here alone."

"Well, Paul. I have to say that these last weeks, since before Christmas, really," Otto said, turning to Hildegard for confirmation, "have been difficult."

Hildegard nodded.

"*Quartiermeister* are constantly knocking on the door, asking for meat. They have soldiers to feed, they say." Otto's hands were on his hips, expressing his annoyance with the persistence of the quartermasters. "What few farmhands we have are staying away. Not that I blame them. We have to do the work ourselves, me and Hilde, and we have provisions for only a few more weeks. It's time to go."

Paul heard finality and acceptance in his uncle's voice.

"I've notified your parents that they can expect us by the end of the month, and your father has arranged our travel papers. And, since we don't use the trucks much in the winter, we've been saving our petrol rations. We have everything we need to get to Bavaria."

"Otto! Don't keep the boy standing there at the door." Hildegard beckoned. "Come in, Paul. Come in."

"Oh, mein Gott! Ilse-Renata! I almost forgot about her. She must be freezing."

"Ilse-Renata?" Otto quizzed.

"A young woman I met last week. I left her in the car while I came to look for you."

Hildegard and Otto exchanged a look that said, "Aha! Finally!"

"Well go and get her! *Dummkopf*! You don't leave someone sitting in a car in the middle of January and forget about them," Hildegard said, scolding him playfully.

Paul did as he was told, running around the outside of the house only to find the car empty. "Ilse-Renata!" he yelled anxiously.

"Here!" She rose from the opposite side of the car, dusting her hands together. "I thought I'd stretch my legs. When I stepped out of the car, this creature came bounding out of the field. I guess he was too late to greet you, but he certainly caught me! Nearly knocked me over." She laughed.

He liked her laugh. It was music to his ears. "His sire's a Schnauzer. That's why he's so big. Good farm dog, though, aren't you, Wolfy!"

Wolfy abandoned Ilse-Renata, and jumped at Paul, planting his muddy fore-paws on the breast of Paul's overcoat.

Paul stepped back abruptly. "Off! You crazy hound." Then he crouched down to greet the dog, ruffling his feathery coat.

Wolfy took the liberty of greeting Paul with his own expression of affection—several slobbery licks to a face that Paul had unintentionally made available to him.

"Bleh! Stupid dog. Keep your tongue to yourself! Off with you now. Go find a rat or something …" He waved his arm, and the dog bounded off into the adjacent field.

He stood facing Ilse-Renata, wiping slobber on his sleeve and brushing long dog hair from his hands.

"Mein Gott!" he said, raising his hand to his chest "Now I have mud on my overcoat."

"Don't touch!" Ilse-Renata raised a warning hand to stop him. "Let it dry and it will brush off easily."

"Of course; you're correct," Paul said, feeling silly. "You'd think I'd remember that! I've spent enough time crawling through the mud these past years."

Her gaze drifted up from his coat to take in the farmhouse.

"Come." Paul extended his hand in invitation. "My aunt and uncle are in the kitchen, but I'll take you through the front. It's muddy along the side of the house."

He led Ilse-Renata up two steps and through the front door, where they doffed hats, coats, and soiled shoes, and padded through to the kitchen for introductions.

⚜

Over a hot lunch of stewed vegetables, fresh bread, and slices of sausage, the foursome chatted amicably in the old farm kitchen.

Most of the packing was done, and some things had already been shipped to the Neue-farm.

"These last items will travel with us at the end of the month," Otto said. "However, we have a few more things to do before we go."

"We want to butcher the last of the animals," Hildegard added. "We'll leave some meat and chickens with our neighbours and the farmhands. Who knows when they'll see good meat again."

"The rest we'll take with us to the Neue-farm," Otto concluded. "Hildegard should have time to make up some sausage too, before we leave."

"That sounds like a lot of work," Ilse-Renata said.

"Have you ever lived on a farm, Ilse-Renata?" Otto asked.

"No. I'm a city girl. I've visited family who owned farms, but I think they're gone now."

"Gone?" Otto asked again.

"Yes. I grew up in Neisse, but my family was originally from the area formerly known as Upper Silesia," she said. "My father was killed in the summer of 1932, during the protests. A random grenade."

She looked at her hands, folded in her lap. "My mother went to live with her sister in München when my brother enlisted two years ago. I haven't heard from him since early last year. I fear the worst."

She raised her head and locked eyes with Otto. Tears trickled down her smooth cheeks. "I'm sorry," she said, the pink on her cheeks deepening. She pushed the tears away with a knuckle and smiled shyly. "That was too much information, wasn't it?"

"My dear. We are saddened to hear of your loss, and your hardship," Hildegard said as she reached to pat Ilse-Renata's hand. "Here, we are family. You must never fret about what is said."

Paul cleared his throat, making a mental note to investigate the whereabouts of

Ilse-Renata's bother, and took control of the conversation. "Speaking of sausage," he said, "I have orders to return with fresh provisions."

He quirked his lips in a half-grin, before continuing sheepishly. "The price of my furlough …" He shrugged and added, "That is, uncle, if you have anything to spare."

Otto smiled, reaching toward Paul, and slapped him on the shoulder with an open hand. "Of course! We'll put together a hamper of fresh produce, some cheese, and cured meats. Such a small price to pay for a visit from our brave soldier!"

Their conversation changed to Breslau and whether it remained safe for civilians to stay in the city. Otto noted that few cities in the east were safe.

"Many folks, especially women, are moving toward Dresden and Berlin, seeking a safe-haven," he said. "Food in those areas is scarce. At least we have food, and we've been shipping the surplus to Bayreuth at every opportunity."

"Uncle, I'm sure everyone in Bayreuth is appreciative," Paul said.

"I wonder, Ilse-Renata," Otto said, clapping his hands together, "could you be talked into a little hard labour? I'm sure Hildegard would welcome extra hands with the packing." He looked to Hildegard and she nodded her agreement. "And Paul, perhaps you'd help me with the butchering?"

"Of course!" Paul and Ilse-Renata answered in unison.

"Then, if you like," Otto said, looking directly at Ilse-Renata, "You can travel with us to Bavaria. If we can't find you work when we get there, I'm confident my brother-in-law, Paul's father, will know what to do."

Ilse-Renata thanked them for their generosity but declined. "I am happy to help while we're here. But, I must return to Breslau and continue my work. I promised Herr Kobelev that I would stay with him so long as we remain safe."

"Very well," Hildegard said. "But you must come to us if you feel you are in danger."

302

✤

In the following days, Paul helped Otto with the slaughter and closure of the farm, and Ilse-Renata worked with Hildegard, packing the last of the household goods and learning how to make sausage.

"Our sausage is renowned, you know," Hildegard said, proudly enlightening Ilse-Renata. "People all around look for our sausage in the shops. We even shipped to Amsterdam four times a year before the conflict started," she said sadly. "If this is to be our last batch for a while, we must make it the best!"

She straightened to a taller self, as if determined to make it happen, and used a corner of her apron to dry a tear threatening to escape her eye.

"How silly of me," she said, appearing embarrassed. "We have no time for emotions. We have work to do!"

✤

When they were not working, the older couple rested or slept. In the afternoon, while his aunt and uncle napped, Paul took Ilse-Renata to explore outdoors.

"I will have to stow my memories deep inside," Paul said with a husky voice and a hand on his heart. "I don't know when I'll see the farm again."

He inhaled deeply, casting his dark eyes about the snow-dusted fields and buildings that had always meant home to him. "The sounds, the smells. A city smells different, and here it is quiet, even at its noisiest."

Ilse-Renata smiled at him, her eyes sparkling to hear him remember.

"So many events: my father teaching my friends and me to be good soldiers"— he pointed toward a small, leafless forest—"planting, harvesting. So many memories. Tucked here." He shook his head and patted his chest again. "I don't want to forget any of it."

CHAPTER TWENTY-EIGHT

They wandered throughout the farm lands and visited a few neighbours who remained. On the last afternoon of his leave, when the sun peeked from behind threatening, grey clouds, he and Ilse-Renata walked down the frosty lane-way toward the yellow standard marking the entrance to the manor. He stopped, stroking the post. Flakes of dried paint fell away.

"What is it?" Ilse-Renata asked. "This post means something to you, doesn't it?"

"Uh huh," Paul answered. He looked at Ilse-Renata then. Looked at her hazel eyes. *So trusting.*

"Come," he said, his voice deep with emotion. Taking her hand, he added, "I want to show you something."

He led her up the drive to the front of the manor, fished in the inside pocket of the brown corduroy jacket that he always wore on the farm, and pulled out a key.

"Paul, what are you doing?" She looked about, as if half-expecting someone to jump out from behind a bush and reprimand them for trespassing.

"This house belongs to my family," Paul said. "It was my family's home, until Papa moved us all to Bayreuth in 1939. He was a soldier in the Great War, and always he worried about our safety."

He closed the door behind them. "Come. I'll take you on a tour."

They wandered through each room, and he shared his family's history and stories. "I could write a book about events that happened in each room. We lived here for so long."

"Since when?"

"My great-grandfather bought the house in 1865," he said, concluding his tour and leading Ilse-Renata back to the front door again. "Every generation since then has lived here. Some married and moved away, like my father's sister, Tante Marie, but always a generation of Langes has lived here: until 1939."

He opened the front door and stepped out onto the landing. "And we still own it, of course," he said, holding up the key. "Hopefully, when the war ends, we'll be able to move back. Or at least some of us." He paused, turning around to look at the crest.

"Why 'hopefully'?" Ilse-Renata asked.

"Well," he answered, contemplating his next words. "It will depend largely on who occupies this land after the war, and whether the house survives any bombings in the meantime."

Paul hesitated, as if deep in thought, then said, "I've told you so many stories this afternoon. Have you space for one more?"

"Try me," she said, encouraging him to continue.

"My grandfather told me that each time a Lange soldier went off to battle, he would place his hand on this crest."

To illustrate, he reached up and put his hand on the crest that rested above the lintel.

"It's as if there's a connection to the past. As if each soldier draws on the experience of the others to keep him safe. To bring him home."

Paul examined her face for understanding. "I'm sure that sounds silly." He dropped his hand from the crest, keeping his eyes focussed on it. "Papa told me that each time he prepared to report for duty during the Great War, he would put his hand on it. Sort of ... take it with him. He said it kept him grounded and focussed during battle. When he'd come home on leave, he would put his hand on it again. Before he did anything else. He said that it wasn't until he felt that crest in his hand that he could believe that he was home, and safe."

"The connection between the soldiers in your family and that crest," Ilse-Renata said, staring up at it, "is indeed a powerful story. I'm glad you saved it for the last. I'll always remember it." She spoke quietly, so as not to break the spell that Paul's words had created for her.

They stood on the doorstep amicably for a minute of heartbeats. Then Paul reached up with both hands, yanked the crest hard, and stepped backward as the fastenings gave way to hold it in his hands.

"Just in case," he said bashfully, realizing his destructive impulse. "I want Papa to have this in Bayreuth. So Lange soldiers will always find their way home safely. I'll ask Uncle Otto to take it with him."

"Paul Lange! You are truly a romantic!" Ilse-Renata said, teasing him.

"I guess I am." He grinned. "Let me show you," he said, stepping down two steps and turning to face her. Then he wrapped his arms around her, the crest in one hand, and kissed her soundly.

Inhaling deeply, they parted and laughed, their breath floating between them on the frosty air, mingling and spiralling upward into the late afternoon light.

"We should get back," Paul said, gazing into her hazel eyes. "My aunt and uncle will be wondering where we are." He took her hand again and led her down the stairs, along the drive to the lane, and back to the Schmidt farm.

Holding Ilse-Renata's small hand firmly in his, he dreamt of his future with her. In his other hand, he held secure the crest that safeguarded his family's past and a future yet to come.

Otto and Hildegard waved farewell to Paul and Ilse-Renata. Their short visit had come to a melancholy end, and the quiet farmhouse would echo emptiness in their wake.

Earlier, Otto had helped Paul load the boot of his military vehicle with the last of the fresh produce, fresh meat, and sausage, the price to be paid for Paul's few days of leave.

"Ilse-Renata is a lovely young woman, is she not, my dear?" Otto asked, still waving as the vehicle turned left onto the main road.

"Indeed, she is! Paul would be wise to keep his eye on her," Hildegard agreed. "And, I'm certainly glad for her help, as I am sure you are of Paul's." She continued. "Come. We're waving like fools, and they can't even see us!" Hildegard turned toward the side of the farmhouse, heading for the kitchen.

"Thanks to their extra hands," Otto acknowledged, "we've completed our work far sooner than I expected. I'll use the rest of today to distribute parcels to the folks hereabouts and to say our good-byes. I think we can finish packing tomorrow and be off the following day to Bayreuth."

"And not a moment too soon, from the sounds of it!" Hildegard said, adding, "I'd like to go with you today. I have some preserves that I'd like to deliver. Won't Gerhard and Emma be surprised to see us in Bayreuth before the end of February!"

An hour later, the old farm truck was loaded with farm goods, and the two set off to say their farewells.

CHAPTER TWENTY-NINE

Five days later, Otto rolled the truck to a halt in the yard of the Neue-farm, where his parents had been residing since the previous fall. Wolfy leapt from the back of the truck and ran, barking with joy, to greet Herr and Frau Schmidt. Frost coated the frozen ground on which he landed and muted the volume of his bark.

"Crazy hound," Herr Schmidt said, ruffling the dog's fluffy coat. "Go find some creatures in the field. Off you go." He swung his arms, shooing the dog out of the way.

"How was the drive?" Herr Schmidt asked. "Did you encounter any difficulties?"

"Not really," Otto advised. "It took longer than we had hoped. We were constantly diverted to back roads and farm roads that were frozen and icy. We couldn't travel much faster than a horse-drawn wagon. The ruts and bumps were challenging. Fortunately, we kept back this last truck: the cabin sheltered us from the wind and weather. And, of course, Gerhard ensured that we had the appropriate papers, so we were never stopped for long."

"Looks like we could have snow in a few hours," his father commented, interrupting Otto's report while he flagged the attention of the farm's manager.

"Yes, sir?" the elderly gentleman said.

"Will you see if you can round up a few helping hands so we can get this truck unloaded before the snow arrives?"

"I think there are some fellows in the barn. I'll find them and return shortly," he said, departing in the direction of the milking barn.

Within the hour, a cream-coloured Rohr, its dark blue convertible roof closed to the elements, rolled into the yard and stopped next to the truck.

"Your mother telephoned to say you'd arrived," Gerhard said, climbing out of the car. He greeted first Otto, then Hildegard, with a welcoming embrace. "You're early! I didn't expect to see you for at least another week."

"Paul stopped by for a few days. He and his friend offered to help, and that sped everything up nicely," Otto told him.

When Gerhard failed to enquire about Paul's friend, Hildegard made a face at Otto as if to express her surprise that Gerhard had overlooked the reference. Otto shrugged his shoulders in response.

"Paul was able to get time off?" Gerhard exclaimed.

"His commander let him take a few days, on the condition that he return with food. Fortunately, we were able to oblige him."

"Good man," Gerhard said, slapping his long-time friend on the back. "I can spare an hour. Let's see if an extra pair of hands can help get this stuff unloaded before the snow starts."

As if on cue, heavy, grey-white snow clouds began roiling over distant hills and two men arrived from the milking barn.

Able-bodied men were hard to find, most having been conscripted, but any man who had left the farm or the estate to serve their country was welcomed back and re-employed, if they were capable. One of the fellows was missing a hand, taken by an exploding grenade. The other had lost most of his sight during a fire-flash, and gnarled flesh scarred the left side of his face.

Together, they worked with Gerhard and Otto, and the truck was soon emptied.

An hour later, the workers were beckoned into the kitchen for a hot meal prepared by Frau Schmidt. Gerhard declined, insisting that he had to return to the office.

Otto followed him to the car. "You look worried. What's going on?"

Gerhard stood next to the driver's door, looking toward the churning snow clouds. He inhaled deeply, as if in resignation, and released a plume of frozen breath.

Quietly, so as not to be overheard, he spoke. "Otto, I am so glad that you are not involved in this military business. My work these days is taxed with worry. The Führer has started conscripting the "Hitler Youth." The poor pups don't even receive adequate training. Sure, they're schooled in a military environment, but they are not taught military disciplines. Most have become young killing machines, without direction or purpose. They have no sense of discretion!

"In addition to the work that I've been doing, I am now tasked with trying to salvage what's left of the ones who make it home. They are so messed up: mind, body, and soul."

Otto braced his gloved hand on the hood of the car and shifted his weight to his right leg for stability. "Perhaps when we get set up here, I might be of assistance?"

"Perhaps. I'll keep that in mind, but … I'd rather you stayed here, focussed on the running of the farm, and ensuring that everyone is safe," Gerhard said. "I can rely on you, and, if I need someone to talk to, you'll always be here."

"I'm here for you, brother," Otto said, placing his hand companionably on Gerhard's shoulder as snowflakes began to fall.

Gerhard hesitated, as if reluctant to leave his friend. "I'm worried about the resisters and what they may have disclosed under interrogation—Ulrich von Hassell, Adam von Trott zu Solz, and the others in the Kreisau Circle," he whispered, waving his arms across his chest; a subconscious gesture used to increase blood flow to his freezing fingers.

Stepping closer to Otto, he said, "My name could be on any one of their secret lists, and that information could be revealed during an interrogation! I'm so worried about it that I've developed an ulcer, for God's sake!" In reflex, a hand rested against his belly and he winced.

Otto noted the deep lines carved in his friend's face, etched there by the worry of the past years. "As could be mine," he said. "I may not be an officer in the Wehrmacht, but I'm always watchful. I've heard that

the *Gestapo* are executing anyone expressing defeatist ideas, not that I share my
thoughts aloud with anyone other than you
and Hilde. Regardless, if the Gestapo find
you, I have no doubt they'll find me, too.
Their interrogation techniques have a way
of helping folks part with information that
they didn't even know they had!"

"Well," Gerhard mused, "we weren't
involved in the attempt to assassinate Hitler
last July, and, so far, I haven't had to resist
any of the Führer's orders. Let's continue to
hope, shall we?"

He gave Otto a feeble smile, then regained
his earnest tone. "I've heard a rumour that,
after the assassination attempt, the Führer
had some of the chief resisters rounded up,
then ordered them to commit suicide. That
man has no compassion for the faith of a
good Catholic."

He shook his head in disgust. "Hassell
left the safety of his home in Bavaria for
his office in Berlin and waited there until
the Gestapo arrested him. Freisler presided

over his trial. Of course, he was found guilty, sentenced to death, and executed the next day. Some may have escaped the country—they're missing, at least—likely thinking that they'd found honour in their resistance and can do nothing more."

Gerhard kicked at the fluffy snow gathering around his boot, then continued. "When Himmler first ordered the Gestapo to pick up resisters, the focus was on members of the Kreisau Circle. But now, diaries are being found that list the names of others, and the round-up has been extended to include any suspected sympathizers and anyone who may have acted against the Gestapo in the past. It's all so sickening … and frightening. I want to wish for Hitler's death, but, as a good Catholic, I can't endorse his assassination. Besides, I had to take that damned Hitler Oath when I was recalled."

Disheartened, Gerhard opened the car door and lowered himself onto the leather seat. "But, I'm here, and here is where I will stay: caring for the lost souls who find their

way home and watching out for my family."
He winked at Otto. "God help them, and
God keep us safe from it all!"

Otto placed his hands on the car door
and closed it gently. "Amen to that! Come
by when you have time. We can talk
more. Until then, keep your head down."
He hopped away from the car as Gerhard
turned the ignition.

Gerhard waved, put the Rohr into gear,
and drove out of the farmyard and onto the
roadway.

CHAPTER THIRTY

Paul's platoon remained in Breslau until early February, 1945, when they were redirected to Italy to join the mountain infantry. They were ordered to assist with reinforcement of the Apennine defence against the push northward from Rome.

Before departing, Paul slipped away from the barracks and sought Ilse-Renata at the laboratory.

"We're leaving soon," he told her, a worried look lining his face. "Don't stay in the city too long."

"We won't. Herr Kobelev has already been enquiring about transportation."

"Good!" Paul said, pulling her into a tight embrace. *I hope I live to see her again.* "Do you know where you'll go?"

"No. I need to find my mother. She was in München, but I think she's moved north to stay with another aunt. I'm not worried. I'll find them," she said confidently.

"And ... I'll find you," Paul said before he kissed her soundly. "Wait for me?"

"I will," she whispered. "Come back to me."

Paul turned to leave, but froze in mid-step. "I have some news of your brother," he said turning to face her again. "It's not really news. Not great news, anyway. He is not listed as injured, captured, or dead." He reached for her hand. "That's the problem. He's not listed anywhere." He hugged her again. "I hope by the time I see you again, you'll know where he is."

"Thank you for looking," she said, her eyes glassy with tears.

Any civilians remaining in Breslau on January 19th received a military command to leave the city immediately. Herr Kobelev insisted that he be allowed to meet with the garrison commander to discuss an extension for the departure time of the lab employees.

"The submarines need the detergent that we've developed," he insisted. "We need more time to finish the latest batch, package it up, and ship it out!"

"Very well," the commander granted, "but you must hurry, and don't stay any longer than necessary. At best, we may be able to hold the Russians back another week or two, but their attack becomes more ferocious every day."

"Thank you, Commander. We'll work as quickly as we can," Kobelev said.

"Be warned," the commander barked before Kobelev exited his office, "if the Russians enter the city before you leave, I cannot promise you any protection."

Kobelev acknowledged his warning with a nod, before closing the office door on his way out.

One week later, the last shipment of detergent was secreted out of the city, en route to the naval dispatch office.

A few days later, the lab was almost empty.

Evidence of the work conducted in the lab had been boxed up and was ready to be shipped to a more secure location the following day.

"I've been speaking with my contacts at the airfield," Prow Kobelev told Ilse-Renata. "I've heard rumours that some aircraft mechanics are planning to depart shortly. They intend to take a few trucks from the base before the city is completely under siege."

Ilse-Renata listened intently, knowing that whatever Prow planned would affect her. *I wish I could telephone home. Mother will be fretting about my safety, but I don't know where she is now.*

"I have some assets," Prow said, breaking into Ilse-Renata's thoughts. "Some money, jewellery and loose gems." Her eyes refocused on his face. "Are you any good with a needle and thread?"

"I learnt to sew in school," she told him. "I'm not very good at it, but I can mend. Do you need something repaired?" she asked, confused that he should mention money and sewing in the same breath.

"No. Just listen to me closely," he said, casting his eyes about the lab and settling on the wall clock. He took her by the arm and led her into his office. "The others will start arriving soon, and I don't want to be overheard," he said.

In the office, he disclosed their departure plan. "Tomorrow, come in early. Bring your sewing kit, a skirt, and a coat with you. I'd like you to sew my assets into the hems of some garments. Do you think you can do that?"

"Yes, of course," she answered, standing a little taller with the trust and confidence that Herr Kobelev instilled in her.

The following morning, Ilse-Renata arrived early, carrying an extra skirt in a tote bag.

"Ah! You're here!" Prow said, greeting her. "Come into my office and we'll work out the details."

She followed him, closing the door

325

behind them, and hung her coat next to his on a wooden coat stand.

"Have a seat," he said, inviting her to sit in the guest chair he had set before his desk.

From behind his desk, Prow lifted a leather satchel and opened it. On the cleared desk that stood between them, he placed two cloth money belts, two leather pouches, and a wallet. He shook out the contents of the two pouches onto a scrap of black velvet—one contained jewellery, and the other contained loose gems.

"Ever since I sent my family away, I've been buying jewellery and gems with my spare cash. Unlike money, they are easier to conceal." He looked up at her, giving her time to consider his words. "I need you to sew the jewellery and gems into the hem of our coats, and your skirt. Sew them in tightly, so they don't rattle. Can you do that?"

Sitting stiffly in the chair, Ilse-Renata nodded her understanding, twisting her hands nervously in her lap. "What about the money," she asked shyly.

"We'll put the money into the belts," Herr Kobelev said, fanning the wallet to show her the contents. "Splitting it so we each carry half. We'll each wear a belt around our waist. You must never do anything to attract attention to the jewels or the money. I will use money from my belt first. If necessary, I will ask you for more later."

"I understand," she said, her voice quivering as she answered.

Having concluded his instructions, Herr Kobelev walked around the desk and placed a calm hand on Ilse-Renata's shoulder. He peered into her teary eyes. "You mustn't worry," he said. "Together, we'll get through this. We just need to be smart about what we do. Yes?"

Ilse-Renata relaxed at his touch and showed him a brave smile. "Yes."

"I'll leave you to your task, then," he said, opening the door. "I'll tell the others that you are doing some paperwork for me and that you are not to be disturbed."

"Of course," Ilse-Renata said, making herself comfortable. She removed the thread and needle from her sewing kit and set to work.

⚜

Some hours later, Prow returned to his office just as Ilse-Renata snipped the last thread. "Finished?" he asked.

"Yes. Now what?"

"Go home. Collect the rest of your things and meet me here tonight at six o'clock. Wear dark clothing and don't use a suitcase. Wrap only those things that you absolutely need into a bundle. If you have portable food like bread and cheese, bring that, too. If we lose our transportation along the way, you must be able to carry what you bring. Pack wisely."

A crease appeared between Ilse-Renata's brows, and her usual smile gave way to a frown.

"Are you afraid?" he asked.

"A little," she answered.

"You are wise to be afraid. Your fear will keep you alive. And I will protect you. I promise: you will be safe with me."

"I do … trust you," she said sincerely. She grabbed up her coat and handbag. "I'll be back by six," she said, tucking her braids into her felt hat and inserting the pearl hatpin.

Taking up her handbag and the tote bag in which she carried her spare skirt, Ilse-Renata asked, "What about the others?"

"I spoke with them earlier," Prow said. "They've all gone home to prepare. I expect them back around six.

"You need to be off." Prow said, encouraging her to leave. "Rest a little, if you can. It will be a long journey."

CHAPTER THIRTY-ONE

At 6 o'clock, Ilse-Renata met her employer in front of the laboratory. She wore the grey, hooded coat into which she had stitched the jewellery—a collection of expensive rings, bracelets, necklaces, and small broaches—and the black skirt into which she had stitched the loose stones.

She also wore a pink pullover sweater and matching sweater coat, hoping to disguise the bulge of the money belt at her waist. The extra weight in her clothing made her feel sluggish, echoing her worry of what was to come.

In her arms, she clutched her small bundle of personal items, including a change of clothes and a swatch of woollen fabric that her friend and colleague, Lieselotte, had insisted she carry.

The weathered satchel that hung from her shoulder held bread, cheese, a heel of

Schmidt sausage, and a bottled beverage. *If I eat sparingly, I'll have enough food for several days. After that, I'll just have to rely on Herr Kobelev.*

"Right on time, Ilse-Renata!" Prow said as she followed him into his office, where a bundle of personal items rested on the top of his desk. "I can always rely on you for promptness. Thank you."

His kind smile reassured her. "The others will be here shortly. Remember, say nothing of what we've done."

Ilse-Renata hugged her bundle and nodded. When he opened the top drawer of his desk and removed a small pistol, she remained mute, but watched wide-eyed as he tucked it into the pocket of his greatcoat and slipped a box of bullets into a secret pocket inside.

By 6:30, most of the laboratory employees had gathered just inside the door.

"Everyone is here except Lieselotte," Prow said. "Where is she? Does anyone know?"

"I spoke with her just before I left the lab this afternoon," Ilse-Renata reported. "She said she planned to go directly to the airfield to ask about a seat in an earlier truck. I tried to stop her, but she was too frightened to wait."

"Why that impertinent little ..." Prow growled, stopping as if reluctant to say more. "Then we'll have to assume that she found a seat! Let's just hope that she hasn't compromised our plans."

He glared at the others. "Leave the lights off. We don't want to attract anyone's attention."

In a stern, quiet voice, Prow continued. "A truck from the airfield will arrive in a few minutes. I have bribed the organizers of this little adventure in exchange for your seats. When it pulls up, you must quickly and quietly board. Please don't speak unless necessary. We don't know who's watching, and we don't want to cause trouble for the organizers. Understood?"

In his hand, he held a torch. He snapped

the switch on as he finished his speech and circled the light around the room. When each of his employees had acknowledged his instructions, he snapped the switch and the room fell dark again.

Moments later, they heard the brakes of a truck squeal outside the door, then footsteps on the road in front of the lab and a rapid knock.

"This is it," Prow said, opening the door.

One by one, he directed each of the men toward the back of the truck. When only he and Ilse-Renata remained, he wrapped his arm around her shoulder and escorted her out the door.

Hands reached out from the truck toward her. She handed up her bundle, which quickly disappeared into the dark interior, then took one offered hand in each of hers. Prow's hands encircled her waist and boosted her up; then he jumped in behind her.

As the last two passengers settled on one of the benches that lined the inside of the truck, the lab workers heard the clutch groan and felt the truck jerk into motion.

⚜

Russian shells had begun falling on the city early in the evening, making the truck's passengers tense on the ride to the airfield. Silhouetted against the munitions flashes, they found another truck loaded and waiting for them. The driver informed them that the other trucks had been departing at thirty-minute intervals.

"We are the last," he said. "As we travel, we will put space between us."

Together, the two trucks lumbered out of the city, into the countryside. The lead truck slowly pulled ahead until it disappeared into the dark. Each truck moved without headlights, to avoid being sighted.

By the time the convoy reached the border between Germany and Czechoslovakia, at least an hour separated each of the trucks.

Near Prague, as the truck carrying the lab workers passed through a forested area, it was stopped by Czech partisans. An argument ensued with the driver, who did not understand their demands. Some of the lab workers expressed their concern to Prow, fearful that the freedom fighters might cause trouble for them.

"Don't worry. I'll take care of this," Prow said as he hopped out of the truck.

Before he engaged the patrol in conversation, Ilse-Renata watched as he discretely patted the right pocket of his greatcoat, as if to reassure himself that the pistol remained stowed there, available if needed.

When, in the language of the partisans, he suggested that they accept two gemstones to help their cause, the truck was waved onward.

As the gears of the truck groaned into motion, Prow climbed into the truck and resumed his seat.

Ilse-Renata immediately released a breath that she had not realized she held. Sighing, she said a silent prayer that use of the gun was not required.

❧

After Prague, the trucks turned south and west, travelling through Pilsen toward *Oberpfalz*, a region northwest of the Bavarian Forest. American planes buzzed overhead when the truck passed along train tracks. Machine-gun fire sparked from the planes, but the truck in which Ilse-Renata travelled with her colleagues was spared.

Not long after, they came upon the remnants of one of the airfield trucks from Breslau. Its shell sat in the centre of the road, badly burnt, flames still licking from under the hood. Ilse-Renata covered her mouth with her hands to stifle her shock.

"What is it?" Prow whispered.

"That's the truck we saw Lieselotte riding in this morning." She gasped.

As their truck passed the burnt-out shell, holes in the sides of the vehicle told them that it had been strafed by the machine-guns of American fighter planes. Charred remains of some of the occupants were still visible, including the driver and two large men who had been sitting in the back. Nothing could be seen of Lieselotte.

"She wanted me to go with her." Ilse-Renata sobbed. "I told her we'd be safer with you, but she wouldn't listen!"

A short time later, as the truck navigated through Oberpfalz, it was stopped at an American check point. On approach to the check point, Ilse-Renata and her truck-mates became more animated.

"I never thought we'd make it!" one of the former lab workers said. "Now we're safe. The Americans will protect us from the Russians!"

"Look at these guys," another colleague exclaimed. "In Germany, we never see so many coffee-coloured men together in one place."

Prow hopped from the back of the truck, and once again Ilse-Renata watched his hand slide discretely over the coat pocket that held the pistol before he approached the American soldiers. He explained who they were, and that they had come to Ober-pfalz seeking American protection from the Russians.

One of the soldiers gave him directions to a Red Cross station further along the same road, where they could ask for food, then used his rifle to gesture them onward.

At the Red Cross station, their names were added to a growing list of displaced persons. In addition to reporting their whereabouts, they were able to learn the whereabouts of family members.

The truck bearing Ilse-Renata and her colleagues continued to travel until they arrived at Weiding, where the first of the men set off in search of his family.

In rapid succession, more of the men left the truck to find their families, until only Ilse-Renata and Prow remained. By that time, the truck had run out of fuel, and no more could be found. Prow had spent all his cash on provisions, accommodation, fuel, and bribes.

⚜

"Wait here," Prow told Ilse-Renata as they walked into a vacated train station. "I'll see if I can find us transportation."

He stopped mid-step and returned. "You'd better give me a few of the stones," he said. "I'll need to show I can pay. Go inside, so no one can see what you're doing."

A few minutes later, Ilse-Renata appeared at his side. She held a closed fist out to him and released five gemstones into his open hand.

"Wait here," he said. "I'll try to find food, too."

Ilse-Renata sat on a bench, fighting against the warmth of the morning sun and the hunger that threatened to lull her into a doze.

Heavy footsteps alerted her to someone's approach. She jumped to her feet and ducked inside the train station, her heart pounding. She crouched inside the doorway and listened to a heated exchange between three American soldiers who stomped past the entrance, rifles slung over their shoulders.

Fearful of their return, she remained inside the station until she heard soft footsteps on the wooden stairs outside.

"Ilse-Renata?" She heard the worry in Prow's questioning voice.

"Here," she said, stepping out into the sunshine with her bundle clutched to her chest.

"Are you all right?"

"Yes," she said. "I was startled by some soldiers, so I hid."

"Come then! I've found us a ride, and some food."

Ilse-Renata hastened alongside Prow until they came upon a farm tractor pulling a trailer.

"Hop on," the farmer said. "We've a way to go."

Prow helped Ilse-Renata hop onto the flatbed trailer and jumped up to sit beside her.

"Where are we going?" she asked.

"North. To find your mother," Prow said. "Once I know you're safe, I can go in search of my own family."

He dug into his coat pockets and retrieved small bits of bread, cheese, and a bottle of ale.

"Eat," he said. "Then you can rest a bit."

The bread and cheese settled welcome and heavy in her belly. The ale quenched her thirst as tiny bubbles found their way down her parched throat. The sun warmed her again and, together with the after-effect of the ale, made her drowsy.

She fought to stay alert, but sleep overcame her. Slipping deeper into slumber, Ilse-Renata leaned sideways, only to be jerked awake by Prow.

"What is it?" she asked, shaken by the abrupt awakening.

"You nodded off," he said. "I was looking at the destruction of the landscape and didn't realize it until you were about to fall off the wagon. I caught you just in time. Otherwise, you would have been under the wheels, and I would have wasted weeks of my time trying to save you from certain death," he said, teasing her. Within his jest, she saw the truth.

"Thank you," she said humbly. "I don't know what I would do without you."

"Nor do I," he mocked, wrapping his arm around her shoulders and holding her close.

"I'm so tired," Ilse-Renata mumbled into his chest.

"Sleep, then," he said, caressing her hair with his free hand.

⟡

Prow continued to find transportation that carried them further north, closer to her mother. At Zeil on the Main River, Prow asked her for more of the gemstones.

"We aren't far from your mother's accommodation, and we can't arrive empty-handed. We will stop at this farm to buy eggs and meat," he said, pointing toward a farm they were approaching.

"Wait here," he said moments later, leaving her to sit on the front steps of the farm's house.

When Prow returned a while later, he carried a basket of eggs, a loaf of bread, and an oddly-shaped bundle wrapped in brown paper. "What's that?" Ilse-Renata asked, pointing at the package.

"The farmer only had one calf left, and he refused to butcher it, so I had to do it."

"You know how to butcher cows?" she asked, surprised at her employer's unusual skill.

"No, but I learnt quickly," he said.

"That doesn't look like a calf," she said, sizing up the package again.

"It's not," Prow said, grinning at her. "I couldn't carry a whole calf, so I only took half of it. I've left the other half for someone else. That clever farmer made me pay for the entire calf, though, and now he will benefit from a second sale of the remaining half. A sly fox, he is. Come on. I also got directions to your aunt's house. It's not far."

When they neared the town's grocery store, Prow pointed. "Your uncle owns that store," he said. "Your mother should be staying there."

"Wait!" Ilse-Renata snapped. "Let me straighten up." She licked her hands and smoothed her wayward hair, brushed straw from her coat, and polished the toes of her shoes on the legs of her hose.

"I don't know why you bother," Prow said, shaking his head. "We've been travelling for more than two months. No one is going to complain about how you look. They will simply be happy to see you!"

Ilse-Renata blushed, realizing the futility of her endeavours. "My mother taught me to be respectful."

She stopped suddenly and turned to face Prow. "Before we go in, I must say thank you. Again. It is only because of you that I am here. You have been so kind to me, and you have fulfilled your promise to keep me safe. I don't know how I will ever repay you." She twisted her hands, feeling at a loss of what to do.

"Don't fuss," Prow said. "You're embarrassing me. If your mother can make a meal of the food we bring, that will be enough thanks to see me to my own family. Come!"

CHAPTER THIRTY-TWO

Gerhard sat slumped on the settee, his
elbows braced on his knees, support-
ing the weight of his head. He looked up
with tired eyes, fingering the throbbing scar
on his brow.

"Gerda. You're home, then." His voice
was flat. Gerda entered the old study and
sat in an armchair opposite.

"Yes, Papa. I'm not needed at the farm
just now. I can stay with you for a few days.
There's things that need to be done."

"I thought we'd be safe here. I promised
Vater that I'd keep everyone safe," Gerhard
lamented, his hands covering his face as he
wept. "I can't believe they're gone."

Gerda dropped to her knees and wrapped
her arms around her father, trying to comfort him.

"Mein Gott!" he said, gently prying
his daughter's arms away from him.

He sat straighter, as if trying to find his self-control.

Moments later, he jumped to his feet and began pacing past the old painting of Mars that hung on the study wall. "The German defence is already forfeit! There's no need for the Americans and the British to continue their air raids! Bombing the city of Bayreuth in the middle of April was not necessary! That stupid, arrogant action obliterated half of the Old City, the area around the train station, and Wagner's Villa Wahnfried. And, thousands of civilians have been killed! For what?"

Gerhard continued his rant. "But not us! *Gott sei dank*. The Lange house stands unscathed. But not the Lange family. No. We have not escaped; death has marked us." His words were heavy with grief.

"Papa, please," Gerda said. "Come and sit with me. I'm afraid that your excitement could cause a heart attack."

"Ha!" Gerhard plopped back into his chair, dismissing her concern. "Otto! He survived the worst war in history, only to be killed by one of those irresponsible bombs! And Hildegard, poor woman. And Marie. My beautiful sister Marie …" He rolled his head in his hands.

"What were they doing in the Old City?" Gerda asked, pouring a brandy and handing a glass to her father. The late morning sun filtered through the stained-glass window in the study, casting colour about the room. A beam of light caught the crystal of the glass she handed to her father, sparking small fires of light on the walls.

"It was Otto's birthday. They went to a tea garden to celebrate. They shouldn't have gone. I told them not to go." He moaned.

"How is Mama?" Gerda asked, changing the topic.

"Wha—oh. She's good. The doctor said she was very lucky. The debris that fell around her protected her. She has a head trauma, but she will recover from that. The doctor said she can return home as soon as the dizziness stops. A few days, perhaps."

Gerhard staggered up from his chair, rising to his full height and stretching his tired body. Gerda noted with surprise that his spiked hair was a mixture of ebony and grey. More salt than pepper since she visited six weeks earlier. She rose to steady her father.

"Papa?"

"I need my ulcer medication," he said, pointing to a prescription bottle on his desk and grabbing his belly. A small gasp of discomfort escaped his lips. "And, we must make the funeral arrangements."

"Yes, Papa. Let's have our midday meal first, shall we?" She snatched the prescription bottle from the desk and hooked her arm through his. "Your medication is to be taken with food, so this is perfect timing. Let's go eat. We can attend to the funeral arrangements this afternoon."

On cue, the cook appeared at the doorway and announced that the meal was ready. Seeing Gerda, she excused herself to set another place in the dining room.

In measured steps, Gerda escorted her father into the dining room, where the cook had set out bowls of hot, vegetable soup and fresh, black bread. They ate quietly, remembering their time lived with the dead.

Over tea, they discussed plans for their afternoon: to visit the *Beerdigungsinstitut* to make funeral arrangements, then to visit Emma at the hospital for her latest prognosis.

"Where are Grandmother and Tante Cook?" Gerda asked.

"They're at the hospital with Mama," Gerhard told her. "It was fortunate that they were unable to attend the birthday celebration. Tante Cook was ill that day and stayed in bed. Grandmother stayed behind to keep her company." He bent his head in anguish, trying to control his emotions.

As they prepared to leave, the cook reminded them that Arthur would arrive later that afternoon. "I'll meet his train," Gerda said, "while you rest, Papa."

"I wish Paul was coming too," Gerhard said. "I haven't heard from him in weeks. He was sent to Italy, you know. I'm worried that he may have been caught." His words evaporated into a mumble, but Gerda heard the last clearly: "Dead."

"Yes, I know, Papa. I pray he's safe, too."

Emma was released from the hospital a few days later, the gash on her forehead the only visible damage of the bombing.

"My head will heal in time," she told Arthur as he escorted her into the funeral service, "but my heart will always miss three I held so dear."

The day following the funeral, Gerhard asked Emma, Arthur, and Gerda to join him in the study for coffee before they each headed off to start their day. As Gerhard closed the study door and invited his son and daughter to sit in one of the armchairs, Emma poured them each a cup of false coffee. Coffee had not been on shop shelves for a very long time.

"We need to prepare ourselves," he said, without mixing niceties. "Either the Americans or the Russians will reach the city shortly, and I don't know what will happen to Arthur and me. At the best, we will be taken as prisoners of war …"

"No! Gerhard!" Emma exclaimed, covering her mouth to stifle the volume.

"Now, my dear," Gerhard said, placing a hand of reassurance on her shoulder. "We've talked of this possibility, you and me. As I see it, we are facing the inevitable."

Looking toward Arthur, he continued. "I can only hope that the Americans arrive before the Russians, and that they are more charitable toward us."

Turning toward the women, he said, "You must be prepared to manage things on your own. Focus on the farm, Emma. Between you and the general manager, I think you can train Gerda to step in wherever she's needed. We need to keep growing food to feed the people, as well as expand the herd. What do you think, Gerda? Are you up to it?"

"Oh, yes, Papa! I love the farm, and welcome the opportunity to learn more about its administration. I used to follow Uncle Otto and Tante Hildegard around. I loved watching them at their work," she said. Sadness appeared to overwhelm her, and she slumped into her chair. "They worked so well together."

"That's my girl," Gerhard said, ignoring her reference to the death of his two friends. Instead, he smiled fondly at his only daughter, hoping to cheer her up.

"Emma, leave the factories for now. The Americans will want to see that our priorities are growing produce and expanding the herd. If my return is delayed for any reason, and you see that the farm is prospering, then you can turn your attention to the factories. You know enough about them to get them organized; just don't do anything that would suggest the assembly of armaments. If any of the employees return, they will help you. If I still haven't returned by then, run the factories—organize the men to make only the parts necessary to repair or rebuild damaged farm equipment."

"But, Gerhard," Emma interrupted again.

"No 'buts,' Emma. With or without Arthur and me, the farm needs to work. Germany needs to be fed. After that, the factories will need to commence operations. Farm machinery will need to be repaired or rebuilt. Ultimately, the factories will be our future, and our primary source of income. Do the best you can. I have no idea how long Arthur and I will be detained, but we must plan for a worst-case scenario."

"Do you think we'll be executed, Papa?"

Emma and Gerda gasped at Arthur's question.

"Not if the Americans arrive first," Gerhard answered. "I suspect they'll want to put us to work, rebuilding the country. I don't have the same confidence in the Red Army. They'll want retaliation."

He sat next to Emma as she collapsed onto the settee, wrapped his arms around her, and held her until she stopped shaking. "Arthur, if you're interrogated, be honest. That's all I will say on that matter. Don't do or say anything foolish, understood? Don't speculate or base your answers on rumours. Facts only. Understood?"

"Yes, sir." Arthur gave his father a sloppy salute. He had vacated the chair upon which he had first sat. As his father had spoken, he had slipped to kneel beside his sister, holding her hands, trying to comfort her.

"If you return before me, help your mother and sister rebuild."

"Yes, sir."

"Pray God that you both return home quickly," Emma said, her voice full of sadness.

"Amen to that," Gerda said, sniffling into her hanky.

"One last thing," Gerhard said. "I expect the detainment to be abrupt, without notice, and so you must, too. I don't want to think about the consequences if the Russians arrive first. I'm truly hoping for the Americans."

He smiled benevolently, hoping to reassure his family. "When you hear that the Americans have arrived in the city, and we don't return at the end of the day, presume that we have been taken prisoner, and pray for our speedy return. If the Russians arrive, we must pray for ourselves and each other."

Within a week of the funeral, American forces arrived in the city. They continued to push north, dispatching troops throughout Bavaria and commandeering any military bases and other facilities that suited them, including the Depot where Gerhard worked in the administrative offices. All military men, including Gerhard and Arthur, were detained for questioning.

Although Gerhard was a senior officer with the Wehrmacht, his interrogators soon determined that he was not a member of the Nazi party, and that his position as an administrator overseeing the well-being of returning troops during the war was non-threatening.

355

When he was finally given the opportunity to inform the committee assigned to his interrogation about the farming operations overseen by his family, and his determination to make the farm fully functional as soon as possible, he was released on one condition. The farm would be inspected on a regular basis to ensure that the operation was as originally described, and diligently managed.

Gerhard took the opportunity to mention that his son was also involved in the farm's operations, and, as summer faded into fall, Arthur was released.

By then, some of the hands who had been injured during the war had also returned to the farm. Those men resumed their former responsibilities as best they could. Adjustments were made to accommodate any disabilities.

Gerhard and Arthur were billeted at the farmhouse to oversee the farm's operations, thereby supplanting the responsibilities of Emma and Gerda. Consequently, the women returned to their home in Bayreuth and made themselves useful elsewhere.

Each day, a truck arrived from a nearby prisoner-of-war camp, delivering able-bodied German prisoners to provide additional labour for the farm. Other than communications necessary to instruct the prisoners, the prisoners were forbidden from any actions or words that might be perceived as socializing.

Gerhard noted that the prisoners were malnourished, and that, as the days passed and the men applied themselves to the physical labour required to run a farm, their health worsened.

When the first inspector arrived, Gerhard complained about the condition of the men and insisted that he be permitted to provide them with at least one hearty meal per day. For that, he would require someone to prepare the meals, and requested the women from his home: his wife, daughter, and the family cook. "A man well-fed will be stronger and more capable of doing the required work," he argued.

The inspector contemplated Gerhard's suggestions, and ultimately agreed to implement the necessary changes, subject to one condition of his own.

"On the occasion of each of my inspections," he informed Gerhard, "I will welcome an expression of your heart-felt generosity, illustrated with a healthy ration of meat and a large basket of fresh produce." He leered at Gerhard, waiting for him to object.

Gerhard almost complied, then decided to hold his tongue. If he could provide one solid meal per day to each man who worked on his farm, those men had a chance at survival. Further, he reasoned, by keeping them well-fed, they would be more committed to carrying out the tasks assigned to them. In the end, the farm would thrive, producing bountiful crops that could be put toward feeding the nation.

It may be a year before everyone involved will benefit, but, God help us, we will! Besides, I'll have my family close by, where I can protect them.

CHAPTER THIRTY-THREE

Paul and his men were caught in the Apennine trap, and transported to a prisoner-of-war camp overseen by an American command. At the time of capture, Paul and his men were stripped of their gear, loaded into trucks, and taken south to a camp near Rome.

They were inspected on arrival for any other contraband, then forced to relinquish their boots. Without boots, they were not expected to escape.

When the war ended, their captors continued to detain the German soldiers, but relaxed their security enforcement. Although the prisoners received food rations in accordance with the Geneva Convention, the rations were meagre, and the men were always hungry, especially after a day of hard labour.

The captives discovered that, with care, canned goods could be secreted out of the American food supplies. They took advantage of the American inattention, supplementing their diet and building their own stash of supplies.

The prisoners were often ordered to unload trucks arriving from the American airfield so supplies could be dispatched to other camps. Some shipments included crates of baseballs, bats, and leather gloves, and the prisoners quickly learnt the value that their captors placed on their national game of baseball.

"Captain?" Private Lothar whispered to Paul one sunny afternoon, soon after their capture.

"What is it, Shoes?" Paul said, hoisting a sack of flour onto a cart. He noticed that the private had pried a slat loose from one of the crates.

"Captain, I can do something with these," Shoes said, fingering a leather catcher's mitt.

Paul raised an inquisitive eyebrow, considered for a moment, then nodded. "Carry on, Private."

Shoes waved to a few of his comrades,

and together they helped the crates of baseball gloves disappear.

The Americans complained bitterly that the baseball gloves they had ordered had not arrived, and promptly placed another order.

"How do they expect us to play baseball without gloves!" the supply officer grumbled.

Shoes ensured that the crates of gloves were stashed out of sight, and, as time passed, he transformed the leather baseball gloves into footwear, a pair for each of Paul's men.

"Shoes, we are very fortunate that you worked as a cobbler before you were drafted," Paul said privately, patting Shoes on the back. "Keep up the good work!"

One by one, as the men received their shoes, Paul instructed them on the best route home. "Follow the road north, by night. Stop at cloisters and beg asylum by day. Hopefully, the nuns will take pity and provide food and shelter for God's loyal Christians."

Adding words of encouragement, he said, "And fill your pockets with canned goods before you leave. The nuns will appreciate a donation for their efforts."

Slowly, the number of men diminished, but not the headcount. Because the American soldiers charged with carrying out the daily headcount did not speak German, they had failed to realize that the number of heads ceased to equate to the final number shouted at the end of each muster call.

As the one-year anniversary of their capture approached, Paul began to worry about their circumstance. Many of the men had already escaped, and he feared their captors would soon realize the headcount deception. He called a secret meeting with the remainder of his men and spread the word that the next escape would be en masse. Private Shoes assured him that, by the targeted escape date, every man would have appropriate footwear and sufficient canned goods to see them home.

Together, Paul and the remaining German officers devised a plan that would guide everyone north. As a distraction, a few small groups of men were to head in other directions first, then wind their way home. They hoped that, by splitting off in small groups, headed in a variety of directions, their captors would be overwhelmed with the resulting search and give up the pursuit.

Paul knew that, because he was an officer, he was a valued captive. He and the other officers expected to be pursued, aggressively.

On the night of the escape, Paul ensured that his men were away safely before he set out on his journey south toward Rome. He deliberately left small clues so that the American soldiers would follow him, allowing the others ample time to travel beyond risk of recapture. When he was confident that sufficient time had passed, Paul disappeared into the dark.

Paul's plan was to seek asylum from the Pope. He was confident that, if he reached Vatican City, the Holy Father would feel compelled to keep him, one of God's faithful servants, safe. He was wrong.

When he finally arrived at the Vatican, Paul announced to the Swiss Guard that he wished to ask the Pope for asylum. The guards laughed at him.

"This is neutral territory, yes," one of them said, "but currently the Pope is not accepting any foreigners, not even devoted ones, into the Vatican. We can, however, offer you a comfortable prison cell once you've been tried for trespassing."

As the guards lunged toward him, Paul raced off in the opposite direction, twisting and turning down cobbled streets until he was beyond the pursuit of the Swiss Guard and clear of Vatican City.

Appalled at the Vatican's closed-door policy, Paul resolved to find his own way home to Deutschland, and to focus instead on finding Ilse-Renata. He had been away too long.

I hope she still thinks of me the way I think of her.

CHAPTER THIRTY-FOUR

Paul travelled north, keeping his distance from the prisoner-of-war camp that had held him for the past year. Until he was well beyond the area, he travelled by night, avoiding the check stops and patrols that continued to search for him.

Paul had no idea of the date, except that it was 1946. The Americans had celebrated the arrival of the new year with a raucous party. *It feels like spring, perhaps early summer.*

One warm evening, he took shelter in a small barn that housed two milk cows, a pig, and some chickens. He burrowed under a stack of clean hay and fell asleep. Early in the morning, he awoke abruptly to squealing brakes, followed by a heated exchange of Italian and English-speaking voices.

Paul pushed hay from a crack in the planked wall, providing a clear view of the dispute. He lay motionless, noting from the uniforms that American soldiers were interrogating the Italian famer—the farmer whose barn he happened to be occupying.

The conversation was stilted; neither party had a particularly good command of the other's language. To each insistent suggestion made by the sergeant in charge, the farmer responded in the negative, insisting that the Americans leave his property.

Having learnt Italian in school, Paul gleaned from the farmer's comments that the Americans were indeed looking for him. He burrowed deeper under the sweet-smelling hay.

The sergeant insisted that the farmer's property be searched. The farmer relinquished finally, and two privates moved briskly from one building to another, looking for their missing quarry.

The private that dared to enter the farmer's house exited promptly, the farmer's wife chasing him out with a flick of her apron, waving a floured arm in protest.

The other private stood at the entrance to the barn, nose wrinkled, and waving his hand before his face. "Sarge, this place stinks like a latrine! No one in their right mind would spend time here, let alone hide."

Five minutes later, the Americans and their jeep drove off the farmer's property in a cloud of dust. The farmer stood his ground firmly, shaking his fist in protest despite the dust.

Paul waited. When he was certain that the American soldiers had left the farm, he crawled out from under the haystack.

Dusting himself off, he walked out of the barn with his hands raised high in the air, then addressed the farmer. "Sir," he said in clear Italian, "I'm sorry to disturb you. I believe those men were looking for me."

The farmer turned and looked at Paul with an expression of disbelief. As a smile of awareness dawned on his face, the farmer said, "Please, *Signor*, come inside. You must be hungry. You can freshen up a little. Yes? And my wife will be happy to cook you a good breakfast from our meagre pantry. Please. Come."

The farmer and his wife were kind and generous Catholics who were happy to provide Paul with a hearty breakfast of warm bread fresh from the oven, a chunk of hard cheese, and a cooked egg. He rubbed his belly in gratitude as he popped the last of the bread, dripping in egg yolk, into his mouth and grinned. "I can't remember the last time I ate so well!" he told them.

The farmer's wife responded to his gratitude by assembling a bundle of extra food for him to take on his journey north.

When he announced that he must leave, his hosts detained him long enough to give him a change of clothes and a pair of sturdy boots. He could see misery in their eyes as they proffered the boots and the clothes.

"These were our son's," the farmer said. "He died of an intestinal illness last fall. He had just turned eighteen." The farmer shook his head in sadness, and a tear escaped his wife's eye.

"He was about your size." The farmer continued. "I think you are thin enough for them to fit."

"I can't accept your generous offer," Paul told them, empathizing with their loss. "Your gesture is greatly appreciated, though. And I am truly sorry to hear about your son."

"No!" the wife said with insistence. "You must take them. Please." She held the folded clothing in her outstretched arms, willing him to accept. "If you don't take them, one day we will have to discard them, or give them away to someone else. We would rather you had them. You too have suffered much, we think."

"Then I'll take them, with thanks," he said, with a small bow.

Steam rose from a kettle sitting on an old, cast iron stove. The farmer's wife efficiently poured the warmed water into a basin and invited Paul to wash, while she and her husband gave him privacy by busying themselves in the yard outside.

Seeing the sun rising higher in the morning sky, Paul quickly washed and changed. *I must be away from here, before the Americans' return. If I'm found here, that will cause trouble for these kind folks.*

Twenty minutes later, with a bundle slung over his shoulder, Paul hugged the farmer and his wife and bid them farewell. Setting steps to road, Paul marched off, thinking, *I should be able to cover a few kilometres before the heat of the day forces me to find shelter.*

⚜

Paul travelled north, through the remainder of Italy and then Austria, mostly by foot, grateful for the heavy boots he had received from the farmer. On occasion, he managed to find a ride with a sympathetic local, who would share whatever food they could and pointed him in the right direction.

Once he reached Austria, travel was easier; a few of the locals even welcomed and fed him. On the outskirts of Innsbruck, he approached a Red Cross unit and asked for shelter and food. He was given another pair of boots and a change of clothing.

Paul gave his name and military information to the office clerk. His name was added to the list of displaced persons, and he received papers for travel.

"Please," he said to the clerk, "I'm looking for a young woman. Her name is Ilse-Renata Chemiker. Is she on your list?"

The clerk flipped through several pages. When she finally stopped, her finger ran down a list of names beginning with the letter C. "I have an Ilse-Renata Chemiker and an Erna Chemiker residing in München. Is she the one you seek?"

"Yes, yes," he said with enthusiasm. "Erna is her mother. She has an aunt and uncle in München. That must be where she is. Can you give me the address?"

The woman hesitated. "Is she a relative?"

"No," he said with pleading eyes. "I'm going to ask her to marry me."

"For your sake, I hope she accepts," the woman said, her voice doubtful. "Young women don't wait around for soldiers these days: especially ones who've been missing for so long."

She hastily scribbled the address on a slip of paper and handed it to him. "Good luck to you."

Paul tucked the paper into his jacket pocket and walked out of the Red Cross office, plopping his cap upon his head. *I'm grateful that Ilse-Renata is in München, not Dresden or Hof.*

Paul managed to catch a ride on a transport truck that took him all the way to München and dropped him just outside a train station, a mere two kilometres from the address he had been given by the Red Cross.

Before he closed the truck door, he asked the driver for the date.

"It's May 8th, of course! The war has been over for one year already!" the driver told him.

Paul thanked the driver and headed into the train station. It was evident to him that the station had been bombed at some point during the war, but repairs had already been made.

In the water closet marked *Herren*, he washed his face and tidied his hair as best he could. It had grown long during the past year. *I need a haircut and a shave.* He fussed, rubbing the dripping beard that bushed around his face. It was only then that he noticed the deep lines etched in his face, evidence of hardship and starvation.

Mein Gott, I hope she doesn't turn and run at the sight of me.

He covered his head with the familiar cap, given to him by the farmer and his wife, and set off in search of his ultimate destination.

On the road outside the train station, he put purpose in his stride and went in search of Ilse-Renata. Since he had last seen her in Breslau he had worried after her safety, hoping that she was able to exit the city before the Russians attacked. *She must have, idiot! She's in München, after all!*

He also hoped that she would greet him favourably. The thought of seeing her again was the one thing that had kept him going. A knot of anxiety formed in the pit of his belly and grew tighter with each step he took toward the address where he hoped to find the woman he loved.

Walking along a main street, reality slowly permeated Paul's press to find Ilse-Renata. The devastation of his surroundings saddened him. Devastation was a part of war. He knew that. But now that the war was over, it all seemed pointless. *Did anyone really win?*

All around him, beautiful, old buildings had been scarred, marred, or demolished. Some of the city lots had been cleared of debris; others showed signs of new construction or repair. The Allied bombing may have broken the city of München, but the people seemed determined to make it rise again.

During his imprisonment in Italy, Paul had begun to realize that he had detached his emotions from his military responsibilities. He had blocked his feelings to protect himself against the horrors of the war in which he had been forced to participate. He tried not to see and feel the harm inflicted by one human being upon another.

Why? What's the point? What was achieved? My questions never stop, and no answers ever come.

He felt an overwhelming sadness and sense of despair when he considered the loss of life, the loss of land and home, the wickedness of war, and the men who governed it. Paul's footsteps slowed with tiredness. He was tired of war, ruin, and loss. Mostly, he was tired of walking.

He was tired, too, of waiting for Ilse-Renata. Paul desperately needed to find her, telling himself that she could help him end the madness that threatened his soul. His anxiety blossomed, aggravating a pain that twisted in his belly.

Paul turned onto a side street that appeared relatively unblemished. The roadway had random craters, more like potholes than bomb damage, and an occasional injury to a wall.

With relief, Paul noted that the house before him appeared to have been divinely protected. The white stone wall that surrounded the property was unmarked, as was the two-story house built of sturdy, red brick.

Standing before the wooden gate in the stone wall, Paul compared the numbers written on the scrap of paper given to him by the Red Cross clerk against the iron numbers nailed to the gate. The paper fluttered between his vibrating fingers.

Paul inhaled deeply to still his racing heart as he replaced the paper in his pocket. His belly fluttered again. *What if she's not here?* He licked his dry lips and ran his tongue around his teeth. *Breathe!*

As he searched for the courage to open the gate, Paul absentmindedly brushed his clothing and polished the toes of his battered boots on the back of his shabby pant legs.

Automaton-like, he reached down, released the latch in the gate, and entered a small garden. Paving stones formed a rose-lined path that led him to a front door of dark, weathered wood. Paul removed his cap and smoothed his hair with trembling hands. *What if she's not here? What if she doesn't want me? What if …? Stop fool! Just ring the damn bell!*

Ilse-Renata had been sitting in the living room reading a book when she heard the hinge of the gate squeak and footsteps approach the front door. *Curious; we aren't expecting anyone today.*

She snapped the book shut and set it on the table next to her chair. Leaning forward, she peered through the window and blinked, not believing who she saw. She took a deep breath and blinked again. Heart pounding, she flew out of the chair and raced to the door. Before the bell chimed its first note, she tore open the door, grinning from ear to ear.

"What took you so long!" she exclaimed as she leapt into Paul's arms.

Paul wrapped his arms around her and twirled in a circle of joy before he set her on her feet again. He gazed into her eyes, only then noticing her lips, parted and waiting. He promptly responded to her invitation.

When they finally separated to catch their breath, he dropped to his knee, holding her hands firm in his. "Marry me," he said. "I can't bear another day without you. I have dreamt of you and only you for more than a year. I would have come sooner, but my men and I were captured and held in a POW camp near Rome. We finally escaped, and I've been walking for weeks just to get here. To you. You must be my wife."

Ilse-Renata met Paul's eyes with sincerity. "I have loved you from the moment I saw you standing in front of that ancient church in Breslau. You could have swept me off my feet that first night."

Taking a deep breath, she straightened, encouraging Paul up off his knee, and continued with sincere confidence. "Of course I'll marry you!"

"Ilse, what's going on? Who is this?" Erna Chemiker asked, standing in the doorway.

Paul took a quick step away from Ilse-Renata as they each guiltily clasped their hands behind their backs. Paul dipped his head, as if embarrassed to be caught canoodling on the door step.

Blushing, Ilse-Renata responded to her mother through a great smile. "Mama! This is Captain Paul Lange, just returned from a year of internment in Italy. Tomorrow, I will be his wife!"

The next morning, as Erna and her sister prepared a wedding lunch, Paul and Ilse-Renata took a bus to a small town outside of München. They had little money and no clothes fancy enough for a wedding. They did not care; they had each other.

The previous evening, while the family discussed wedding arrangements, Paul stated that, for reasons he would rather not elaborate on, he preferred to be married at a town hall, rather than in a Catholic church.

I don't want to be involved in a discussion about religion, and how the Pope let me down.

"You can't just march into the München town hall and expect to be married on the spot!" Ilse-Renata's uncle had told them. "You must make an appointment. It could take days."

"Then we'll find another, smaller town to help us," Paul said, determined to be married the following day.

"Yes!" Ilse-Renata agreed. "We must be married tomorrow!"

CHAPTER THIRTY-FIVE

Hand-in-hand, Paul and Ilse-Renata walked briskly from the train station to the town hall. It was early. Most employees had yet to report for work. Paul and Ilse-Renata approached a desk, over which hung a sign reading: "Marriage Licences".

"May I help you?" a middle-aged woman, dressed in a neat brown suit, asked, looking up from a typewriter.

"Yes," Paul responded eagerly. "I've walked all the way from Rome to marry this young woman." He looked lovingly at his betrothed. "I'd appreciate it if you could ensure that we don't leave here today until it's done."

Ilse-Renata smiled back at him. "And I've been waiting for more than a year for his arrival," she said.

"We can help you," the woman assured them, "but the marriage commissioner hasn't arrived yet."

"Good morning, Mrs. Vogel!" a kindly-faced gentleman with white hair greeted the clerk.

"Good morning, Mayor," Mrs. Vogel replied.

"And who have we here?" the Mayor asked, smiling at the tall young man with long, blue-black hair and a bushy beard, and the petite blonde at his side, their hands tightly clasped.

"Mayor Schulze, this young couple is hoping to be married this morning," Mrs. Vogel said, before introducing Paul and Ilse-Renata.

Paul shook hands with the mayor and explained their urgent desire to be married.

"Ah! I understand," said Mayor Schulze. "I saw military service as well. I appreciate what you've been through, and how long you've had to wait."

When Mrs. Vogel explained that a

marriage commissioner would not arrive for another hour, the mayor said, "Then, Hannah, I must do it! I am the Mayor, am I not!"

Mrs. Vogel gave the mayor a fond smile. "Yes, sir! We will finish the paperwork and attend at your chambers in a few minutes."

The mayor nodded toward the three and departed, walking smartly down the hallway toward his office, whistling a popular wedding tune.

Paul and Ilse-Renata stayed with her family long enough to enjoy the celebratory wedding lunch, then caught the last train heading north to Bayreuth, where they arrived at dusk. Hands tightly clasped, they walked to the Lange family home from the train station. Paul carried a small suitcase with Ilse's few possessions neatly packed inside. He had none.

By the time they reached the home of Gerhard and Emma Lange, it was dark. The newlywed couple stood at the threshold of the home that Paul had last visited more than two years prior.

Pausing to collect themselves, Paul noticed that his father had mounted the crest over the lintel. He reached up, placing his hand on the worn crest. *I'm home and I'm safe.* He felt the shape of the crest pulse in his hand.

"I hope no other Lange will have to place a hand on this crest before setting off to war," he said.

"I agree absolutely," Ilse-Renata said brightly.

He left his concerns hanging on the crest, opened the door, and led his wife into the dimly-lit hallway.

Paul sniffed the aroma of food being prepared for the evening meal, trying to identify it as it wafted from the kitchen.

"Oh, good," he said, "We've arrived in time for dinner! Smells like Schmidt sausage and sauerkraut."

It was quiet in the foyer, but Paul could hear a soft noise coming from within the study. He set the suitcase on the floor inside the front door and walked toward the tuneless humming, still holding his wife's hand.

Standing in the doorway of the study, he tore his gaze from her eyes, squeezed her hand, and said, "Hello, Papa."

Gerhard swung around, the force of his turn jerking the glass in his hand. Small drops of brandy jumped free of the crystal vessel, spatting on the silver tray below it.

"Paul!" Gerhard exclaimed, setting his glass on the tray. "You're home!"

Paul stepped into the room and his father's welcoming embrace. Looking over his son's shoulder, Paul added, "and who is this lovely young lady?"

"Papa," Paul said bashfully, "this is Ilse-Renata … my wife."

Caught unsuspecting, Gerhard searched his son's face, then Ilse-Renata's. As their news permeated his thoughts, he grinned broadly.

"Ilse-Renata. A lovely name," he said reaching beyond Paul to take her hands.

385

"Welcome to our family," he added, before enveloping her in his embrace.

The introduction made, the three of them stood silent and grinning for a moment. Suddenly, Gerhard jerked his head toward the doorway and bellowed into the foyer. "Emma! Gerda! Arthur! Come quickly. Paul's home!"

Footsteps and squeals came from every direction of the house. They arrived one by one, greeting their wayward family member and welcoming his wife.

"You've arrived just in time for dinner," Emma said. "Gerda, run along and tell the cook that we'll have four more for dinner. Arthur, go tell the old ladies that Paul is home, and that they should join us for dinner."

Then she turned to Paul. "There is time enough before dinner; would you like to rest? Are you hungry? From where are you coming? How long have you been travelling?" Her questions flew at them in rapid succession.

"We've just arrived from München, Mama. We are a little hungry, but we can wait." He turned to his wife for affirmation and she nodded. "I wouldn't mind the opportunity to properly bathe and shave," he said, running his fingers through his beard.

"For the past year, I was imprisoned by the Americans in a camp near Rome," he summarized. "I arrived in München yesterday and Ilse and I were married this morning. We had lunch with her family, then caught the last train home."

"Oh, my!" Emma said. "So much news and so many more questions! Ilse, dear. May I call you Ilse? Or do you prefer Ilse-Renata?

"Please call me Ilse," she said shyly.

"Very well. Ilse, would you like to wait here while I sort things with Paul, or would you like to come along?"

"If you don't mind, I think I'll come along. Herr Lange, will you excuse me?" Ilse deferred to Gerhard.

"Of course," he said, shooing them out of the study. He took a sip of his brandy and sat with ease in the chair behind his desk.

"Well," he muttered to his glass of brandy, "so much for the priesthood!" His face radiated pleasure and confidence that the Lange family would have a fruitful future.

❖

Before she left her son and new daughter-in-law, Emma hugged them both and congratulated them once more. With her hands resting on her son's arms, she said, "Paul, dear, you are so thin. It breaks my heart to think what you must have suffered while you were interned."

Her eyes filled with tears. Brushing them aside before they slid down her cheeks, she smiled and said encouragingly, "We'll just have to fatten you up! Won't we, Ilse?"

Ilse smiled at her mother-in-law and then at Paul. "We will, indeed."

Emma left the newlyweds in Paul's room

while she ran down the oak staircase in search of Gerda and Gerhard.

"Gerhard, my dear. This night is their wedding night! They must have our room. Do you think you can manage one night in Paul's room?"

"In a single bed. With you?" he leered at her. "I would be delighted to try …"

She grinned at his mischief. "You … are … impossible!" she said, wrapping her arms around his waist with her face turned up in anticipation of his kiss. He obliged.

Emma pushed him away. "I must find Gerda. We need to prepare the wedding suite," she said, floating out of the study. "Ger-da!" she hollered into the house.

During dinner, the conversation stayed to family topics, notably the rash on Ilse's cheeks and the absence of Paul's beard—which caused crimson blushing each time someone commented on one or the other—and life in Bayreuth since the end of the war.

They talked about the bombings in the

city and the death of Otto, Hildegard, and Marie, but otherwise avoided any discussion of the war. Ilse enjoyed the banter and felt as though she had always been part of the family.

When they retired to the study afterward to relax with a glass of brandy, Emma announced that their bedroom had been prepared for Paul and Ilse.

"It won't do to have you share Paul's small bed on your wedding night," she said.

"Thank you, Mama," Paul said, feeling his scalp prickle with embarrassment, "but we'll manage." He looked at his new wife, who, pink-faced, nodded her agreement.

"Nonsense," Emma said. "Gerda and I have already prepared the master bedroom for you. We insist. Don't we, Gerhard," she said, appearing to defer to her husband for agreement.

"But what about you and Papa?" Paul asked.

"Well, that was my ques—"

Emma jabbed her elbow in Gerhard's rib,

ending his comment. "We will manage just fine in your bed. Just fine," she said looking intently at Gerhard, a small grin beginning on one side of her mouth.

Gerhard raised his glass. "To the newly-weds!" he said looking over the rim of his glass at Emma, a glint in his eyes meant for her alone.

"Do you think you can learn to tolerate my crazy family?" Paul asked, watching Ilse remove the braiding from her hair and brush out the dark blonde tresses that fell in waves below her breasts. Her pale, pink cheeks gave her creamy complexion a healthy glow, causing the three freckles on the tip of her nose to darken.

Her hazel eyes searched the mirror until she found his dark ones. "Of course! They're wonderful people. It's easy to understand you now. Seeing how your family is at ease with one another."

"I wish we could have had a big wedding in the cathedral," he apologized, "but it will be a while before I have money that can be used for anything other than necessities. Besides, I'm not particularly fond of the Church just now."

"I presume you'll explain your comment about the Church at some point, Paul, but please don't apologize," she said, placing the brush on the low dresser and rising from the stool where she had been sitting. "There is nothing simple or ordinary about a quick, shoe-string wedding at the end of a war. We may have nothing now, but we can build a life together. Family is what is most important."

"*Ja*, but we can't even have a wedding night in a hotel, let alone a honeymoon!" He moved toward her.

"None of that is important. We are together now. 'Till death us do part'," she said, mimicking the words the mayor had said that morning. "That is what's important."

She smiled up at him, raising her arms to embrace him.

He bent his knees and lifted her lithe form off the floor. His apple-flavoured lips lingered on hers while he carried her the three steps to their wedding bed.

"We'll have to find our own bed soon," he said. "My parents are generous by nature, but I don't want to take advantage of the situation."

"Agreed," she mumbled, kissing the pulsing notch at the base of his neck. As she traced small, butterfly kisses to other tantalizing parts of his anatomy and inhaled his maleness, they forgot about war, church, and family, and focussed only on themselves for one glorious night.

CHAPTER THIRTY-SIX

Over a late breakfast the following morning, the Lange family made plans for their future. A new wing would be added at the far end of the house to provide sleeping quarters and other private rooms for Paul and Ilse. In the meantime, Paul and Ilse would purchase a new, bigger bed for his room so Gerhard and Emma could have their own room again.

Gerhard, Paul, Emma, and Ilse took their coffee into the study. Gerhard and Emma sat side-by-side in a pair of worn, leather armchairs, leaving the settee for the newlyweds. A discussion followed regarding the design of a new addition to the house.

"Son," Gerhard said, "since you don't appear to have any imminent plans to enter the priesthood, I'm wondering whether you have discounted university studies?"

The question caught Paul unawares, and

Ilse even more so. "Priesthood?" she said, her eyes wide with questioning surprise.

"It's another long story," he said quietly, smiling back at her. "May I tell you later?"

Emma giggled. Leaning toward Ilse, she efficiently shared what Paul wished to avoid. Paul rolled his eyes when she concluded the story with their arrival the previous evening.

"I see," Ilse acknowledged with her own giggle.

To end the embarrassing discussion, Paul made a small cough, and took control of the conversation. "Well … I hadn't given university much thought in the past," he said. "However, it has a certain appeal now. But I'm not alone any longer." He wrapped his arm around Ilse and lost himself in her eyes momentarily. "What I really need is a job."

"Consider this," Gerhard urged. "Come to work in the factory with me, part-time. Earn the income you need. The two of you should be able to live here frugally." He looked at each of them, then continued. "Attend to your studies the rest of the time."

Paul heard his father's words and turned to Ilse. "We can certainly discuss this, Papa. Do you need an answer right now?"

Ilse placed a small hand on his arm. "Paul, I think your father's offer is generous. If you're looking for my blessing, you have it."

"Then it is done!" Gerhard announced, rising from his chair to pour more coffee. Emma assisted by passing a bowl of sugar.

"A toast!" Gerhard said, raising his coffee cup. "To an early and successful renovation and a happy future to you both."

"Hear, hear," Emma said in agreement, raising her cup in good cheer.

"Perhaps, sir, you might help me find employment, too?" Ilse asked, looking to Gerhard. "I'd be grateful for any help."

"Of course, if that is what you wish," Gerhard answered. "On one condition …"

"A condition, sir?" Ilse said, looking puzzled.

"Yes, a condition." Gerhard grinned mischievously and elaborated, "You will call me 'Papa' or 'Gerhard.' No more sir!"

"I can do that. Thank you. Papa," Ilse said shyly.

Paul looked at the happiness surrounding him, feeling the weight of his emotional isolation slip slightly from his shoulders. *I must speak to Papa soon. I need to know how he handled his fears and nightmares at the end of the Great War.*

When discussions of the new addition concluded, Paul and Ilse excused themselves, anxious to be off in search of a new bed.

Gerhard set himself to make some phone calls to facilitate the pending construction.

Arm in arm, Paul and Ilse walked into town, stopping at shops along the way, looking for a new bed. They finally found the one they wanted, paid for it, and arranged to have it delivered later that day. With free time on their hands, they went looking for a restaurant where they could share a quiet meal and talk.

"So," Paul said after the waiter had taken their order and cold glasses of a Riesling wine sat before them, "I told you of my year in Italy. Now you must tell me how you got from Breslau to München. It can't have been easy. I know what Breslau was like when I left. And after I heard about the convent, I worried about you constantly. Did you stay much longer?" He reached across the table and held her hand.

"No. We didn't," she said, looking at the large hand that covered hers, a band of gold gleaming on the ring finger of his right hand. "What did you hear about the convent?" she asked, delaying her story a bit longer.

"Do you recall the story that I told you about Nayda and the other young girls?" Paul asked.

Ilse nodded in her recollection.

"As we were moving out, we heard of another raid by the Reds. One of the other platoons had gone out to investigate. Fortunately, by then, Nayda and her classmates had been removed to safety in Dresden. But the nuns were still there, of course.

"When the platoon arrived ... well ..." Paul hesitated, not knowing what to say next.

When he found the words, he continued. "The story we heard from some of the men in that platoon was that every nun had been raped and beaten, regardless of their age. None were spared."

He paused, taking a sip of his wine. "The story resembles the one we heard from Nayda, does it not?" It was a rhetorical question for which he expected no answer, then continued.

"Apparently, two of the nuns were so distraught that they ran into the river as soon as the Russians left. The weight of their soaked habits pulled them under the water. The current pulled their bodies into the fast-moving water, and they drowned." Paul shook his head in disbelief.

"Oh yes! I know what you mean," Ilse interjected. "No women were safe, including nuns and children. We heard on the wireless that several convents were attacked. Many women, including nuns, fell pregnant. Apparently, the Communists justified rape as a means of eradicating the German race. In addition to murder, that is. Few, if any, of the women kept their babies. Hospitals reported that so many babies were abandoned that they had insufficient supplies to care for them all. And no one wanted half-German, half-Russian children."

Ilse took a deep breath to steady her shaking hands. "I even heard one announcer say that nurses took babies to the river's edge and drowned them." Her words were hushed and miserable. "Can you imagine! Drowning a baby! How desperate they must have been." A sob issued from her lips as a tear escaped her eye.

Minutes passed quietly, neither knowing how to continue. Moisture pearled on their wine glasses and trickled down the stems to the white linen table cloth.

Finally, Paul said, "That is an ugly side of war. Not that there is anything pretty about it." He shook his head. "We can pray for their souls. Otherwise, it's in the past, and there's nothing we can do about it." They hung their heads and were quiet for a few more minutes, then he tugged on Ilse's hand.

"And what of your brother? Have you heard from him?" Paul asked, trying to find a safer topic.

"Ah! Now that is a strange story," Ilse said. "Many months ago, my mother received a letter—if you can call it a letter. The envelope had been forwarded to several addresses before it reached Aunt Kaethe's house, and it had no return address written on it. Inside the envelope was a small piece of paper with short note written on it. The note said: *Am alive. Don't worry. Your son.* A faint thumbprint covered the words 'your son.' It looked like a bloody imprint, but we aren't certain."

"And you've heard nothing more?" Paul added.

"Nothing."

"I'm sorry," he said.

"Me too," she said. "On the cheery side, it gives us hope."

"Indeed," Paul agreed, reaching for his wine. "Now, tell me about your adventure. How did you get out of Breslau?"

Sipping her wine, Ilse told the tale of her escape with Prow Kobelev.

"What happened to the jewels?" Paul asked.

"Oh! I gave them all to Herr Kobelev, of course." She lowered her eyes, as if embarrassed. "He insisted that I should accept two emeralds. I used one to buy train tickets to München for Mama and me, and to pay something to my uncle in gratitude for my mother's keep.

"We left soon after for München, where we stayed with my Aunt Kaethe and Uncle Hans for the past year. I gave them the second emerald." She folded her hands on the table in front of her and looked at Paul. "And that is where I found my husband," she concluded, her smile bright. "Or should

I say, that is where my husband found me!"

"I'm glad you were there," Paul said, taking her hands in his and kissing the knuckles of each. "I was so afraid that I wouldn't find you. Or worse: that you wouldn't want me."

"Not possible," she asserted.

"Excuse me, sir," the waiter said, dishes of food balanced precariously on his hands and forearms. Paul released Ilse's hands and they both leaned back to allow the waiter to set the plates on the table.

"Mmm. Smells wonderful!" Ilse said. The waiter lifted the bottle of Riesling from an ice bucket near the table, offering to pour. "Yes, please," Ilse said. "I'm very thirsty this afternoon."

The conversation lightened as they shared their meal together, until Paul asked, "Say, whatever became of the woollen fabric that Lieselotte asked you to carry for her? It sounds like an odd request to make of someone, especially since you were fleeing for your lives."

"Oh!" she said. "Lieselotte had just bought the fabric. She had no space left in her bundle and refused to leave it behind. She asked me to carry it for her. I didn't have much in my bundle.

"There was little to do in München for the longest time. Curfews, tight security, and limited food and other supplies kept us close to home. Everything was so topsy-turvy when the fighting stopped and the opposing military forces moved in. So I borrowed my aunt's sewing machine and used the fabric to make myself a pair of trousers. I'd never had a pair before then."

Teasing, she added, "How wonderful and freeing they are. Now I know why men have kept them a well-guarded secret!"

⚜

"Come in, son," Gerhard said, beckoning Paul into the den a few weeks later. "Join me in a brandy before dinner?"

Paul nodded and turned to close the door behind him. "Papa, I think I need some help," Paul said. "May we speak privately?"

"Of course! Sit! What is it?"

"Ilse is worried, and I don't blame her," Paul answered as he settled into one of the old armchairs. "I don't recall, but she says that I cry out in my sleep and thrash the bed covers. All I know is that I can be fast asleep one moment, and the next I am sitting up, soaked from sweat and totally disorientated, my heart pounding."

Gerhard said nothing and motioned for Paul to continue.

"I must be dreaming about war experiences," Paul said, appearing to contemplate the apple fumes rising from his glass. "But I can't remember. The fact that I can't remember worries me."

Gerhard relaxed in the chair across from his son.

"It is the trauma of war. I have seen it many times, and I have had my own experiences," he said. "When I returned from the Great War, my father helped me deal with my nightmares. There was no help for him when he served. He had to learn to live

405

with his memories. But, when the Great War ended, he and I worked with others to set up a system of help for battle-weary soldiers. In time, we helped ourselves, also.

"I can help you find the guidance you seek, but you'll never be free of your memories. You will learn only to manage them in a manner that doesn't interfere with your life and your relationships. Let us enjoy our brandy, now. The women will be looking for us in a few minutes. Tomorrow, we will find you some help. Yes?"

"Yes, Papa. Thank you."

"And while we're at it, you can investigate what is required to get you a seat at the university."

"Yes, sir," Paul said, raising his glass in salute.

CHAPTER THIRTY-SEVEN

"Come in, son." Gerhard beckoned from the bed he had shared with Emma for more than half a century. "I've said my good-byes to everyone else. I saved you for the last. We have much to discuss."

"But, Papa, you've had visitors all day," Paul cautioned. "Why don't you rest for a while?"

"No time," Gerhard replied, rubbing the scar of an old battle wound on his forehead. "Open the top drawer there."

Paul opened the first drawer of an ornately-carved walnut dresser.

"Bring me the rosewood box from the back corner, right-hand side."

Paul easily found the small, wooden box with three stalks of ripe grain carved into the top.

When he placed it in his father's outstretched hand, Gerhard stroked it lovingly, then handed it back to Paul.

"What is it?" he asked, his brow creased with curiosity.

"Something that I should have given you a long time ago. Open it."

Paul flipped the brass clasp and the lid popped open. Nestled in a bed of black velvet sat a man's ring. Paul pinched it free and held it to the light.

"*Grossvater's* ring," he whispered reverently. The Lange family crest, carved in a blue cameo, was as brilliant as the last time he had seen it. "I'd forgotten about it."

"No doubt," Gerhard said. "I've never worn it. It's been in that box since the day my father died. He wanted me to make copies for you and your siblings, but I couldn't bring myself to open the box. I loved him, you know. Respected him. And each time I took the box from the drawer, I felt the pain of his loss."

Gerhard swiped a tear from his eye, his thumb rasping against a day's growth of whiskers. "That ring has been passed down from father to eldest son for more than two hundred years. It's yours now."

Paul opened his mouth to respond, but words failed him.

"Promise me that you'll make copies before it's too late."

"I will," Paul muttered, trying to clear his flooding vision. He sat in the armchair next to his father's bed, and the two men were quiet for several minutes.

"Now, back to business," Gerhard wheezed, interrupting the silence. "You must have a backup plan. There's too much unrest all around us. The Russians could march through this country and tear it apart." His grip was firm and steady as he squeezed his son's hand, emphasizing his concern.

"I will, Papa," Paul responded. "You and I saw the worst of humanity during the wars. I promise to do whatever I must to ensure the safety of our family."

Together, the old soldier and his son talked into the small hours of the morning. They shared their experiences in the military and the ongoing nightmares that haunted them. Then they discussed the growth of their family and the ongoing success of their businesses.

After a while, Gerhard lay motionless, his eyes closed. Although his breathing had become shallow and raspy, Paul felt firmness in the clammy hand that still grasped his.

When he closed his own eyes to contemplate the past, a vision of a fortune-teller flitted through his thoughts. *'Eyes the colour of melted dark chocolate,' she said. Everything else she told me that day came true, but I haven't seen those eyes since the day ... since the day on the dock at Schinawa. Is her warning to haunt me for the rest of my life?*

Startled by his thoughts, Paul sat erect in the chair and jabbed his fingers through his short black hair. When he looked up, his father's shadowed eyes glimmered back at him.

"Let's talk about that backup plan," Gerhard whispered. His breathing was shallow. "I'm beginning to fade, and I need to know we have a plan before I go."

As the predawn sun turned the sky blood-red, and small birds chirped in welcome of a new day in 1975, Gerhard closed his eyes one last time, twitched his fingers to alert his resting son, and released his last breath.

Salty tears traced a path on either side of Paul's nose, and he dashed them from his eyes. Licking moisture from his lips, he rose from the chair where he had kept his vigil and stood rigid at the foot of his father's bed. He snapped a crisp salute to the old soldier whom he had loved for a lifetime.

"Farewell, Papa," he choked. "Safe journey."

Then he turned to the door that would lead him into the hallway, the bearer of sad, but expected, news.

NOTE TO READERS

Thank you for reading The Crest, Book I of the Prophesy Saga. I hope you enjoyed the adventure as much as I did.

Other readers find reviews helpful for locating books they prefer to read. All reviews are appreciated.

Don't forget to visit my website: jerenatobiasen.ca, to read about my other works and inspirations.

Turn the page
for an exciting excerpt from
The Emerald,
Book II of the Prophesy Saga —
coming soon!

Turn the page
for an exciting excerpt from

The Emerald

CHAPTER ONE

Nicolai Kota led the caravan along the outskirts of Liegnitz toward a small lake where the city hosted its annual fall festival. Sycamore leaves were fading from summer greens to the yellow and orange of early death. He reined in the horse to halt his *vardo* and raised his arm to stop the other wagons trailed behind.

"I'll head into Liegnitz from here," he said. He kissed his wife's creamy cheek, noting how the sun glinted off the emerald dangling above her breast, suspended on a heavy gold chain. He handed the reins to her and hopped down. "Lead the caravan into the grove. Assume that we'll be assigned the same location as other years."

"All right," Rosalee said, tucking an

errant curl of dark hair under her kerchief. "We should be circled by the time you catch up."

"Give me a few minutes to saddle Bang," Nicolai said, walking to the rear of the vardo. Rosalee set the brake, prepared to wait.

Nicolai beckoned the driver of the next wagon to join him. Hanzi, the band's *kris*, set the brake of his vardo and dismounted gingerly. He limped along the side of his horse toward Nicolai, obviously aching from the hours of inactivity.

As kris, Hanzi was responsible for overseeing the laws and values of justice for the *vista*, the name given to a community of nomads. He had become kris the same year that Nicolai's father was elected *voivode*, more than twenty years ago. Hanzi leaned on his walking stick, his gait encumbered with arthritis. He stopped and stretched, running his gnarled hand along Bang's flank, straightening the saddle blanket as he did so.

"Rosalee will lead the vista into the old grove," Nicolai said. "I'd appreciate it if you could keep an eye on everyone. Some of the young fellows have been a bit rambunctious lately."

"I will, Chief," Hanzi said. "Do you want anyone to accompany you?"

"No need," Nicolai answered.

Hanzi tipped his hat and returned to his own vardo.

"Papa, can I go with you?" Punita asked.

Startled out of his thoughts, but not surprised to hear the question, Nicolai turned from Hanzi's departure to see his nine-year old daughter nuzzling the horse's muzzle.

"I can't imagine you'd allow otherwise," he said, grunting as he hefted the saddle in place. "Make yourself useful, my love. Get the bridle. Watch your fingers with the bit. You know he likes to nip."

"Yes, Papa," Punita said, skipping to the back of the wagon where the bridle was stored.

A moment later, Rosalee appeared at his side. "You're taking the imp, I hear."

"Yes. Can you manage alone until we get back?" he asked, tightening the cinch.

"I'm sure some of the other girls will help," Rosalee said, watching her daughter coerce the bit into a resisting mouth.

Nicolai walked around his prize racehorse checking the tack before mounting. When he was seated, Punita passed the reins up to him and waited for his hand. He reached down, and she clasped both hands around his wrist. As he lifted, Punita used her legs to scramble behind him, onto the horse's rump.

"Hold tight to the saddle, Punita. He's going to prance."

"I'm ready, Papa."

Nicolai settled in the saddle and touched his heels to the barrel of the horse. As predicted, Bang began dancing sideways before lunging forward.

"We'll be along in a while," Nicolai said to Rosalee, reining Bang in a circle. "I plan to visit with Alexi Puchinski once I have our business licence and confirmation that the usual grove is appropriate."

Nicholai gave Bang a nudge with his heels, and the horse leapt forward eagerly.

Rosalee watched the horse canter toward town, raising her hand in farewell. When the horse and riders disappeared into the small forest ahead, she returned to the front of the vardo. Perched on the bench, she released the brake and snapped the reins. The horse leaned into its task, and the other wagons rolled in line behind hers. When she was certain all of them were in motion, she clicked to her horse and its pace quickened. As one, the caravan snaked toward the grove.

She led the caravan to a grove situated on the edge of the lake near the fair grounds. As she entered the grove, she guided the horse to the right of the clearing. The others followed. She continued until her horse closed in on the last wagon, completing a circle of privacy and protection.

Those who were driving wagons that would be used during the fair formed a semi-circle outside the grove along the side that edged the fair grounds. Some wagons carried goods that would be emptied, so they could be set up to create a stage. Ornate wagons would be used for telling fortunes, reading futures, and selling potions.

The Kota family had two vardos: the twelve-foot high *ledge*, which was used for day-to-day living, and the *kite*, a modified Reading wagon that Nicolai had had built for Rosalee soon after they married, from which Rosalee conducted her business. Built in the town of Reading, the kite was ornate on the outside, but simple on the inside. The berths and cooking facilities had been replaced with a table and chairs for guests who came to have their fortunes told.

Rosalee set the brake, climbed down from the bench and began unhitching the horse. Before long, one of the men arrived to lead the animal to a holding pen for grooming and grazing. Thanking him, she set about organizing the space around her ledge for family use during the time of the fair.

Three young girls—friends of Punita—ran up, offering to help collect wood and build a fire. Accepting their help, she left them and walked through the camp to ensure that everyone was satisfied with the locations of their respective vardos.

Soon the smell of campfire smoke wafted through the enclosure. A current of voices rose as folks bustled to and fro, organizing the glade that they would call home for the next few days.

Rosalee paused as she approached the fifth wagon. A group of boys—not yet men—had gathered away from the vardos. They lounged against trees and teased one another.

"Excuse me, gentlemen," she said, looking at them sternly, "When you have finished your break, would you mind filling the water barrels? I think you'll find that most of them are empty, and we'll need fresh water to prepare the meals."

As she spoke, they straightened themselves and walked toward her.

"We'll start on that straight away," the oldest, a boy of seventeen, acknowledged.

"Thank you, Helwig," she said, continuing on her tour. Approaching the next vardo, she noticed three other boys lingering behind it. They moved into the vardo's shadow when they saw her. *These are the boys who concern my husband. I'll ask Hanzi to keep an eye on them until Nicolai returns.*

"Samson! Where are you?" a woman's voice bellowed from within the wheeled home.

"Your father will be back soon," she warned them. "You and your brothers best get busy."

ABOUT THE AUTHOR

"The thrum of city life runs through my veins, and I draw energy and inspiration from my west coast lifestyle. I've had stories swimming in my head my entire life, and when I returned to the west coast, those stories surfaced with a determination to be heard."

Jerena Tobiasen grew up on the Canadian prairies (Calgary, Alberta and Winnipeg, Manitoba). In the early '80s, she returned *home* to Vancouver, British Columbia, the city in which she was born.

Although Jerena has occasionally written short stories and poems since her return to Vancouver, it was not until 2016 dawned, that she began writing her first full-length manuscript, which was set primarily in Germany during World War I and World War II. When that draft was complete, she travelled to Europe and traced the steps taken by the story's primary characters. Then, she rewrote that manuscript, embellishing it with experiences and observations. The manuscript evolved into three volumes, the first of which tracks a family of German soldiers through two world wars *(The Crest)*. The second volume tracks a family of Roma who are forced to flee Germany during the early years of Adolf Hitler's round-up of undesirables *(The Emerald)*. The third volume reveals what can happen when the paths of two very different families collide *(The Destiny)*. Together, these volumes became the saga *The Prophecy.*

CPSIA information can be obtained
at www.ICGtesting.com
Printed in the USA
LVHW112237161118
597443LV00001B/1/P